W9-ATY-573

Lady
LAS VEGAS

ALSO BY SUSAN BERMAN

"Driver, Give a Soldier a Lift!"
(PUTNAM)

Easy Street
(THE DIAL PRESS)

Fly Away Home
(AVON)

Spiderweb
(AVON)

Lady LAS VEGAS

THE INSIDE STORY BEHIND AMERICA'S NEON OASIS

SUSAN BERMAN

Jacket design by New Video and Michael Hornburg.
Book design by Michael Hornburg.
Type formatting and picture layout by Bernard Schleifer.
Printed and bound in the United States of America.

ISBN: 1-57500-020-2
CIP data available.
2 3 4 5 6 7 8 9 10

TV Books publishes books developed from quality television. The company is founded on the principle that books naturally extend the excitement, enjoyment and entertainment benefits inherent in television.

TV Books, Inc.
Distributed by Penguin USA

TV Books titles are available at special discounts for bulk purchases for sales promotions, premiums, fund-raising or educational use. For details, contact:

Special Sales Director
TV Books
61 Van Dam Street
New York, NY 10013
http:\\www.tvbooks.com

This book is published to accompany the special presentation telecast on A&E Network.
The series was produced by MPH Entertainment, Inc.
Executive Producers Jim Milio, Melissa Jo Peltier and Mark Hufnail.
Co-producer Susan Berman.

PHOTO CREDITS

SB: courtesy of Susan Berman; NSM: Nevada State Museum; UNLV: University of Nevada-Las Vegas, Special Collections. TV Books would like to thank Susan Berman and the photo research department at MPH Entertainment for providing photographs and for permission to reproduce copyright material. While every effort has been made to trace and acknowledge all copyright holders, we would like to apologize should there have been any errors or omissions.

pg. 15, SB; pg. 16, SB; pg. 18t NSM; pg. 18b, NSM; pg. 23, SB; pg. 25, UNLV; pg. 27, SB; pg. 30, UNLV; pg. 31, NSM; pg. 34, UNLV; pg. 39, NSM; pg. 40, NSM; pg. 41, NSM; pg. 45, NSM; pg. 46, NSM; pg. 49, UNLV; pg. 51, NSM; pg. 53, NSM; pg. 55, SB; pg. 57, SB; pg. 59, SB; pg. 61, SB, pg. 64t, NSM; pg. 64b, NSM; pg. 67t, NSM; pg. 67b, SB; pg. 69, SB; pg. 73, NSM; pg. 75, SB; pg. 77, SB; pg. 78, NSM; pg. 80, NSM; pg. 83, SB; pg. 87, NSM; pg. 88, UNLV; pg. 90, NSM; pg. 92, NSM; pg. 95, NSM; pg. 97, NSM; pg. 99, NSM; pg. 103, NSM; pg. 105, NSM; pg. 109, SB; pg. 110, UNLV; pg. 112, NSM; pg. 114, NSM; pg. 116, UNLV; pg. 119, NSM; pg. 121, SB; pg. 127, UNLV; pg. 131, NSM; pg. 133, NSM; pg. 135, NSM; pg. 138, UNLV; pg. 139, NSM; pg. 141, NSM; pg. 145, NSM; pg. 146, NSM; pg. 148, photo by Gerardo Somoza; pg. 151, courtesy Mirage Resorts, Inc.; pg. 153, NSM; pg. 154, NSM, pg. 157, NSM; pg. 159, courtesy Mirage Resorts, Inc.; pg. 160, courtesy Mirage Resorts, Inc.; pg. 165, UNLV; pg. 169, photo by Gerardo Somoza; pg. 171, UNLV; pg. 175, NSM; pg. 178, NSM; pg. 181, NSM; pg. 183, UNLV; pg. 189, NSM; pg. 193, photo by Gerardo Somoza; pg. 195, photo by Gerardo Somoza; pg. 198, UNLV; pg. 202, NSM; pg. 207, NSM; pg. 209, photo by Gerardo Somoza; pg. 213, NSM; pg. 215, NSM, pg. 216, NSM; pg. 219, NSM; pg. 220, NSM.

CONTENTS

ACKNOWLEDGMENTS

I'd like to thank the following people, without whose vision and support this book would not have been possible: Jed Baron, Nyle Brenner, Deke Castleman, Burton Cohen, Fred Doumani, Bob Evans, Nina Feinberg, Danny Goldberg, Mark Hufnail, Neeti Madan, Alvin Malnick, Thom Mount, Deni Markus, Tom Padden, Raleigh Padveen, Melissa Peltier, Hal Rothman, Charlotte Sheedy, Diana Ungerleiter, Michael Ventura and especially Jim Milio, who had faith in me from the very beginning. I would like to acknowledge thanks to the publishers of *Easy Street*, for allowing me to use of some recollections I first wrote about back then. And I would like to express a most special thank-you to publisher Peter Kaufman and TV Books.

—S. B.

October 1996

ABOUT THE AUTHOR

Susan Berman is a journalist, novelist, screenwriter and playwright. She is the author of a classic, critically acclaimed memoir of growing up in Las Vegas, *Easy Street.* Her Father, mobster Davie Berman, was Bugsy Siegel's partner in Las Vegas and took over the Flamingo Hotel after Siegel was slain. Her access to personalities new and old in Las Vegas is without parallel.

She lives in Los Angeles, California.

Lady
LAS VEGAS

SANDBOX IN THE DESERT

In the beginning I adored her, that Lady Las Vegas, my fantastic, world-famous, older sister—who could ever compare? Even though my father, the famed Las Vegas hotel-casino pioneer Davie Berman, had her just one year before my birth, she had 40 years of sophistication, glamour and class on me. As I grew up, I began to envy her. Did my dad like her better, prefer her? She intrigued him, magnetized his interest, and earned his constant praise.

By the time I was eight, I wanted only to grow up fast so I could give her a run for her money in my dad's eyes. I began to resent her deeply. The most famous designers dressed her in beads and silk, jewelers bestowed diamonds and rhinestones on her, and her dancer's feet were encased in satin high heels. She smelled expensive; her eyes, never faded, were always neon bright, her lips a tantalizing red.

I was short and scruffy, wore jeans, a Western shirt, and cowboy boots; my knees were always skinned, my nose was sunburned from living in the Flamingo Hotel pool, my hair was in pigtails, and the only time I smelled good was when I could swipe some of my dad's Zizane cologne. The resent-

ABOVE: MY FATHER, DAVIE BERMAN.

MY PARENTS, DAVIE AND GLADYS BERMAN, AND ME AT MY COUSIN FRED SHORR'S WEDDING AT THE FLAMINGO HOTEL, 1950.

ment turned to deep hostility. By the time I was ten, I refused to go to her events, honor her civic pride.

If she was mainstream, I would be fringe; if she was popular, I would be antisocial; if she was a people-pleaser, I would be withdrawn or strident. If she was a femme fatale, I would be a tomboy. If she was valued for her body and her sex appeal, I would be valued only for my mind. By the age of twelve I hated her with every fiber of my being and I held her responsible for the terrible tragedy that befell my family and orphaned me.

My parents had loved her, nurtured her, rescued her when she was down. My father spent nearly every waking hour with her, sometimes working both swing and graveyard shifts, so proud was he to own her hotels. First he ran his downtown clubs, then the Flamingo Hotel, and finally the Riviera. My mother adorned her New Year's Eve parties, her floor-show openings, her pools. I sent my parents out to her every day and every night, confident that they would be returned to me unharmed.

My father died because he could not leave her alone, even for a weekend. His friends said, "Davie, go to the Mayo Clinic for the surgery, go to Cedars of Lebanon in Los Angeles." He said, "No, if I don't go to a doctor here, who will have faith in our town?" That faith killed him. My mother could not go on without her Davie and took her own life in sorrow.

If Lady Las Vegas had been less seductive, less appealing, if she had been anyone other than herself, my parents would have been able to live out a normal life span and I would have been with them. She was heartless, harsh; and like her gambling tables, she never takes the blame.

As fate would have it, I was left to my father's black-sheep younger brother, Chickie Berman, as his charge. I thought, at least with him I won't be in competition with Lady Las Vegas. He didn't live there, as we had.

But I was wrong. My father had picked her because his only trade, gambling, was legal and holy within her boundaries, and he based his empire on her charms. He had had a life of operating beyond the law, had done his time in Sing Sing, and now had a beautiful wife and a tiny baby, and he wanted a new life that only Lady Las Vegas could give him.

She was the trophy daughter that bestowed respectability, that let him be the godfather of a booming town. My Uncle Chickie did not seek respectability; he craved action. He ran to her for a different reason, to fuel his addiction. She had the edge. Me, I had only boarding-school uniforms, sweet smiles and homework. I lost again. He too died for her; she drained him of every penny, every ounce of blood.

Nothing is ever enough for her.

In the way of siblings who are raised much too closely, I was so threatened by her very existence that I had to move halfway across the nation, then the world, to escape her. And it was only from this distant vantage point, many years after I had fled from her, that her overwhelming presence did not threaten me any longer and that I finally came to appreciate her again.

As I think about her over the half century that I have known her well, I have both loved and hated her. No one can deny that my hometown, Las Vegas, is unique. Of that I'm proud. The cacophony of the slot machines, the caw of their slippery, silvery mouths when they pay jackpots, and the constant litany of "Place Your Bet" were my nighttime lullabies. At first, all anxieties cease when I drive toward that neon oasis; my heart thrills to the mileage signs—just 150 miles, just 29 miles, and still no sign of her! I can't wait!

THE FLAMINGO HOTEL IN THE 1950s, WHILE MY DAD WAS RUNNING IT.

BELOW: THE POOL AT THE FLAMINGO, WHERE I GREW UP.

She is not the dull end run of a milk-train route, filled with forgettable houses, the result of careless urban sprawl, the unplanned offspring of exhausted parents. No! She is the result of deliberate, loving creation—she was wanted, she was treasured! In the midst of the harsh, rejecting desert on all sides, protected by sloping purple mountains, she conceals her secrets until the last possible minute, because surprise is in her arsenal. Then, miraculously, because she was born and sustained by miracles, she rises majestically out of the desert! She knows how to make an entrance!

I see her now, for the first time after many years, as we drive toward the Strip. It is nighttime, her time; she lives by night, and because of her, so do I. As hazy and slow-moving as she is in the morning; as bored and somnolent as she is at three in the afternoon, when the sun blankets her with a paralyzing heat; as restless as she gets at five in the afternoon, when her yellow fireball is more lovingly dressed in pink and ready to sink behind the mountains—so am I, waiting for darkness as minutes creep by, anxious like her to come alive at night. It has been so long since I have been here, I wonder how I will find Lady Las Vegas, how I will feel, and, more important—whether I will survive her intact.

My strange Vegas pedigree allowed me to be raised in wealth and glamour by a man who owned the town—this is how Lady Las Vegas honors winners, which we all seemed to be in those early Vegas years of the Forties and Fifties.

She can be so grand when she loves you! Our public life was enviable, but things were sad at home. In the Vegas way, we were in denial, covered up our secrets, denied rumors, kept smiling. Many years later, when I lived on the low side in dives with Uncle Chickie, I saw how Lady Las Vegas treats her losers. She can be so cruel! I vowed to live my life far away from her clutches because she had an in to me that was lethal.

In a final bid to win me back, when I was in my 30s, she presented me with one of her fine sons and made him so spectacular that I had to marry him. He was another Vegas child trying to escape her bonds. But her hold on you is so deep that although your body may be elsewhere, your thoughts don't leave her for a second.

In 1983, I met my future husband Mister Margulies (Yes, that was his name) in the Writers Guild script-registration line in Los Angeles. I had moved there from New York just two months before. He wore a faded T-shirt and jeans; a gold ID bracelet on his left wrist that said "Mister"; a gold, square clunky pinkie ring; Ray-Bans; and a light-blue golf cap with "Dunes Country Club" in a yellow, threaded scrawl. He was young, tan, healthy-looking, immaculately clean, and somewhat shabby (for want of funds, not of style).

He immediately removed those Ray-Bans. His 1,000-kilowatt, dark-brown eyes met mine with a laserlike intensity, and then, as if his glance had been too intimate, too penetrating, he averted his eyes.

"I know you," he said, in a distinctive, soft, low voice, the phrase punctuated with just a hint of a question mark, connoting uncertainty, a Vegas "anything-is-possible-the-sky's-the-limit" vibe. The hook immediately involved me, seductively drew me in, demanded that I give him permission to go on by uttering some encouraging phrase of my own.

He stood squarely in a determined fashion, upper body thrust slightly forward. At first glance he looked like a boy just on the edge of manhood, but on second glance he looked like a man who had never really had the freedom to be a boy. Had Vegas stolen his childhood as it had mine?

"I recognize you from the pictures on the back of your books, my dad has them all. My dad is Jay Margulies. He worked for your father. He loved your dad, in fact my Hebrew name is David Abraham, I was named for your dad. I'm from Vegas," he concluded, in that same low, confidential tone Vegas people have, as if all this were top secret or, at the very least, terribly important and not to be trivialized or squandered by loud sound.

How else to compete with the constant casino noise? How else to compete with the endless flow of cash? How else but to speak in low tones when Lady Las Vegas's shrill cry is so high?

"You're from Las Vegas?" I asked, incredulous, but in those same low tones. How could that be? It defied the law of chance. You don't meet Vegas people, town-without-pity people in a screenwriters' registration line; you meet them, smelling of Shalimar and Bijan, in fancy Italian restaurants in Beverly Hills and New York and Miami, restaurants with red wallpaper and real Sicilian waiters and more than just a vague smell of the Mob.

You meet them in La Costa, on golf courses all over the country, in homes in Chicago, and they tell you they knew your dad way back when, and what a tragedy it was that your parents died so young, and how you look just like your dad—too bad, I mean he was "one handsome fella, but your mother was so beautiful, such a dish, and you're a girl. Luck of the draw."

Yet, Mister was from Las Vegas, a decade younger than I, raised in a different era. Could Vegas be different from what I remembered? Could Lady Las Vegas have grown and changed as much as I had? How long had I avoided opulent homes with that wallpaper with the big green leaves, and hotels with it, too, like the Beverly Hills Hotel (pre-Sultan of Brunei), because that was the Mob wallpaper they had in my dad's hotels. The Mob decorator was everywhere in L.A., and the sight of that Mob wallpaper brought me down.

How long had I avoided my dad's friends in Trousdale Estates and in Beverly Hills, with their walk-in closets full of tennis clothes and their leather backgammon sets, because only they were left to tell me tales of my own childhood? I "was a handful for Davie," and "at four you could play gin rummy better than anybody, but Davie, boy, was he crazy about you!" It made me so sad.

Don't people who grow up in Vegas worship silver-dollar Mammon, crave jobs as card dealers, think of floor shows as high taste? Don't they aspire to live in Spanish Trails and have a condo in Beverly Hills so their wives can come down here to shop? My dad's friends had their refrain, "Yeah, she did a lot of damage, Susie. Cash business, gotta spend it, you know. " No, Mister wasn't like that. His soul reflected purity and intellect.

"Yeah, I'm from Vegas, and I'm a writer," Mister said, noting my puzzled expression. A pause, a beat, instant empathy, mutual credentials of pain.

"Tough town to dream in, isn't it?" I asked. He nodded and in that holy moment we exchanged a look, a look of two dreamers who dreamed of a life outside of Las Vegas, and who were raised on children's bedtime stories in a town where the heat was so stifling, so limiting, that we had nightmares in the air-conditioning when we were three. Circumstances beyond my control had freed me from her clutches. How had he gotten away on his own?

"I guess you and I are the only ones to have made it out of Vegas alive," I said, being from a town where people died "unfortunate deaths" and where, when you said your dad died, you quickly added "of natural causes" and hung your head in shame because you could not bestow the same honor on your lovely mother. He looked at me, then looked quickly away, far away, four-and-a-half-hours-to-Vegas away.

Did he look down because he saw the future? Mister didn't make it out of Vegas alive. Just on the brink of Hollywood success as a screenwriter, he died at 27. Did he meet the doom meant for me? Is there a curse on Vegas parents and their children—is it the sins of our fathers, or is that just an old wives tale? His father committed no sins. Mine did, was reincarnated and cleansed. Am I to suffer for the sins of his youth?

I married Mister for the brilliant, loving, unique person he was, but did I also marry him so I could experience Lady Las Vegas through him and not have to face her directly? Did I need his protection from her relentless glare? Did I want her but not want her, long for her but fear her, want to drink her in indirectly from his life source?

As life progressed, I knew that at some point to be whole I would have to go back to my hometown, not for my usual hop, skip, jump, and funeral—but for an extended time. I had to determine her impact on me. It was not

"*J'accuse*," but more "What happened?"

In the way of people who have had cataclysmic shocks in their emotional lives over which they have no control, I approached the threatening situation intellectually. I would study her, detach myself from her, then judge, and maybe, if I had the strength, at last go back to experience her.

I began to think about hometowns: How much did we have the right to expect of them? Anything at all? My hometown was an emigrant's paradise, a town my father and his friends willingly came to, to start over. So my town was a place to come to, not to leave from. Most of my friends left their hometowns to escape the drudgery of their parents' lives, many of them from hometowns that people flee. My hometown is everyone's fantasy and my reality.

I am from a hometown that everyone desired, that they insisted was better than their own. Although visitors usually granted her only three days, it was with great regret that they left, vowing that they'd like to live in Vegas forever. They never left saying, "Vegas was great, next time we'll try Hawaii"; no, they always promised they would repeat their Vegas trip soon, lamenting that it would be too long—at least a few months—before they could come back. "Davie, whatta town, you've got it made," they'd say to my dad when we dropped them off at tiny McCarran Field to begin their journeys home.

Our phone at home would ring, my dad would answer, exuberant: "Hi Morrie, when do you arrive? Hey, it's 80 degrees here every day, how bad can it be?" I felt special to live in such a hometown, as if I had been specially selected, specially blessed. When we traveled as a family we traveled to New York or Miami or Los Angeles, people reacted with surprise and envy when they heard we lived in Las Vegas: "People actually live in Las Vegas? Wow, You're so lucky!"

Lucky—that's what I thought we were; even though I had a love-hate thing going with Lady Las Vegas, I felt we were lucky to live there, and that my special luck would last forever because I was a part of her. Maybe my expectations were too high, maybe I expected too much of her and was let down too harshly. Maybe one does not have the right to have such high expectations of one's hometown.

I think now about how she formed me, unconsciously. There was a feeling of unlimited possibility about her—her vistas and boundaries expanded constantly—there were no limits. Every year that we drove down the strip, the 20 blocks from our house to the hotel, my dad would say, "Look at her, look at how she's growing! There's no stopping her."

First a small strip grew out of a scrappy, dusty downtown, where before there had only been sagebrush and desert. Then there were more hotels on the

Strip, then the subdivisions, then the first shopping malls. She was growing in every direction; a new hotel or building cropped up where empty space had been just yesterday. More people, more cars, more schools, more glory for Lady Las Vegas.

All things were possible when you were part of her; all risks were worth taking, because they turned out okay. It was right to be unstoppable: Tenacity paid off; go for it! I didn't know that my father and his friends were refugees from small, poor, cluttered cities; I didn't know that Las Vegas opened a window for their claustrophobic souls and let in the first fresh air. This is all I have ever known: big, airy, open, unlimited, make your mark, stake your turf, don't hold back!

Lady Las Vegas had spirit; she celebrated life, she lived large. She did her floor-show openings up in gold wrapping paper with big satin bows. Her New Year's Eve celebrations were luxurious. I was too young to go but spent half a lifetime watching my mother dress for the events.

First, we'd go to Fanny's Dress Shop at the Flamingo; it was outside the hotel, in the back across from the pool. My tall, beautiful, former-dancer mother would select a long, satin, scoop-necked, beaded gown. I still have her gowns. They were rose-colored or, maybe tonight, light green, with clear and white beads. She didn't like white because she didn't like to tan, and she didn't like black—"too depressing."

MY MOTHER, BEFORE SHE WAS MARRIED, DANCING IN HER "PENNIES FROM HEAVEN" TAP NUMBER IN MINNEAPOLIS, 1938.

The gowns would be strapless or with spaghetti straps, but no cleavage showed; my mother was modest. The size-eight dress would have to be taken in at the waist—she was fashionably thin. She'd charge the dress to my dad, and we'd leave the shop just as the wives of my dad's partners, Millie Alderman (Willie Alderman's wife) or Marie Simms (Chester Simms's wife) would come in to get their gowns. Tall, thin, red-headed and so delicate, Marie had been a model in New York, and she was gorgeous. She and my mother liked each other; they laughed about the time Chester was working for Meyer Lansky in Havana and Marie called my mother and had her fly over with a suitcase filled with canned food. Our fathers and their friends were always running through the dress shop. As it turned out, the bookie joint was in the back room.

The day of the New Year's Eve party or the floor-show opening, my mom and I would get our hair done at Gigi's Hair Salon at the Flamingo, and we'd have manicures and pedicures, Revlon's bright red Jack O' Diamonds. I was going to be staying home with the baby-sitter because I was only six, but my mother groomed me as she groomed herself.

I watched my glossy parents ("See ya later, little kiddo," my dad would croon) go out into the starry night all dressed up as I prepared for a dull evening of beating our bodyguard, Lou, and the baby-sitter at gin. The baby-sitter was always a shutout, what a bore! I hungered for the moment in the early morning when my parents would come home, wake me, and give me the gifts the hotel had bestowed on the lady guests. These gifts were not for children, but I got them because I was their special child. I still have the velvet beaded purses, the watches, the silver trays with the flamingo in the center.

As I got older, my parents took me to celebrations appropriate for children: the opening of the Dunes, the Stardust, many dinner and floor-show openings. Our town had a fabulous, civic-pride Western parade, the Helldorado Parade; I was a butterfly on the Flamingo Hotel's float. We had massive Easter-egg hunts on the grounds of the Last Frontier and idiosyncratic Passover celebrations in the showroom there, too. Life was to be enjoyed with major events, orchestrated perfectly, planned to the smallest detail, no expense spared.

And because the gangster/mobsters and their wives were so happy at last to have a place to throw respectable parties, they went all out; no one was ever as proud or as fine hosts as they were. Life should be careful, full of purpose, deliberate, no part of it overlooked or given short shrift.

Just as it appeared to me that planning produced wonderful results, so it was apparent that hard work brought success. My father was thrilled to

AN EARLY VIEW OF THE DUNES.

work sixteen hours a day, as were his friends. There was no other life—this was the life: casinos, families, golf, occasional vacations cut short because "gotta get back to Vegas, miss her. " Even the year my father died at 54, when he had enough money to retire comfortably, retirement was never an option.

When my mother pressured him to move to Los Angeles, he said, "But I can't, Betty, L.A. is just another town to me, it's not Las Vegas. Here I have work, I have worth." Las Vegas bestowed worth on him, as well as on me. But if your town can bestow worth, then when she frowns on you and you lose everything, can she take it away?

All our patrician casino families looked alike, seemed alike. Our fathers were dark, Jewish or Italian, compact men around 5 feet 8 inches in height. Our mothers were beautiful Presbyterian "girls," tall, but not as tall as our dads, thin, white-skinned. We looked upon the tall Mormon men with suspicion; they were too tall, they could fall on you.

No one had big families—one, two children at the most. These men from dark pasts had married their fairy-tale princesses late in life; many had to adopt. Our mothers all seemed to have trouble getting pregnant or staying pregnant; hysterectomies for "depression" were common in our town—my mother had one when she was just 29. Once again, the Mormons, who ran the managerial end of our hotels and who were the only people, besides themselves, that our dads trusted, seemed like alien tribal members with their families of five and six—from a different planet. Did those children have to share a room? How terrible! Did they wear hand-me-downs? How shameful!

The dark side of many of our families' lives was our mothers' deep unhappiness. Vegas is not a woman's town. Our mothers had left their families in the Midwest and the East to follow their men, and they led isolated, lonely lives in my hometown. Their men worked night and day, they saw them for dinner and at the shows and on Sundays, and their men called hourly to check in, but Vegas was a man's town.

Many were former dancers or models like my mother, with no desire or need to work; they just wanted to be wives and mothers. The shadows of their husbands' former and present Mob lives were always hanging over them. Men died "suddenly" in my dad's business—Ben Siegel, many others—would their man be next? Would their children be kidnapped? Would they be harmed? Life was just too precarious, too spooky to give our mothers any real sense of security, which money, even "cash money," cannot buy.

My mother was the wholesome type: her life revolved around me, she was the Brownie leader, the room mother at the Fifth Street Elementary School. She took the neighborhood kids to Hebrew School at Beth Shalom and to the Saturday-morning matinees at the Huntridge Theater.

She made all my clothes on her shiny, tan Singer sewing machine; took me to dancing lessons; arranged for the piano teacher. But it wasn't enough. She didn't turn to drink, but she suffered nervous breakdowns. Life, without structure and a core of family, did not smile on her as it did on my dad.

My parents were passionately in love. As my mother lost more and more touch with reality, my father, saddened beyond words and suddenly old, almost overnight, could only say "Susie, with these hands I'm going to work and work until we get that girl well." Famous psychiatrists were consulted; she was sent to Minneapolis and Los Angeles; massive amounts of tranquilizers were consumed; appointments were kept; electric-shock therapy was given. But his hands couldn't get her well; all the money, skimmed or made legally, couldn't get her well.

My town gave me the message that there is safety, not at home, but out of the home. I wanted to be strong, like my father, and have a career. Home

MY MOTHER AND I AT MCCARRAN AIRPORT IN 1948 ON OUR WAY TO L.A.

was associated with breakdowns, accidents, long afternoons spent in bed in a darkened room.

No matter how successful my father became, when he was speaking at civic events, elected head of the Temple, honored by City of Hope and the Variety Club, somehow there was always the message that we were still a little different from other successful people in the nation, that we could only trust our own, that one has to make one's way outside the structure of America as a whole, because, even though the word never left my father's lips, we were Mob.

To this day, I see myself as an outsider, even though I have gone to some of my nation's finest schools and colleges, done well, and achieved a career. I am distrustful of the mainstream. I dislike team players, preferring individualists who do it "their way." After a childhood of hearing "Trust your gut," because that was how my dad decided how much credit to give a gambler, I do the same. He would stand in the pit, a dealer would nod toward a gambler who wanted his credit extended, and my dad would make the call just by looking at the guy. He was never wrong.

Like him and like my town, I run on instinct, immediately like or dislike someone, make snap judgments, and never change my mind. My loyalties to my friends and family run deep and true, but I know I am not easy to know. I am on guard. The Lady taught me that.

Vegas and the Mob, the Mob and Vegas, Vegas and the Jews, the Jews and Vegas, Vegas and its showgirls and dancers, and its showgirls and dancers and Vegas: I am from that, part of it. People say I am "a fast study" and "people smart"—that's how Lady Las Vegas has always been, so maybe some similarities between sisters do exist as they grow up.

I knew my town was in America, but I thought we were located in the center of the nation. When I learned that we were way over by the West Coast, I was stunned. How did so many people hear of us? Oh, Lady Las Vegas, you are fantastic! Somehow America made it possible for my town to exist. In the last year of my father's life, the Hungarians were being murdered by Russians in tanks, and he'd say, "We are so lucky to be in America, Susie; that could never happen here." I didn't know that his parents had fled Russian pogroms when he was three. I didn't even know he had been born in Odessa; I thought he had always lived in America and in Las Vegas.

As I reflect on my life, I see now why I had to go to places very different from Las Vegas to grow and develop. She could annihilate me, that Lady Las Vegas! I felt at ease in Portland, Oregon, where I went to the well-known Oregon Episcopal Church boarding school. There was rain, rain, rain, greenery, old stone and brick buildings—very far away in spirit from my insomniac older sister.

San Francisco was as far removed in sights, smells, and temperaments from Vegas as you could get. It had fog, bridges, and Victorian homes, and New York had, well, it had indescribable New York with its closer-than-this masses of people, feelings of oldness, and decay and snow. I even went to Israel for a year to write a novel, in my way looking for my family and my heritage because my father had been a Zionist who raised money for the War for Independence and I was very proud to be Jewish.

But the deserts of Beersheba made me nervous, deserts like Vegas. I ran into friends of my dad's at the Dan Hotel in Tel Aviv; too close for comfort, memories threatened the edge of my existence. It was fetid and hot like Vegas, heat that could burn your hope. I had to flee.

Lady Las Vegas, what can I say about you for sure? That you taught me always to eat out, to stay only in the best hotels, and to appreciate a good sense of humor? My dad and his friends, which included many famous comedians, were hilarious, their takes on life grounded in mirth and irony. I can say that, like you, I expect people to be well-groomed and not too tall.

I'm trying to make light of the only close family relationship I have left, perhaps to neutralize it so I can get closer. I have only one sister, Lady Las Vegas, and she is you. Our parents are dead—our two, and all your founding mobster-godfathers of the Forties and Fifties. When I turned my back on you, did I do it out of terrible hurt—or was it shame?

Lady Las Vegas, we share special memories that only the two of us have. I'm 51 and you're 91. Neither of us is getting any younger. For years, I've had no forgiveness in my heart for you. I thought you did me wrong, but was it your fault? Has your life been as easy as I imagined? Who are you, really? Was my family your victims, or were they responsible for their fate? How much influence does a city have on its residents, or do no rules apply when that city is Las Vegas?

Can we finally love each other again, or is it too late for us? How have you survived and prospered against tremendous odds all these years? Where do you get your strength, your tenacity?

Can we give each other a second chance? We've got to try, because life is for the living, and Lady Las Vegas, you're all I have left. You're my sister and my hometown. I need to know you.

*THE FIRST SIGNS
OF LIFE IN THE DESERT.*

BEFORE THEY THREW THE DICE

My town was young when I was. Although the Lady was 40 when I was born, she had the youth and vigor of a teenager; she had been revitalized by her affair with my dad and his friends. Other cities were already creaking with age. Cities in the east were crumbling, ready for gentrification, but my town was just getting started; expansion was in her soul. She was so accepting, so affirming with sunny weather every day. I could hardly believe that other cities punished you with tears and snow and ice half the year, made you fight for your survival. Life was supposed to be easy, relax, enjoy!

All of Las Vegas's early history was still evident when I grew up there in the late Forties and Fifties. Looking back through my dusty memories, I can see the connection between the Vegas I knew and her geological origins. I can feel the importance of the Native American Paiutes to the land and the old Western forts and trails that abounded from wagon-train days. When I was living there, the Mormons ran the casinos for us and sold the real estate.

The city still had a very real connection to its past and the people who had tamed her. In 1950, walking with my mother in the area where the Strip is now, as part of a field trip for my kindergarten class, we would find arrowheads and unusually beautiful rocks that looked like they had come from some bygone era. My favorite rock was purple crystal that refracted into a million sparkling bolts of lightning when I held it up to my lamp. My favorite shop in the town was the rock shop at the Last Frontier Hotel. It never seemed strange that I lived in the desert; it was all I knew. Kangaroo rats and the fear of scorpions were part of my daily life.

Every Christmas, I remember, my dad would put my mom and I on the train to go to her home in St. Paul. The Twin Cities looked strange to me; tall, old buildings; no desert; and snow, which I was scared of. I'd come back home and tell my friends about snow but no one could fathom it. It finally snowed for a day when I was seven. We stayed home from school to gaze at this wonder of the world. We tried to catch it as it glided to the ground, barely sticking around in such unfamiliar terrain. It was the biggest news in town for months.

In the early Fifties, my father took my mother and me to New York for a week. He wanted to bring "Guys and Dolls" to the Flamingo; it was the beginning of the production shows. In New York City, I saw skyscrapers, the Empire State Building, subways; my father took us everywhere.

I loved it but it wasn't real. This was an imagined city with animated people, and once we left I was sure it existed only in my mind. No, real cities were open and never-ending like my hometown, with flat, pink endless skylines in the afternoon. In real cities, at nine in the evening you could go into your backyard and see a big yellow searchlight from a Strip hotel and run in and out of the flickering beam. Real cities had desert dust and cottonwood blowing off the trees in your face and were surrounded by deep purple mountains. A feeling of comfort suffuses me when I am in open desert; the cities of our childhood are the cities of our heart.

Before Lady Las Vegas developed her permanent dark allure in the Forties, before the gangsters and mobsters bestowed on her that mantle of timeless fascination, she had had trouble with all of her suitors. It had caused her no end of pain—because what good is a lady who can't hold on to her man? Various peoples and economies flirted with her but never spent the night. No wonder she was so happy to see the mobsters of the Forties. They were solid men, men you could count on. They valued her for who she was, and more important, who she could be.

"Paris is on a river, New York is on the Atlantic, San Francisco is on the Pacific. Chicago's on a lake. There's reasons for everything. There's no reason for Las Vegas—no reason the place should be there," says writer and director Rod Amateau.

Half a billion years ago Nevada was under water. During the Paleozoic era 340 million years ago, violent episodes of uplift raised the ocean floor, drained the sea, and left towering mesas and level plains. Over the next 260 million years the shape of Nevada's land was continually altered by cataclysmic extinctions, volcanic activity and climatic crises. Seventeen million years ago, tectonic forces created the general landscape of the basins and ranges that can be seen today.

Four great ice ages, roughly two million years ago, carved out Nevada's geography. By the end of the last ice age, Las Vegas valley had the shape it retains today, long and flat, cutting a diagonal 18 by 26 miles across Clark County at Nevada's southern tip.

Throughout these formative years, Las Vegas had been above and below water many times, as evidenced by the marine fossils in the hills and mountains surrounding her. Thousands of years ago there were the great inland lakes, and the White River was a huge fresh water river that ran through the area. But the water left, and that has remained a problem for her to this day. Did her water evaporate as a result of global warming or did something magical, mystical, very Vegas happen?

Author and Vegas expert Michael Ventura visited Nevada's Natural History Museum. "They have this wonderful relief map of what Nevada was like 30,000 years ago. That's not a long time geologically, but the Atlantic coast was almost exactly the way it is today, the Midwest is the way it is today, but Nevada had all these lakes and all these animals. And all these lakes 'drained suddenly,' quote unquote.

"All these lakes 'drained suddenly'. This is a very threatening fact as far as I'm concerned. What does that mean, drained suddenly? They don't know. Did the developers do it? Was there a hole in the ozone? Something to pin on a bad guy? No. The planet just said, `I'm tired of all these mammoths and camels and giant sloths and saber-tooth tigers and vegetation. I'm draining all this suddenly.' That means to me that this place was wild, this place was strange before we got here."

Strange, but perhaps the only city in America where we wouldn't be surprised to see mammoths and sloths walking around. We'd just figure Vegas impresario Steve Wynn found them and, with the sheer force of his personality, talked them into signing a contract at the Mirage. "We've got tigers, we've got a volcano, we've got a circus, you'll love it, I'll give you your own habitat. Why do you want to remain extinct? That's no fun. Where are you going to get a better deal?"

Now her sun is so cruel that even leathery lizards hide from its glare. Her wind is hot, relentless, her air is sandy and parched. Only skeletal remains of that primordial time testify to the original watery birth of this

THE PAIUTE INDIANS HAVE SHARED THE HARSH TERRAIN OF NEVADA WITH SPANISH MISSIONARIES, MEXICAN FUR-TRADERS, AMERICAN EXPLORERS AND, EVENTUALLY, THE MORMONS.

valley. A nurturing, lush lake region with thick greenery that nourished ancient beasts seems almost a dream.

She was hot, dry, and inhospitable to guests. Her isolated existence proved too lonely for her. One who has been loved and abandoned always seeks that love again. Men had marveled at her lush beauty, but could she win back that love now that her physical appearance was lackluster? She seduced a lake to move right in with her, under her valley, recharged by rain running off the ranges. Underground pressure forced the water up as a series of tantalizing springs.

She was queen of the desert now with no nearby competition, the only oasis for miles. She simply bloomed with all the attention, based in part on the fact that she is one of the most geographically isolated major cities in the continental United States. Los Angeles is 270 miles to the southwest, Salt Lake City is 420 miles to the north, Phoenix is 290 miles to the south. Except for the Las Vegas Wash, which drains into Lake Mead to the east, her valley is an enclosed system protected by mountain ranges.

These artesian wells created an oasis of tall grass, cottonwoods and creeks. The first Spanish explorers who discovered this life-giving oasis called it "Las Vegas," which means "The Meadows." But even with her comely attributes and charms, she had trouble getting a commitment. The first insincere lovers to leave her were the Clovis people, nomadic hunters and gatherers who lived throughout North and South America at the time. They hunted those mammoths and sloths until they became extinct. Expeditions to Tule Springs, an archaeological site in eastern Las Vegas valley, have uncovered relics from this culture.

She had a series of affairs with various Native American tribes after the Clovis. Human habitation varied with the climate; sometimes she was just too hot to handle. One of her memorable paramours was the Mojave Desert people, but after promising her the moon, they decided she was too much trouble. They left her for a valley they deemed better endowed and took the moon with them. After that a few more Native American cultures made a date with her but stood her up.

Way back when, no one remembers the exact year of the first date, the Southern Paiute came to stay. They were easy-going with low expectations of comfort. In fact, approximately 66 of them still live there today. They pride themselves on being adaptable and being survivors like the city they chose to live in.

The Paiutes moved back and forth between ecological zones according to the time of year. They preferred to be vegetarians but hunted rabbit if necessary and deer or sheep in high country. In low country, they ate tortoises and lizards. Whatever Las Vegas gave them was good enough. They weren't shopping for a better deal.

The Paiute religion has no structure, no deity; everything natural is considered sacred. The religion focuses on celebrating the dominant seasonal conditions. Lady Las Vegas liked their laissez-faire ways. They believe in living with the land rather than conquering it. They survived by flexible, seasonal gathering and even cultivated small plots of land when it was possible. They were a gentle people, in contrast to the warlike Apache and Sioux.

"The Las Vegas Paiute tribe has been in the area since time immemorial. We had a fairly large land base that extended from Death Valley all the way down into the Colorado River, into the southern part of Arizona and southern part of California. We were a migratory people," says Alfreda Mitre, the Charitable Chairperson of the Las Vegas Paiute tribe.

"We are famous for survival. It takes a lot for people to survive in a very harsh environment with little water and very low vegetation, and we had a very good command of the environment. We used the environment in a sacred way."

"The Paiutes were very tough, very hardy; they could endure through the heat. They had certain cultural habits that enabled them to avoid the heat of the day," says Dr. Martha Knack, professor of anthropology at the University of Nevada, Las Vegas.

"They were up at dawn, working, and rested in the shade during the highest point of the day. During full moons, they'd work all night long gathering food or traveling from one place to another. They built alliances with other tribes that included periodic exchange of resources. They were very surprised when the Euro-Americans arrived and wanted not to move in and share, but to move in and take over, which was an entirely different philosophical approach to life in the desert."

The Paiutes' first contact with Europeans was in 1776. Two Franciscan friars from Mexico, a Spanish colony, blazed the Old Spanish Trail. The leader of the expedition was Father Silvestre Escalante, who established the eastern end of the trail from Santa Fe, New Mexico, to the southwest corner of Utah. At the other end, Father Francisco Garces traveled toward him through California and Arizona. Garces encountered the Paiutes, who treated him very hospitably.

In the 1820s, explorers like the American fur trapper Jedediah Smith followed the trail and established Nevada as the new gateway to Southern California. It was frequented by the Spanish and Mexican explorers of the late 18th and early 19th century.

Mexican trader Antonio Armijo's 1829-1830 expedition went along the Spanish Trail from Santa Fe to Los Angeles. It was during this expedition that a young scout, Rafael Rivera, left the group and became the first non-Indian to find the springs of Las Vegas.

This discovery opened the Old Spanish Trail as a trade route. Traders could make the journey more frequently because of Lady Las Vegas's life-giving springs. The traders and travelers camped at Paiute homesites, and their stock damaged the delicate plant life. They shot game and depleted the land's resources; they shot at the Paiutes and even kidnapped their children and sold them as slaves in Mexico and California.

The famed explorer/surveyor John C. Fremont led an overland expedition west and camped at Las Vegas Springs in 1844. It was now a popular watering hole for wagon trains going west. He considered the Paiutes "humanity in its lowest form and most elementary state." He insisted they stole food and ate roots, giving them the derogatory term, "diggers."

In the early 1850s, the only other people besides the Paiutes who could tolerate a lasting relationship with the sultry city came along, but even they abandoned her for a time before settling in. They were the Mormons, who had a hard time getting along with their neighbors. They believed theirs was the only true church. They practiced what was looked upon by outsiders as a form of communism and dabbled in alternatives to monogamous marriage. After persecution drove them out of Ohio, Missouri, and Illinois, and after the murder of their prophet, Joseph Smith, the Mormons turned toward the unsettled West.

They came in the 1850s to settle and had a policy of identifying certain men to act as missionaries with the Indians. They were bent on religious conversion but also had a secondary function of political pacification. They wanted to make certain the Indians stayed friendly. They served as intermediaries every time a squabble broke out between Indians and settlers.

"By the time the Mormon Fort was established in Las Vegas in 1855, there was already a well-established Mormon settlement in San Bernandino, California. The Indians were glad to see the Mormons because they had a commitment to them and considered them the chosen people. After the Indians' contact with other white men, especially Spaniards, they needed the protection of the Mormons. They listened to the preaching of the Mormons and stole whatever they could," says Dr. Leo Lyman, a history instructor at Victor Valley College in Victorville, California, and a ninth-generation Mormon.

Settling Las Vegas was part of Mormon President Brigham Young's master plan to establish the great state of Deseret, with boundaries that would enclose the Southwest from the Rockies to the Pacific. He hoped his missionaries could colonize the Las Vegas valley. But the U.S. Congress thwarted the plan, and the state of Deseret never took place. It turned out that the Mormon colony in Las Vegas was more successful at irrigating the land than converting the Indians. The desert was more willing to cohabitate with the Mormons than the Indians were.

"The Mormon leader John Steel organized an expedition to look for lead. So the Mormons discovered a lead mine and got into mining. But Brigham Young did not clearly distinguish between missionary work and mining, and the mining began to dominate. They discovered silver but gradually the whole enterprise was disbanded with Brigham's last order being to bring back as much lead as you can," Lyman says.

When the Mormons disbanded in dissension over how to run the nearby Potosi lead mine, the first colonial attempt to tame the Meadows had failed. But there were lasting benefits of Mormon occupation.

"They proved that people can live here. They proved that the Indians can be coexisted with. There was then a mining rush to Potosi," Lyman says.

Southern Nevada's mines then prospered. Starting in 1859, the precious silver in the Comstock Lode lured hundreds more fortune-hunters to the desert.

"People came pouring over the border from California in the fashion that they have ever since Nevada was created as a result of the Comstock Lode. It was created to serve a colonial purpose," says Hal Rothman, historian at the University of Nevada-Las Vegas.

"Abraham Lincoln needed a state to assure his reelection in 1864 and boom, presto, they created Nevada. That's why they called it the 'Battle Born State,' because it was created during the Civil War. They needed the silver money in Nevada for the Civil War," says Michael Ventura. "Now you need something like 200,000 signatures or 200,000 people in a place to be a state. They kind of waived that for Nevada. They broke the law to make Nevada a state, and Nevada has been breaking laws ever since."

The miners stimulated a ranching economy since they did not want to grow their own food; they were willing to exchange their food for beef and grains. The new ranchers were Las Vegas's first permanent settlers, and these ranchers struck pay dirt by selling goods to the miners.

"When a lot of the land grabs occurred, there was a tremendous amount of conflict because water was very important," says Alfreda Mitre. "Once settlers came into the area they fenced off springs, they fenced off major water sources for our tribes. It changed the whole way of life."

When the reservation was created, the migratory Paiutes were prevented from traveling. They were kept like animals in a zoo, dependent on their caretakers, the federal government, to feed them. By 1900, the number of Paiutes in the Las Vegas area was only a fraction of what it had been before the arrival of the whites, because of fighting, white man's disease, and disruption.

Their ancestral lands taken, their sacred watering sources gone, some Paiutes went to work for ranchers. One of these, Helen J. Stewart, would later play an integral role in the tribe's future by deeding them 110 acres of her land in 1911. It would be their only legal land base until 1975. She sold the land to the Bureau of Indian Affairs for $500, wanting to insure that the Indians would have a place in the expanding city of Las Vegas.

One gold miner became famous. Octavius Decatur (O.D.) Gass settled near the big springs in Las Vegas valley in 1865 and built a ranch and shop inside the decaying Mormon Fort. The Gass family farmed 640 acres, and by the 1870s Gass had bought most of the homesteaded land in the valley and owned the rights to most of the water.

Mining and ranching changed the face of the valley, but the greatest force of change for Las Vegas was the advent of the railroad. After years of bitter rivalry between cutthroat railroad tycoons, including a scuffle with sticks and shovel handles at the mouth of a contested tunnel, Montana Senator Williams Andrews Clark inaugurated his San Pedro, Los Angeles, and Salt Lake Railroad on January 20, 1905, and began laying plans for a train-stop town. It took 35 years and six railroad companies to complete the track that linked Salt Lake City to Los Angeles built on the old Mormon trail.

FIRST TRAIN TO VEGAS FROM L.A., 1905.

AUCTION OF VEGAS TOWNSITE LOTS AT N. MAIN AND OGDEN STREETS, 1905.

Ed Von Tobel, Jr., owned the lumber store when I grew up. My dad and all his friends were far too citified to do any improvements on their own homes so they drove their hotel workmen down to Von Tobel's Lumber Store and purchased the goods. I remember the store well; we were always there when my parents built me a separate playroom in back of our house on South Sixth Street. My dad was tired of coming home from the graveyard shift at 4 a.m. and falling over all my "dress up" clothes in the living room. There was barely any room left for Lou to sit in his chair since my room had expanded into the living room. My play area was moved to my own house out back.

"My father was born and raised in Illinois but came out to California in 1905. He saw these full-page ads in the *Los Angeles Times* that the railroad was forming the town and that there were lots for sale at auction," says Von Tobel, Jr.

"So he and his buddy decided to come up on that train just for the excitement of it. They visited the tent city that was just forming at that time. The train was parked on a siding so they were able to stay overnight in the railroad car."

The railroad wasn't the only organization offering lots for sale. Some residents wanted to cash in on the coming boom. One was railroad surveyor John McWilliams, who discovered and laid claim to 80 untitled acres. He advertised lots for sale, which he dubbed the "Original Las Vegas Townsite" (between Washington and Bonanza bounded by "A" and "H" streets).

An ad running in the *Las Vegas Age* on May 6, 1905, nine days before the railroad auction, stated that "The first regular train on The Salt Lake Route, Tuesday May 2nd, brought scores of investors to Las Vegas, Nevada. The real rush for lots has now commenced. Splendid climate and pure water. Our prices are from $100 to $200 for first-class business lots, $250 for corners." By the time the first train arrived, the Las Vegas townsite called Ragtown had 1,500 people, weekly newspapers, a tent hotel, and merchants.

Von Tobel, Jr.'s dad was swept away by the enthusiasm of the railroad auction held at the north corner of Fremont and Main, where today's Plaza Hotel stands.

"On the second day, they were offering a bargain on the sale of lots, and their railroad fare, which was $25 dollars roundtrip, would apply to the down payment on a lot. At those auctions, it was 105 or 106 degrees. There was quite a crowd of people there. Most of the men were wearing string ties and suits and hats. It must have been miserable for them the first day they were selling lots on Fremont Street, which was the main area, then the second day they started selling off other lots."

FREMONT STREET.

The auction sold lots for as little as $900 an acre. Within 24 hours new owners began building, announcing tent stores open for business. After two days, it was all over. Las Vegas had became a boomtown overnight.

"My dad thought, 'Heck, I got nothing to lose,' so he signed up for a business lot and later he decided this would be a good town for him," says Von Tobel, Jr. "He set up a little lumber yard on the lot. There were going to be customers there, the railroad was starting to build a town. He met my mother at an Elks dance, they both spoke German, his parents were from Switzerland. After a while they got married and started a family here.

"When I was growing up we knew everybody in town. It was only a couple thousand people. It was dusty, and when the wind would blow, why my mother'd almost blow her top, because there was so much dust. There were no paved streets. The town had some businessmen that were trying to stir up business. They were trying to get better roads into Las Vegas so that we could get some tourists in here. The year 1924 was the year we had the first paved street. I was only about ten years old, but that was a great day for me because I could ride my bike on the pavement."

The boom of the young railroad town peaked in 1915 when round-the-clock electricity was supplied to residents. The town was totally dependent on the railroad for economic survival. Population had doubled between 1911 and 1913; it was now 3,000 people. But in 1917, the Las Vegas and Tonopah Railroad suspended operations, and the town went into a slow decline as workers were laid off. By 1920, the population had dropped to 2,300. In 1921, Union Pacific bought the railroad.

The old management ran the town like a company store, but the new management in New York barely knew Las Vegas existed. The railroad workers joined the national railroad strike in 1922; scabs were brought in and violence erupted many times. When it was settled, the railroad punished the town by closing its repair shops and eliminating hundreds more jobs.

Somehow, Las Vegas survived. But with a lack of agricultural resources and mines, no industry, and the loss of so many railroad jobs, the town had to have something else to attract people. Las Vegas tried routing a highway through town connecting Los Angeles and Salt Lake City. It brought tourists to the town but that didn't do the trick. The town's first airport, Rockwell Field, was also completed in the 1920s.

The town was at a low, still without long-distance telephone service. Telegraph messages had to be sent along the railroad's private wires. To travel to the state capital at Carson City or go to Reno, residents had to take the train as there wasn't even a proper road for cars.

The key to Las Vegas's reincarnation was Hoover Dam.

I remember how it looked so gigantic, the sounds of rushing water so loud. Our 1950s adrenaline soared as we went down into the dam in the elevator much like this generation of Vegas's five-year-olds must feel as they experience the theme park rides.

We Vegas kids knew from all the photographs that there was history attached to the dam, but it was not until many years later that I realized Hoover Dam was Lady Las Vegas's man of the moment when she desperately needed one.

After the railroad strike of 1922, the impatient drifted away from the seedy little town, seeking their next opportunity to get rich quick, but die-hard Vegans hung on, pinning all their hopes for salvation on the federal government and Hoover Dam. If the dam was approved, it would be the only economic opportunity in a town of hardscrabble drifters and grubby prospectors.

"It was in 1905, 1906, 1907 that the Colorado River jumped its banks and began flowing into the Imperial Valley. It began damaging property—millions of dollars in damage, crop destruction, people drowned," says author and historian Dennis McBride.

"That's when they began sending more serious expeditions to the river looking for a spot to build a dam."

The original site for the dam was Boulder Canyon, hence the name, "The Boulder Canyon Project." But Boulder Canyon was fractured with faults. Just down the river Black Canyon was a safer site, much closer to Las Vegas. After years of surveys and endless red tape, President Calvin Coolidge signed the dam bill into law on December 21, 1928. The next day Las Vegans trekked through the desert to the banks of the Colorado River to give a mass prayer of thanks.

"The chances are very strong that Las Vegas could have become a ghost town in the 1920s," says Hal Rothman. "Without air conditioning Las Vegas is almost uninhabitable in the summertime." The key to that air conditioning was the electricity from the dam.

While the rest of the nation choked in the grip of the depression, the party town that Las Vegas would become was beginning to take shape.

Gambling had prospered in Nevada since its territorial days. After Nevada became a state in 1864, it instituted gambling license fees for all gambling houses in 1869. As mining gradually died at the end of the 19th century, Nevada became more dependent on gambling. At the turn of the 20th century, mining boomed again with new discoveries of gold, silver, and copper ore. Nevada, amid a wave of national reform, seeking other states' respect, outlawed gambling in 1910.

Gambling then boomed, illegally, and a brotherhood of drinkers (it was during Prohibition) and gamblers emerged. The state suffered from the lack of gambling revenue and payoffs, and corruption flourished.

A movement to legalize gambling again gained momentum. This was done partly as an answer to the nationwide depression and partly to control the unsavory atmosphere that had arisen since it was outlawed. Nevadans were tired of the rigged games, cheating, and back-room gambling that was the rule.

According to Deke Castleman's *Las Vegas*, "On February 13, 1931, Republican Philip Tobin, a rancher from Winnemucca, introduced the bill that provided for the licensing of gambling houses, and the collection of fees ($25 per gaming table and $10 per slot machine) by the county sheriffs. Professional gamblers then took charge of Nevada's gambling." And they have been running it ever since.

In 1931, the year dam construction began, another landmark event occurred—divorce laws were liberalized, making Nevada a mecca for spouses with regrets. At the same time, her most infamous neighborhood, a legend since the city's 1905 inception, the "Red Light District," also known as "Block 16," became a huge attraction.

"North First Street was the only street where you could sell liquor. And it just happened that when they put in the saloons they also brought in some of the girls. The girls were regulated and they had to go to the city doctor once a week for examinations and so forth," remembers Ed Von Tobel, Jr. "We lived on North Third Street and quite often in the night time we could hear the rinka-dink piano playing."

Block 16 soon became one of the most famous centers of prostitution in the West, and its notoriety spread all the way to Washington, which prompted Hoover's Secretary of the Interior, Raymond Lyman Wilbur, to personally investigate the den of iniquity called Las Vegas before he would commit to lodge 5,000 temptation-prone dam workers there.

"The city fathers in Las Vegas said, 'Look, we're gonna shut down Block 16. We're gonna close up the saloons and the bars when he comes because we don't want him to think that we're as loose and wide open as we are,'" says Dennis McBride.

"Their little ploy didn't work; Ray Lyman Wilbur wasn't fooled," says Guy Rocha, Nevada State Archivist. Wilbur announced, "The dam workers are not going to live in that sin hole called Las Vegas. We're building Boulder City."

The government built Boulder City ten miles from the dam site and declared it a federal reservation—under federal, not state, law. A

THE "GIRLIES" OF BLOCK 16.

man couldn't drink, couldn't gamble and, if he was single, had to bed down alone. But the dam workers flocked to Block 16, where the red-light cathouses promised relaxation and release in exchange for those Hoover Dam paychecks.

Hoover Dam was referred to as the eighth wonder of the world, but the architectural masterpiece took its toll in sweat and blood. The tortuous life-threatening work was often inhumane and cruel.

CONSTRUCTION BEGINS ON THE HOOVER DAM, 1931.

"The heat ordinarily in this part of the country can easily go up to 115 or 120. Down in the canyon between those rock walls where the heat is trapped they took temperature readings upward of 140 degrees, and the men were working in that and many of them passed out and died," says McBride. "The workers in those first two years were really living and working like slaves."

Conditions improved somewhat as construction continued, but dangers lingered just the same. Highscalers, hanging precariously by a rope on a fragile bosun's chair, plunged 600 feet to their deaths. Boulders fell, cables snapped, and poisonous exhaust fumes in the diversion tunnels destroyed the lungs of hundreds who never figured in the death rosters.

After President Roosevelt dedicated the dam in September of 1935, a monument was raised to the 112 men who died on site. That was the official number—but hundreds more probably died dam-related deaths.

"That was the depression, and you had a good job and it was payin' you and you had a good bed and a place to eat," says John Stafford, who worked on the dam. "What more could you want to ask for? We was all kind of hatin' to see it end."

When the dam was finished, Vegas went into a decline again. Fair-weather flirts deserted Lady Las Vegas for less hostile environments and more civilized cities. Lady Las Vegas used her imagination to attract tourists. First she created the wild and woolly "Helldorado Days" in 1935, an "anything goes" kind of revelry invoking the spirit of the lawless Wild West.

The Helldorado parade survives even now. It's a big town parade with hotel floats, high school marching bands, and many organizations, some with horseback riders. Every year when I was growing up, I was on the Flamingo Hotel's float, then later the Riviera's float. One year I was a butterfly, attached to big wire wings, feeling faint as the float crawled down Fremont Street, searching the windows of the El Cortez until I saw my parents waving from a room. Another year the float had a bathing beauty motif, and I was a diver.

More divorcées than ever flocked to the town, waiting out the six-week requirement at the dude ranches on Highway 91. Among the famous to untie the knot were Clark Gable and his wife Ria in 1939, and by 1941 the city was hosting over a thousand breakups a year.

But the town needed a strong economic base again. World War II solved the problem. America needed raw materials and manpower to win the war, and southern Nevada found access to both. Proximity to magnesium ore made Nevada home to mines that became BMI, Basic Magnesium Incorporated. Outside Vegas, virgin land became a gunnery range, later Nellis Air Force Base that churned out 4,000 soldiers ready for combat every six weeks. As part of the war effort, in an attempt to protect our boys in uniform, the U.S. government pressured Vegas to close down Block 16.

"If Vegas wouldn't cooperate, and if Clark County wouldn't cooperate, they would have declared the town off limits to military personnel. It was a hostage situation, they held the community hostage," says Guy Rocha. "Las Vegasjust said, well, for the sake of the war effort, we need that economy. We'll stick it out through the course of the war."

"There was a final big party, one last fling, champagne, a lot of the old-timers," he continues. "Everybody saying good-bye, the sun comes up, the girls get on the train, the men wave good-bye and we go off and fight the war."

"The end of the World War II brought the same set of questions to Las Vegas as it brought to everybody else in the nation. What could this little town really do?" asks Hal Rothman.

Ben Siegel, my father, and all their friends had an idea just what Lady Las Vegas could do, and they knew how to make that happen. It was these mobsters and gangsters that would finally give her the stability she so desperately craved. Even though the war years had fueled the economy, the war was now over. The casino owners downtown were the richest men in town. Siegel and his partners were no fools; they saw that gambling worked well in Las Vegas. My father and many of his friends returned from war service to towns that were reform-minded, bent on cleaning up gambling and racketeering within their city borders.

Men who were open to anything needed a town that agreed. Jewish and Italian gamblers heard the cry of Lady Las Vegas, got out their maps, located Nevada, and made room reservations at the El Rancho on the Strip. They took silver and canvas suitcases full of cash and told their wives they would call within a week about when they would return home. But a month later, when they called, it was to tell their shocked wives to pack up and get on the train, they were moving to Las Vegas.

A SUNNY PLACE FOR SHADY PEOPLE

The Las Vegas pioneers of the Forties came not by stagecoach, but by shiny black Coupe de Ville Cadillacs with "swamp coolers"—sandbag air-conditioners—hanging out the windows. They worried more about getting horse manure on their immaculately shined black-and-white wingtips than about danger from the dwindling Paiute tribe who looked on as they parked their fancy cars next to the horses at the downtown hitching posts.

The mobsters and gangsters who were the godfathers of Las Vegas were men in their 40s, seasoned men, dark men, Jewish men, Italian men, men with cigarettes held in their manicured fingernails and hanging from their lips—even the ashes stood at attention waiting for permission to fall off, because these men were powerful men, big bosses, and you didn't disobey.

These rough-hewn men were careful about their appearance; they hid their rough edges by always smelling of Zizane and dressing fashionably in brown or gray pin-striped suits with wide lapels. These men changed their shirts three times a day to keep dry in the heat.

Back home they were tarnished, they were soiled, and they had only this one chance, this one last chance to make a legal living; and they were determined to do it right. They came out here to the wild, Wild West, where the land was considered wilder than they were, where the "bad guys" were the climate, the black widows, and the scorpions; and they were the good guys who would bring cash to a dying town.

They came because Las Vegas was their Holy Grail. The only trade they knew was legal here. Gambling was sanctioned; there were no political payoffs, no busts. Here and only here they could make gambling pay and pay big. The whole country might legalize gambling after the war, and they wanted to be at the center of the action.

These were men who greeted each sunrise with surprise that they were still alive, men who lived precarious, dangerous lives, men who never thought they would live to retire. They fought poverty and the concomitant illnesses and sadnesses that always accompany life at the bottom of society. Somehow, they survived, blaming it on God or fate since most of their families and friends had not been so lucky, and remarked that each day could be their last and that you had to live life with "no regrets."

They had tossed a good turn of the dice, and maybe they would make it for a few years longer. They had wives now and some had babies; they needed a whole new life. These were men who grew up in the Mob and learned how to back up their business with a gun, but they were tired of that now. They were tired of killing and being killed, tired of arguing, tired of going to prison.

They were middle-aged Americans, although they called themselves "the Boys," and they wanted a piece of the American pie. They came from distant shores and knew that this was a land of opportunity. That was the thing about America, anything was possible; they could reinvent themselves by guts, determination, and hard work. This was their America, and they wanted to own it. Their earlier lives had been as harsh as the prairies and as ugly as the tenements in which their immigrant fathers had struggled in vain to make a living.

They had grown up with no opportunity, fighting to grab someone else's territory for their own. They grew up fitting not into the country's rules but into Mob rules where they were one level under their strict and unforgiving bosses—Meyer Lansky, Frank Costello, Joe Adonis, and Lucky Luciano—who had the advantage of being one generation ahead of them.

These men proved their mettle; they did what they were told. They were watched and had to watch their backs; and loyalties ran deep, and commitments ran true. Always they were the young guys, they were the lieutenants who did their bosses' bidding. But Vegas was open, a place they could make the rules as long as they gave their bosses the skim.

The desert heat with its sun was too strong for Lansky's asthma. At first he thought Siegel was crazy and said he should concentrate on developing dog-racing in Omaha before Bugsy changed his mind. Luciano and Adonis didn't want to leave New York for even a minute to work this wide open desert town, and Costello was not leaving Chicago. Let the young guys give it a whirl, give 'em some freedom; they would make money anyway by financing the deal.

There was one problem with the future mecca of gambling—location, location, location. Would dusty dice in an isolated town draw action? Not to mention climate, but could that Vegas sun ever cook! One of the Boys actually tried frying an egg on the sidewalk in 110-degree heat; it cooked sunny-side up. But after all, Vegas was a straight shot down the highway from Los Angeles; if the mobsters gave a continuing party there, surely everyone would come. There had been a recent crackdown on vice in Los Angeles, and vice had moved to Vegas so they had a monopoly on nighttime entertainment. The Mayor elected in 1938 in L.A., Fletcher Bowron, outlawed gambling, which started the L.A. gamblers' exodus to Vegas, where there were a few sawdust joints with donkey acts in the casinos downtown.

The future godfathers of Vegas looked at these and said, we wanna give this place class! Let's lose the Western vibe, the sawdust! Plus, with all this open desert, a major airport could be built so that Western Airlines can fly thousands of tourists into the gambling mecca.

THE FIRST AIR DEPOT, BUILT IN 1926 ON PARADISE ROAD.
IT IS NOW THE SAHARA HOTEL PARKING LOT.

The mobsters looked up—blue sky, bright sun—they could build up! And they looked around—they could build out—all they needed was a financial foundation. And all they needed was respectability. They could only get it here.

So they'd buy their suits and shoes in New York and Los Angeles, and they'd go to doctors back in Minnesota's famed Rochester Clinic or at Cedars of Lebanon Hospital in L.A. Sure, there were no creature comforts here but hell, who cared? There was gold and silver in that there desert, and it was going to come calling. They'd import salami and bagels and lox from Los Angeles restaurants and delis and get their cigars from Cuba. If they wanted to see the ocean, they'd fly to Miami; they'd be in Hialeah for the races anyway, and maybe they'd try Del Mar Race Track closer to home in La Jolla soon. Yeah, it could work!

So they rented the navy-blue-trimmed white stucco bungalows in the El Rancho Hotel on the Strip where divorcées had recently been shedding their worst halves. It was the only place where you could get a phone during World War II in 1944, and the hotel operator was named Pearl. They picked up a black phone and asked Pearl to reach their beautiful shiksa Protestant wives in New York, Chicago, Minneapolis, Detroit, St. Louis, Omaha, and other spots due east. Jubilant and high on the future, they shouted into the phone, "Baby, get yourself on a train or a plane and come out here. This is where I'm gonna build you Paradise."

The character of Las Vegas was formed by these tough dandies who came from the streets and moved to a town that barely had any. They traded dark days of soot-colored snow for sunny cactus and kangaroo rats. They brought *sechel* and urbanity to a town that was being run by a few smart locals and a couple of imported Texas gamblers who walked around in cowboy boots and six-guns. Add several parts Paiute, lots of Mormon influence, and California emigrants who came in the Thirties to work there, and you have the modern town.

My dad, Davie Berman, owner of the Flamingo and Riviera Hotels and part owner of five more Strip and downtown hotels in the Forties and Fifties, was one of these Vegas visionaries. He had been a gangster and a mobster in his youth, and by the time I knew him he was a legitimate hotel owner in Las Vegas, as legitimate as he could be. Famous for his brains and diplomacy, he was known as the "Kissinger of Vegas" in the town where he chose to raise his family.

Born in 1903, in Odessa, Russia, to a poor rabbinical student, David Berman, and his wife Clara, a demanding Jewish princess and daughter of a lumber baron, my dad arrived at age four with his mother and three siblings,

EL RANCHO HOTEL ON U.S. HIGHWAY 91.

Lillian, Max, and Deana, at Ellis Island just like millions of other immigrants grateful to reach New York harbor. That lady with a torch spelled freedom from anti-Semitic Russian pogroms, and a place where Jews could own land.

It didn't matter that his mother Clara suffered a miscarriage on the ship, or that his father David hadn't struck it rich yet, working in a laundry in New York. He took his family, as part of the Baron de Hirsch assimilation experiment, to Ashley, North Dakota. The Baron hoped that Jews mingling with Gentiles in the great Midwest, learning to farm the soil side by side, would be an answer to the Jewish "problem."

My Zada (grandfather) only knew that it was a place he could borrow money from the Hebrew Aid Society and buy land. Bubbie (grandmother) Clara packed her steamer trunk full of crystal and china from her disenfranchised family in Russia, which would do her well in her hoped-for wealthy life.

The first few years in Ashley were anything but kind to the Berman family. Immigrants who preceded them to the Dakotas by 20 years had already claimed the better soil. The hardscrabble land they bought didn't grow crops with ease. David couldn't farm and became a *shochet*, a holy man who blessed chickens when he could find any to bless. Food was scarce; Clara and David buried two infants who died of malnutrition before they finally birthed a healthy third, baby Essie, later called Chickie because he played with the chickens they found.

Anti-Semitic German immigrants taunted them as "kikes" and burned down their farm. By the time my dad was eight, he and his four siblings were scattered to the shrill North Dakota wind living with foster families as their parents couldn't feed them.

My grandfather, trained in Talmud, able to do little else, now couldn't even feed his family; he felt terrible shame. He turned to drink and his wife to despair. The burden to reunite his family fell to my father, so he hopped a train to the nearest big city where he heard Jews could find jobs and hopped off in Sioux City, Iowa, in the dead of winter.

There, he found out that little Jewish boys could sell newspapers on cold snowy corners and, even better, could run errands for gangsters who came down from Chicago to gamble and hang out when the heat was on in the big city. It took him three months to save up the money to rent a horse and buggy and go back to Ashley and get his family back, lock, stock, and no barrel.

Displaying the strength, aggression, and pioneer spirit that would later enable him to help found Las Vegas, my father became the gangsters' favorite runner, their first pick to ride shotgun when they ran rum to Canada. The Dakotas and Iowa were stomping grounds for bootleggers. On almost any night Highway 75 north from Sioux City to Winnipeg was filled with long black cars, loaded with whiskey, making the three-day journey, and often as not there would be at least one hijacking attempt.

He was also the favorite to provide "security" for their crap games at the town hotel. As a teenager my father went to Chicago with them and saw men in fine clothes with plenty to eat. These men were mobsters. He wanted to be one.

So began his mob career. He rented his parents a home in the Jewish section of Sioux City and had his Bar Mitzvah at the brown shul. By age thirteen, he was attending school sporadically but getting straight As. The teachers told his parents he was brilliant. His dad worked for low wages in a bakery, and his mother kept them poorer than poor by buying furniture on time. By age sixteen, he had gotten kicked out of Central High for running crap games at lunch, but not before he distinguished himself as the class poet, writing an elegy to all his classmates who had left to fight in World War I.

By his early 20s, he was a full-time mobster who showed promise; he had already done time in the county jail for coordinating card-game

PLEASE POST.

Post Office Department
OFFICE OF INSPECTOR IN CHARGE
CHICAGO, ILLINOIS

Case No. 79571-[illegible]

October 20, 1926.

REWARD - $8,000.00

Wanted for Hold-up and Post Office Burglary

DAVE BERMAN, alias Dave the Jew; WILLIAM KANNER, alias Dutch Kanner, alias Jack C. Hooper, alias Dutch Hooper; CHARLES P. CLOUSE, alias Curly Clouse, alias Paul G. Hanford, alias [illegible] and REUBEN D. LILLY, alias Blackie Carter.

These men are wanted for the hold-up of the Assistant Postmaster and the fireman-laborer, with deadly weapons, and [illegible] burglary of the Post Office at Superior, Wisconsin, on the night of November 20, 1925. An indictment has been returned and [illegible] pending against these men in the Western District of Wisconsin.

DAVE BERMAN, alias Dave the Jew. Description: Age, 22; height, 5 feet 8½ inches; weight, 177 pounds; complexion,

WILLIAM KANNER, alias Dutch Kanner, alias Jack C. Hooper, alias Dutch Hooper. Description: Age, 27; height, 5 feet 9½ inches; weight, 170 pounds; complexion, [illegible] Black hair, brown eyes. Good dresser. Born in St. Paul, Minnesota.

MY DAD'S EARLY GIGS DIDN'T WORK OUT. HERE HE IS ON A 'WANTED' POSTER FOR POST-OFFICE BURGLARY.

holdups for the big Boys. In a "Wanted" poster for a Superior, Wisconsin, post-office robbery, there was a price on his head of "$8,000." The poster referred to him as "Dave the Jew." It described him as age 22, height 5 foot 8 and a half inches, weight 177 pounds, complexion, medium dark, black hair, brown eyes, born in Russia. At 22, in graduate school at the University of California at Berkeley, I looked almost exactly like he did in this poster but my hair was down to my waist.

In his early 20s, he was known as Frank Costello and Meyer Lansky's favorite boy, and he did their bidding well. This included fencing stolen bonds and kidnapping bootleggers for ransom. He was finally captured in a shoot-out in Central Park in which the FBI shot at him and killed his companion; he shot back, wounding an FBI man. When the FBI wanted him to cop a plea, he said, "Hell, the worst you can give me is life." He was 25.

The case continued to capture headlines as my father was questioned for 72 hours straight and didn't break. The tabloids yelled Berman can't be broken. He was sentenced to life in Sing Sing and did seven and a half years of hard time there. He got out for "good behavior and high IQ." He had been rehabilitated.

Meyer Lansky and his main man Little Moey Sedway sent their men to pick up Davie at Sing Sing and took him to a hotel in midtown Manhattan. There, they opened a safe, which contained a million bucks, and told him to take it; he had earned it for not turning in his bosses.

My dad said, "I don't want any of it, I just want money from your pockets to take a train home to my parents in Minneapolis, and I want to run the Twin Cities for you." That's exactly what he did, running the rackets for Lansky and Costello in Minneapolis and St. Paul for many years and making his bosses very happy.

When World War II broke out, he bribed his way into the Canadian Army; he wanted to kill the Nazis who were killing the Jews. He was too old to enlist in the U.S. Army, and he was a convicted felon.

He became a war hero, returning to Minneapolis after his near mortal wounds had healed and he was honorably discharged. But what to come home to? Minneapolis was cracking down on gambling, and his old friend Ben Siegel told him of a place out West where gambling was legal. His young wife, Gladys Evans (her tap-dancing stage name, born Elizabeth Lynell Ewald), soon became pregnant and he wanted better for his family.

So in 1944 he drove to Vegas with Ben from L.A., leaving his pregnant wife in Minneapolis with her folks until he scoped out the town. He got out of Ben's caddy on a hot November day; it was already freezing in Minneapolis. "Ben," he said, "it's 85 degrees out here, how bad could it ever be?"

Men just like him from all over the nation soon followed. In 1941, before my father came to Vegas, Ben Siegel's advance man Sedway and his men established the Trans America Wire Service, their race-wire service downtown.

By the time my dad and his friends Gus Greenbaum, Joe "Bowser" Rosenberg, Sam "Baby Shoes" Prezant, and others came to town, Lansky and Costello knew that their race-wire service was so lucrative that they needed a monopoly. The competing service, the Continental Wire Service, had to go. The boss of Continental, James Ragen, was gunned down in classic gangland style as he left his office in Chicago: A panel truck (what else?) pulled up and kaboom. But he didn't die and wound up in the hospital. My dad and

MY MOTHER, GLADYS EVANS, AND HER COUSIN LORELEI HJERMSTAD IN THEIR "ALPHABET SOUP" DANCE NUMBER.

his friends owned the Las Vegas Club downtown, and Gus Greenbaum, upon hearing the news that Ragen had lived, furiously walked to the phone in the pit.

"Solly," he said, "you didn't finish the job. Either Ragen dies or you do." Subsequently, Solly or others climbed five stories up a parapet in a Chicago hospital and shoved bichloride-of-mercury tablets (a metallic poison favored by the Mob in the Forties) down Ragen's throat. Then Solly called the club in Vegas.

Bowser took the call and crowed happily, "Ragen's dead, they slipped him the salt," to loud cheers and applause from my dad and his partners. This was cause for celebration. Three hours later all the Vegas mobsters gathered at the club for a celebration dinner; black chefs with high white hats brought silver tray after silver tray of buffet food into the pit. Ah, life in Vegas was good, and it was going to be even more lucrative now.

When my dad got there, in addition to the race-wire service, Ben had three clubs downtown, with big gambling profits now and a source of big-time money laundering for the future. All the clubs were near the train depot, the center of town. Other mobsters heard the cry of Vegas and began to stake their claim. One of the first was Benny Binion, the Texas gambler, who bought the Las Vegas Club and the Westerner Club, and later bought the Eldorado Club and renamed it the Horseshoe in 1951.

Gambling had been legalized in Nevada in 1931, and the first real nightclub, the Meadows Club along Boulder Highway on the outskirts of town, was started by L.A. gambler Tony Cornero, who had specialized in offshore gambling in L.A. Other locals staked a claim: Kell Houssells opened the Golden Camel; and Captain Guy McAfee, Commander of L.A.'s vice squad, gambler, and operator of many L.A. illegal gambling clubs, resigned and followed the cash to Vegas, purchasing the roadhouse, Pair O' Dice Club (later renamed Club 91). He and his brother built the Pioneer Club in 1946.

My dad's first club was the El Dorado Club, which he bought with his partners Joe Rosenberg and Baby Shoes Prezant. Then he went back to Minneapolis, raised more money and bought the El Cortez with Rosenberg, Baby Shoes, and Louis Hershenberg from Chicago. Siegel bought into the El Cortez with Davie, and then the two of them bought the Las Vegas Club and a few other clubs.

Davie's deal was usually the same in every club he owned downtown with Siegel. He was the pit boss, the manager, the "hands-on" boss; and he took 11 percent, Siegel had 25 percent and the east coast Mob bosses took the rest. He went back to Minneapolis on May 18, 1945, for my birth, and all his friends accompanied him. My grandmother Florence dutifully recorded each man's name and his present in my baby book.

My father met my mother when he was 36 and she was 18. She was a tap dancer, one half of a sister act in his Paradise Club in Minneapolis. Never a ladies' man like his younger brother Chickie, he hardly glanced up when Chickie said, "Davie, get a load of this next dancer," and my mother's feet started to fly across the stage in "Pennies from Heaven." When he did look up, he took a good look and said, "Chickie, I'm going to marry that girl." His word was always his bond, and a year later he did.

Six weeks after I was born, my mother and my grandmother Florence brought me to Las Vegas on the Southern Pacific. When the train stopped, my father and all his friends roared up in their caddies spewing dust everywhere. My beautiful 26-year-old mother, with her long shiny black hair and her matching black eyes, got off the train, shielding me from the hot July heat with a white baby blanket. She wore a white linen suit, black patent sandals and a white picture hat.

Her makeup was perfect: She had vaseline on her long black eyelashes, Revlon's Jack O'Diamonds red lipstick on her lips, and the same color on her fingernails and toes. She looked around at the parched sand; the only building was the small train station, the only vista that of endless desert. A piece of sand blew in her eye, and it began to water. My dad thought she was

MY PARENTS ON THEIR HONEYMOON IN SLOPPY JOE'S BAR IN HAVANA, CUBA. ON THE FAR LEFT IS CHARLES "CHICKIE" BERMAN, MY UNCLE. 1939.

crying and whipped out a monogrammed white hankie to wipe away that little tear.

"Baby, don't cry, you're gonna love it here," he said as she laughed and explained that it was just a grain of sand.

"But, Davie, is this all of it?" she asked, expecting, perhaps, something more like L.A. where she had been an Earl Carroll dancer on Sunset Strip during the war. He assured her that this town was going to be everything she could ever want; and he was her Davie and could do anything and so she believed him.

As much a part of my town as the Jewish and Italian fathers who raised us were our high-spirited shiksa mothers—gorgeous, thin, milk-skinned women from the Midwest, who followed their husbands to Vegas full of hopes and dreams. The reality of the town was as much a shock to them as the prairie of North Dakota was to my Russian grandmother. But our mothers gamely adopted Western attire, learned to ride horses up and down the strip, helped our dads start the first synagogue, and took part in town-pride events.

The first order of business for our mothers was finding homes that looked like the ones they had left behind in the Midwest. That was a very tall order since most of the houses available were little wood structures; there were no suburbs. There was simply a small, dusty city with a raggedy downtown, where 16,000 people lived and everyone knew each other; a new hotel Strip; and a ramshackle west side where the black employees of the hotels were forced to live in imposed segregation under an underpass called the Cement Curtain, after the Iron Curtain of the day.

In this cowboy town, men with grizzled beards, perpetual sunburns, sweaty underarms, and silver stirrups walked the streets. Grubby prospectors and down-on-their-luck gamblers looked up in amazement as my father and his friends brought their fancy suits and city manners to this cowpoke town. Gambling was rivaled only by the action at the Western Union office where cast-off mates waited for reprieves from their estranged spouses or at the wedding chapels that lined each end of the town.

There was plenty of open space in which to build if they so desired, but our mothers were used to cities and wanted to live close to each other. The word "ranch" did not exist in their vocabulary. Many residents lived in trailers and cinderblock houses, and there was an Indian reservation on the outskirts of town.

There was no opulent Spanish Trails area like today where Vegas millionaires live and the Sultan of Brunei is building his main residence. There were no luxurious gated golf course developments. There weren't even any

721 S. SIXTH STREET, THE HOUSE IN WHICH I GREW UP.

two-story houses that represented the Midwest stability my mother craved. My father and his friends would have been content to raise their families at the El Rancho; after all, there was room service. But the good wives said no, we need homes to raise our babies in.

So their husbands, running the town from the downtown clubs, said to find houses midway between downtown and the Strip, because any day now, as soon as the opportunity arises, we are going to be Strip hotel owners; that's where the real money will be.

They moved to South Sixth Street, bought little houses side by side, block by block, hoping to find a sense of community through proximity. My mother called the realtor—there was only one in town—and found the only Tudor-style house: small, brown-and-white, with two bedrooms and two baths, which my father paid $7,000 cash for in 1945. It had a fireplace in the living room, maybe the only available fireplace at that time.

They stayed in the El Rancho bungalows while the contractors renovated the houses based on the identities the men had left behind and the shadows they had always lived under. There could be no windows in the baby's room below eye level and only one door. Until the mobsters made the town safe, they wanted to take no chance of gangland bullets in their windows.

Full-length mirrors on the bathroom doors and huge closets were added because these people cared about appearance; no worn jeans and perspiration-stained cowboy shirts for them. Mobsters and mobsters' wives had ready cash that they couldn't show, ready cash that had to be spent, so they were able to buy the high style to fit their expensive taste.

The day they moved in, I was eight months old. My father had bought my mother her dream home in Minneapolis just two years before so she had furniture and china to die for, but she stored it in her parents' St. Paul basement until she was sure she could live in this new town. Now she had her mother bring all their belongings out on the train, and they worked for weeks to make perfect curtains for the little dream house.

Our mothers were warned about the black widows ("they have a red spot on their underside and they are poisonous!"), the scorpions, and the heat ("sunstroke" a definite possibility!). Mothballs were everywhere because silverfish could eat your mink coats.

Hotel gardeners were dispatched to seed instant grass, and it magically appeared only a few weeks later. What had been crabgrass and dirt patches was now dewy, soft-green grass. One of my mother Gladys's main concerns was landscaping options—happy families had brightly colored flowers. What would grow here? After various failed experiments, roses, Birds of Paradise, and purple irises responded to her green thumb. She exulted in the gigantic, gnarled cottonwood tree in our backyard: It was old and like the trees in Minnesota, sturdy and true.

She ordered two white stucco bird baths from a gardener, and within a year robins took their daily baths in our yard. Her father, my Grandpa Jerome Ewald, a contractor in St. Paul, came out for a visit, and in between his fascination with the downtown slot machines, she asked him to build her a birdhouse for that cottonwood tree.

While our mothers were overseeing the domestic front, Ben Siegel was shaping modern Las Vegas. Born in 1905, his watchwords and aspirations were "swank" and "class." Highway 91, now called the Strip, had just a few lackluster Western hotels dotting its landscape: the Last Frontier, the El Rancho Vegas, and the day-glo turquoise Thunderbird Hotel across the street. These were the casino ranches and cowboy casinos populated by divorcées shedding their spouses and out-of-towners sampling the wares of this three-day town.

Bugsy Siegel looked at the structures and said, "I can do better." And boy, did he ever! Raised on the Lower East Side in Manhattan, he had co-founded the Bugs and Meyer Gang with Meyer Lansky that grew into the heinous Murder, Inc. Ben ran all major Mob concessions; he was smart, and he was tough.

But from a personnel standpoint, there had been problems with him from the beginning. Yes, he was charming, but also an unpredictable megalomaniac (hence the nickname he loathed, "Bugsy") who suddenly decided in 1936 that he wanted to move to Los Angeles with an agenda other than Mob business. He wanted to be a movie star. If his good friend George Raft (who used to be his schlepper) and guys like Jimmy Cagney could do it, why not handsome Ben, with his coal-black hair and his piercing blue eyes?

His Mob partners knew they should have tried to talk him out of it; there was never much of a Mob in L.A. But they were glad to get rid of him; he was responsible for much bloodshed. So they told him to set up offshore gambling, consolidate what Mob there was, infiltrate the Mexican narcotics ring, and eliminate the competition for Lansky's bookmakers, National Wire. Luciano had other things on his mind; at the time, he was fighting the U.S. government's attempt to deport him to Italy and figured there were no big fish for Ben to fry on the West Coast. Little did they know that Ben would come up with a stupendous idea of his own and name it the Flamingo Hotel.

Before this, my father frequently had to protect Bugsy from payback, so he knew him well. In the thirties, the Twin Cities were declared safe cities by the Mob. Any mobster could go there and not be killed by their own while their problems were worked out elsewhere. But while they were safe from the Mob in Minneapolis, the FBI and the police were another matter.

When Meyer sent one of his Boys to the Twin Cities to cool down, he sent him to my dad to hide him. Meyer sent Ben there in 1936 after he had erupted in fury and killed two associates. My dad put him in the Radisson Hotel downtown under the name Mr. Cohen. He told my mother, his girl-friend at the time, to grab a friend for Mr. Cohen, that the two of them would double date for a few days. They ate at Charlie's, the finest restaurant in the city, went to my dad's Paradise Club, and had breakfast at my Uncle Chickie's home in St. Louis Park. Meyer worked out the problem, and Ben went back to New York a few days later.

The next year when my parents were honeymooning in Miami Beach, they were strolling along Collins Avenue one night after dinner. My mother

INSET: BEN "BUGSY" SIEGEL.

THE FLAMINGO HOTEL, 1948.

stopped at a newsstand and saw a picture of Ben Siegel in *Confidential* magazine.

"Davie!" she said, upset, "Look who Mr. Cohen really is! How could he lie to you like that? He's a gangster!" Just married at 20, she would later get to know that term all too well.

During those early days in Minneapolis, Ben mentioned Las Vegas to my dad and talked of its potential. When he called my dad to join him in 1944, he knew Ben was a visionary and was ready to follow his dream. My father had come back to Minneapolis from the war, and the city was cracking down on crime; the new mayor was making more political hay than usual by busting mobsters. My dad and his associates in the Kid Cann gang were looking for greener pastures, but sandy ones in Vegas would do just fine.

Ben put them to work in his downtown casinos, which weren't enough to hold his interest. He was mixing with Hollywood high society in Los Angeles where he was known as a "sportsman," and whispers of his gangster background just added to his allure. He had moved his wife Estelle and twin girls from Scarsdale in New York to a huge home in Beverly Hills, but now there was a complication.

He had fallen in love with Southern belle and mobster moll, would-be actress Virginia Hill, and domestic relations were strained. He wanted to build a whole new town for his sweetheart and leave his family behind.

Deferring his goal of acting for now, he fixated on a half-finished hotel down the Strip way out of town, owned by Los Angeles publisher Pete Wilkinson, who had run out of money. Ben and his partners bought in. Soon Wilkinson was out. My father was waiting to see how the hotel did before moving his base of operations to join with Siegel on the Strip. Siegel envisioned a Hollywood-type resort with the finest movie-star clientele, many of whom he had already befriended in L.A.

Actor and comedian Alan King met him then. "I was just a young boy, and he looked up and down the main drag in Vegas which had tumbleweeds on it and said, 'Kid, someday there'll be 50 hotels here.' I turned aside and said to myself, 'No wonder they call him Bugsy.'"

Psychopathology aside, Ben was a fabulous promoter and managed to raise millions from his Mob bosses to hire Del Webb from Phoenix to build the hotel. Lansky and especially Luciano were worried that the investment wouldn't pay, but Siegel said, "Trust me," and so they did.

He named it the Flamingo because Virginia was a redhead who reminded him of the beauteous flamingo birds that decorated the Hialeah racetrack. He and Virginia had a passionate, tumultuous love affair, full of sound and fury and not a little larceny.

Actress Anne Jeffreys, famed for her "Topper" TV series among other acting roles, remembers meeting Virginia.

"We were actresses, and a mutual friend told me I should meet her; since we were both from the South he thought we'd get along. So I went to a party at their house in Beverly Hills. She was very friendly, very nice, light-spirited, kind of casual. I didn't know who her boyfriend was.

"Then she gets a phone call and talks for a while before she says, 'Talk to my new friend Anne, I have to see to my guests,' and she put me on the phone. It was Ben Siegel. He was charming and invited me to Vegas where he was building a hotel."

And build he did, furiously. He had Luciano ship him marble from Italy. There was talk of slow-moving contractors getting killed in the desert, but he denied it. That said, not that many contractors were anxious to meet him and preferred to talk only to Webb. Building materials were scarce nationwide, but he got them from Mexico or anywhere he could.

He was $5 million over budget just before the hotel opened the day after Christmas 1946, a day on which he would have moved heaven, if he had had access, and Earth to meet his deadline. That night he lit up the pink neon Flamingo sign that was to make his hotel famous.

Ben's Mob credibility plummeted when the hotel stayed open for only six weeks. It was a colossal flop. His budget had gone from an original $1 million to $6 million. Critics at the time would decide that Siegel had not created a need before he tried to fill it. Nobody had ever heard of a fancy carpet joint operating in Vegas. It was a town of locals, men with string ties and cowboy boots, and he invited them to a hotel opening for which they had nothing to wear.

Although he imported illuminati from Hollywood, his hotel was only half-finished. Guests had to stay at the déclassé El Rancho. Maybe because he came from a closed-in ghetto, he had no feel for distance and didn't realize that the hotel was too far from the center of town, even though it was but a mile. Boondocks doesn't play if you're aiming for glamour.

The city that invented sunshine decided to pour down rain on his opening. Even the casino, Siegel's sure bet, suffered heavy losses. Del Webb feared for his life—and calming him at the time, Ben issued his famous line about the Mob, "Don't worry, we only kill each other." Too true, in his case.

Jimmy Durante, Rose Marie, and Xavier Cugat opened the Flamingo that night. "Plane loads of stars came in," Rose Marie remembers, "Lana Turner, Joan Crawford, Cesar Romero, Esther Williams, everybody was on that plane. The Flamingo was beautiful, very European-looking, no rooms,

JIMMY DURANTE PERFORMED AT THE OPENING OF THE FLAMINGO HOTEL. HE AND MY FATHER WERE GOOD FRIENDS.

THE GALA OPENING OF THE FLAMINGO HOTEL, A "$5,000,000 RESORT," DECEMBER 26, 1946.

just a dining room, a coffee shop, and the casinos with the croupiers on the high chairs like in Monaco. It was fantastic, jewels and diamonds, everybody was there.

"The third day all the stars went back, and we were working to nine or ten people in the dining room. The people were afraid of the hotel. To see Jimmy Durante work to nine or ten people was really strange. But we finished out the two weeks and then went home."

Ben was not ready to give up. Some say his Mob bosses sealed his death warrant the day the hotel closed. They were sure that he was skimming huge profits from the casino and even from the building costs and that Virginia was frequently dispatched to Switzerland to hide the dough.

He denied any wrongdoing, closed the hotel, raised more money, and told his bosses he would turn a big profit for them. The croupiers in tuxedos were canned the second day, and they were reincarnated wearing those string ties. This time, the hotel was finished and ready for occupancy, and he took out ads in L.A. By March, he reopened it, turning a profit by May.

The character of Las Vegas began to gel. It was never the tables, the gambling; it was the image, the aura of dark excitement, gangster glamour, limitless entertainment, the satiation of desires, and no moral judgments. Party, party, party "the greatest midway in the world," according to a city builder 40 years later—Steve Wynn.

No one who met Ben Siegel ever forgot him. Charisma, power, call it what you will; he simply captivated others. Rod Amateau, Hollywood television writer and director, started his career as Humphrey Bogart's stunt double. Siegel admired Bogart's screen persona and came to the movie set one day.

"He was brought to the stage by George Raft, a friend of his, and he was very courteous and very nice," Amateau remembers. "Later on, somebody told me, 'you know, he's a gangster.' And I said, 'Well, you know, as long as he doesn't shoot me, I'm not gonna judge him; everybody's gotta make a living!'

"His handshake was very soft, as if he didn't want to hurt anything, didn't need to prove anything. It's later on that I realized he was building this hotel in Las Vegas, and I cracked up because nobody can build a hotel in Vegas! We became friends because he was taking acting lessons; he was very diligent, very serious about it."

Kay Starr, who had the big hit "Wheel of Fortune" in those early Vegas days, was often a headlining star at the hotel and met Siegel. "I'd never met a more courtly, more gentlemanly man in my life than Bugsy Siegel. I was invited to sit down at the table, and he was the first one to jump up and pull

AT THE FRIARS CLUB. L TO R: GEORGE RAFT, MILTON BERLE, IRVING BRISKIN, PHIL SILVERS, DANNY GOODMAN, JONNIE TAPS.

out my chair and I thought to myself, 'Well, if this is a gangster, I'd like to know more of em.'"

Rose Marie has her Siegel story, too. "One night I was sitting in the lounge and Ben says, 'I want you to go over there and play some baccarat,' and he hands me $10,000. I said, 'I am not a shill, I am a performer.' He said, 'You're just sitting on your behind doing nothing, go over there and play some baccarat, maybe you'll draw some attention.'

"So I go over and start to play—and so I win about $25,000 and I look at my watch and it's five to twelve, and I have a second show to do. I'm looking around for Mr. Siegel and I can't find him; so I take the money and I shove it in my pants, and I go out and do my show, and when the show was over I went outside.

"I look for Siegel all over the place and finally I found him and said, 'Here's your money. Don't ever ask me to do this again.' He says, 'I wasn't worried about you, I knew you were all right.'"

Finally, with the second opening, Siegel's hotel was a smash, and he was a phenomenal success, raking in huge silver dollars for his big bosses. My dad had cautioned Siegel that he was opening his hotel too soon. When Siegel offered him a cut of the action before the second opening, he wanted to be on board. The problem was how to come up with the ante. Siegel offered him a partnership for a million dollars. It had cost him $160,000 to get a piece of the El Cortez from Lansky just a few months earlier.

My dad did not live large; every penny earned was plowed back into Vegas, and he was down to his last $100,000. In classic Mob tradition, my dad went on the hunt for silent partners, men who wanted the money the Mob could make them but no association with it. He flew to Minneapolis, where many of his colleagues had made big bucks in the rackets but as silent partners, scoured the Iron Range (northern Minnesota) for dough, and came up with exactly one million dollars—a fortune in those days.

He and his younger brother Chickie (his other brother Max had contracted tuberculosis from working with cattle in Sioux City and died in his 20s) flew to Vegas with the money in a suitcase. Uncle Chickie, who raised me after my parents died, was a dapper dandy, a handsome Peter Pan, totally devoted to my father and me but a problem gambler.

Craps was his mistress. His gambling addiction exacerbated his severe diabetes and ulcers, and he was frequently hospitalized and in fragile health. My dad had been his protector since they were children. He always worked for my dad running clubs and restaurants and was a champion bridge player—a life master—but gambling pulsed through his veins and took priority.

My father would not allow him to work in Vegas. He was the black sheep of the family, but my dad adored him and treated him like a son rather than a brother six years younger. My Uncle idolized his older brother, Davie, and wanted to be exactly like him. But he couldn't be; his addiction to gambling ruled his life. My father had stopped gambling when he was in his teens, saying, "Gambling is for rich men or suckers, and I'm neither one."

In one of the only false steps of my father's career, he left Uncle Chickie with the suitcase containing the one million bucks in a room at the El Cortez while he went down to the Strip to cut his deal with Ben. Prior to Ben's death no papers ever needed to be signed; all the Boys were part of the Nevada Projects Corporation—which had been the name of the corporation through which the mobsters and their silent partners began to build the casinos. After Ben's murder, everyone would get a lawyer hoping to protect their assets for their wives if they met a Ben Siegel fate.

Three hours later, my dad returned to the hotel elated. Ben had been in a good mood; everything was set. He walked into the room—no Chickie and no suitcase. Davie feared the worst, since nothing was ever for certain in Mob life even though they were determined to keep rival Mob kidnappings and Mob shootings out of Vegas. The rule was, in fact, that nobody gets killed in Vegas. Just six months previously, two 22-year-old greenhorns, just released from jail in Reno, had actually robbed one of my dad's casinos downtown. My father and his friends watched the robbery, astounded. The ex-cons walked in, pulled out shotguns, and told the cashier to put the money in a bag.

My dad told the two sheriffs who may or may not have had real bullets in their guns to cool it and just let the crime take place. What morons would rob the men who ran Murder, Inc.? Talk about a death wish.

As soon as the unfortunate crooks left the casino, my father and his friends turned to two of their henchmen and said, "Follow them, as soon as they cross a state border, kill them. And bring back the money." They were killed one mile over the California border, and no one ever tried that again.

Had a rival gang kidnapped Chickie and taken the money? My father's blood ran cold; he loved his baby brother. He called his colleagues; no one had seen Chickie. Frantic, he was ready to scour the town when Chickie walked in.

Normally an elegant sport, with dark, olive skin and jet-black hair slicked back shiny with Brylcreem, Chickie wore Sulka silk shirts with "CMB" monogrammed on the pocket and hand-tailored silk suits. He usually had an English Oval in his manicured fingertips and a smoky halo around his head. He was probably the only soldier in the U.S. Army in World War II who had his uniforms made by his tailor for a perfect fit.

That day, Chickie was a mess, drenched in perspiration and dazed. He staggered to the bed sans suitcase, mumbled "I'm sorry" and passed out. When Davie revived him, a tearful Chickie told him he had lost the million dollars in a crap game out at the ranch owned by Benny Binion. He told his brother he'd kill himself if Davie chose never to speak to him and disowned him over his behavior. He begged Davie's forgiveness.

That wasn't all. Chickie had angered a rival mobster from Texas out there, and now that gang was after him and wanted to kill him. In fact, they were watching the airport to grab him if he boarded his flight that night for Minneapolis. Stunned, my father took a deep breath.

He could never bail on family, not on his little brother whom he loved so dearly. He called a doctor to see Chickie, then three friends to drive him under guard to Minneapolis. He sent two other men to the Las Vegas airport to dispatch the menacing Texas mobsters. Three hours after the crisis, he got on a plane for Omaha and Kansas City and raised another million dollars before his deadline to turn it over to Siegel two days later.

When my father became a partner at the Flamingo, he found a situation he was unprepared for. Ben was deeply depressed and seemed not to care about the hotel anymore. The daily operation fell to my dad and Moe Sedway, Gus Greenbaum, and Willie Alderman, my personal favorite, a big lumpy man who adored his son Billy, a towheaded friendly kid who was like my younger brother. Greenbaum, who was number two under Siegel, was a heroin addict, so my father had the full responsibility for the hotel. The FBI files describe Augustus Bertrand Greenbaum as "developing a big-shot complex; the persons under him are having a difficult time to keep from being fired as he is unreasonable and difficult to work with. He does heavy gambling and incurs heavy losses. He squints continually, has a prominent nose and hunches his shoulders forward. He is crude and wears a bow tie."

So much for the FBI's news-gathering ability. Greenbaum was a junkie shooting up in the counting room. Lansky and Costello wanted him dead, and my father had to promise to keep him in line or Greenbaum was going to be taken out. He was rarely straight enough to get that bow tie on. My dad quickly sobered Gus up about his future if he continued using drugs, and Gus gradually behaved.

Siegel's hotel was a hit. He should have been on top of the world, but he wasn't. He seemed emotionally paralyzed at times. Did he know his days were now numbered? His Mob bosses whispered that he had been stealing for years, that he might suddenly sell his shares after robbing them. They wondered if he was planning to go straight and turn them in to the feds.

In a world where your word is your bond, he couldn't raise bail on his. Nobody trusted him; his friends melted into the desert night. At the end of his life, he didn't even care enough to guard his own security, throwing caution to the wind. Maybe he had lived too hard and too fast and just didn't have the energy to survive in his precarious world anymore. Maybe he was enveloped in a dark depression and acted without thought.

On the night of June 20, 1947, Benjamin Siegel was gunned down by the Mob for real or imagined transgressions as he sat on Virginia Hill's couch in her Beverly Hills home. He was 41 years old. There was one man with him, his friend Allan Smiley, who some say was a geologist. Supposedly, Smiley is still alive, but no one knows where he is. He sat on the couch next to Siegel as he was riddled by bullets, but he was not hit. Most of my father's friends say they never heard Smiley had anything to do with the hit, he was just in the wrong place at the very wrong time.

Only his ex-wife Estelle and his two small daughters attended his funeral. The town he fathered, although in shock, did not mourn. Las Vegas is a town that never takes the blame; it owes allegiance to no one except its own

POOLSIDE AT THE FLAMINGO. MY DAD'S PARTNERS IN CASUAL OUTFITS, L TO R: BENNY GOFFSTEIN, MOE SEDWAY AND GUS GREENBAUM.

image, its own soul. It doesn't take the blame if you lose your fortune, and it doesn't take the credit if you get laid by the woman of your dreams, because the town is about entertainment and about the projection of your desires. Before Siegel was dead 24 hours, his former friends in Vegas were heard to say that he was a "New York gangster, his rubout had nothing to do with us."

"I'll never forget how I was told that Benny Siegel was killed," Alan King said. "Somebody said to me, 'Benny took a cab.' That was the line, 'Benny took a cab.' See, nobody ever died. They took them out, they were eighty-sixed."

"We were told that Mr. Siegel went back to L.A. evidently to try and get more money, and that's when he was killed," Rose Marie remembers.

"I felt it was a pity that he died just when he was starting something new. I would feel that for anyone, especially for him because the contrast was so great between his former life and the life he wanted to live," Rod Amateau says. "It wasn't that he was moving a step or two to the right. He was making a complete change, and I felt sad that he got snuffed like that."

Before Ben Siegel's body was cold, Gus Greenbaum, Moe Sedway, and my father walked into the pit of the Flamingo, where they already worked, and said, "We're in charge now."

The Mob was about money, the Flamingo was a cash cow; and the big Eastern bosses wanted their due. The world wondered if Las Vegas could survive without Bugsy, her main architect and godfather.

But Vegas was already a product as much as a city, an event that owed its allegiance to no one person. It never made the mistake of investing its entire image in anyone. It was like a Broadway road show; the town was the thing, not the players. The collective image and history of the players was what the town was based on—gangster glamour—but no individual player owned her.

My father forged his Vegas career with the Flamingo Hotel as his foundation. He was 44 years old, in big action at last, never working less than 14 hours a day. Partners Moey and Joe were old friends but Greenbaum had been a Mob blind date, someone Lansky put my father together with first, for the El Cortez deal. Gus's drug addiction always caused my father severe problems. But nothing diminished Davie's enthusiasm for his town.

The life he gave my mother and me was glamorous, but it seemed ordinary to me. I lived with them, my dog Blackie, and intermittent middle-aged Jewish bodyguards my father referred to as "best friends." When I was four I'd hear, "Susie, please let Lou win a gin game occasionally, you've upset him. He's my best friend."

My father had my portrait painted in oil and hung it near the Flamingo's reservations desk. There I was, a tan little tomboy in jeans, hand-tooled black cowboy boots, a sweater, my pigtails capped by plaid ribbons, and a stuffed animal in my grubby little hand. I was posed against that green, leafy palm-frond wallpaper that all Mob hotels had.

I lived in Las Vegas, the center of the world, and my dad owned it. Our home filled with song and laughter. My parents were up at 7:30 to get me ready for school. My father usually got home just a couple hours before the graveyard shift ended at the Flamingo so he read until I got up. After he dropped me off at school, he'd head for the Desert Inn Golf Course to play with his foursome.

When did he sleep? Seldom. Every three days he didn't work the graveyard, and on those nights, he was in bed by midnight as soon as he took the

MY MOTHER AND I IN THE FLAMINGO POOL, 1950.

counting boxes off the tables. He was the pit boss of the casino, meaning he was in charge of money for the hotel.

When they came into my bedroom to wake me up, they fought hundreds of toys getting to my bed. Daddy was either in his pin-striped suit or already in yellow golf clothes, or sometimes light blue. My mother was gorgeous in a long, blue, satin robe, her black hair perfectly curled even though she had just woken up. She looked as beautiful without makeup as with it, and my dad always told her that.

Sometimes I just couldn't get up—too big an afternoon the day before in the hotel pool, these things could tire a five-year-old. Fifth Street Elementary School was not exactly my idea of a good time. I preferred watching the "ponies" (chorus girls) rehearse their dance numbers at our hotel.

"Susie, sweetheart, it's time to get up," my gentle mother said, tousling my hair. I opened one eye and saw my black Felix the Cat clock wag his tail onward to 7:30. I closed that eye.

"Kiddo, I'll give you a silver dollar if you make it to the table in five. Edderay, etsay, ogay," my father said in pig Latin, our special language (Ready, set, go!).

That was it! I jumped into the clothes my mother had laid out the night before. As I sped into the living room, they would be sitting at the small brown piano, playing "Melancholy Baby" or "You are my Sunshine" and singing. She could actually play the piano and he said he played "by ear," as in "I play by ear, Susie." I tried to see if his ears touched the keys but they never did; they seemed to be uninvolved.

Their ever-present cigarettes—she smoked Chesterfields and he Lucky Strikes—were always smoldering in ashtrays if they were not in their mouths. Lucy Brown, our black maid, who lived on the segregated west side with all the other blacks, got to our house at eight to make breakfast. My mother couldn't boil water. My father called her "Mrs. Brown," and my mother and I called her "Lucy."

We loved her; she kept the home scene going for us. Her son Curtis worked for my dad as a porter at the hotel. When he had a daughter he named her Susan after me, but my dad nicknamed her "Atomic" because she was born during the atomic blasts.

Lucy had breakfast ready for me. My parents rarely ate anything; they drank black coffee and smoked cigarettes. Occasionally my mother nibbled on a piece of toast in the morning. My father, a ritual eater, was always worried about his weight—he was a jock, loved sports, and had flown his own plane at Minneapolis's Wold Chamberlain airfield and gave up flying only after my mother begged.

He lived on "butterflyed" steaks, sliced tomatoes, and coffee at the hotel and occasionally cottage cheese and cantaloupe. Once in a while he shoved down a bagel, lox, and cream cheese.

My father was strict about only one thing, my education. I had, evidently, tested "gifted" when I was three, and my father liked to tell people I was a "genius" who took after him. He told me I was going to be the first Berman to go to college. When he said that in front of his partners, they chuckled. They had been to "college," their nickname for prison, as had he.

The school wanted to skip me two grades in kindergarten but my mother said no, I was "shorter than anyone anyway, had no friends and being the smartest wasn't the most important thing, being a happy child was the goal." In fact, my mother was always trying to make friends for me.

MY MOTHER AND I ON OUR WAY TO A FLOOR SHOW.

One day three granddaughters and their mother came to live with the old Italian lady who lived on the corner in our neighborhood. My mother promptly went down to the corner, introduced herself, and asked the granddaughters, all in elementary school, to come over Saturday and meet me. She bought them all dolls and Lucy cooked a big lunch. I barely remember the details because the day before my dad had brought me my very own slot machine, and I was otherwise engaged.

Two weeks later, my mother invited them back. Their mother told her that they loved her but hated me. "Susie is just like an old man," they said, "she's very bossy, and she chews cigar stubs. But Mrs. Berman is beautiful; if Susie's not there, we'll go." My mother explained that I was with my father and all his middle-aged friends constantly, the only child and a girl, but nothing cut mustard; they weren't coming.

My father was undaunted by my lack of social success. "You have to think about your education, Susie, that's the one thing they can never take away from you," he'd repeat often. Who were "they?" Why would "they" want to take anything away from me?

He'd drill me on my spelling words at breakfast. He did such a good job that I won the Las Vegas Spelling Bee in second grade. He taught me my numbers in the counting room, using the dice, the coins, and the cards. I still remember he and his friends dividing the money—so much for them, so much for the government, so much for Meyer.

DEAN MARTIN AND JERRY LEWIS MADE US LAUGH WHEN THEY PLAYED THE HOTEL.

Most of the floor- show stars came to our home to hang out with my dad. He loved entertainers, especially Jimmy Durante and Jack Benny. He had silver dollar pendants embossed with their names, the word "Zion," and a Star of David. And they wore them. Jimmy Durante must have done it for interfaith reasons.

We were there for every floor-show opening at a ringside table with a host of my dad's friends and guests. He never stayed for the show; he came in at the end, after working the pit.

I can still remember how my heart stopped in anticipation when I heard, "And now from the fabulous Flamingo Hotel, here's our lovely line of dancers." And the chorus girls would parade out in glory.

Sophie Tucker, Pearl Bailey, Liberace, Kay Starr (loved her white dress appliquéd with red dice when she sang "Wheel of Fortune"), Rose Marie,

Danny Thomas, the Mills Brothers, the Andrews Sisters, Spike Jones, Ken Murray and the Blackouts, Jerry Lewis and Dean Martin, Peggy Lee, Xavier Cugat, Ben Blue, Lena Horne, the Ink Spots, Betty Hutton, and so many others were the entertainers in early Vegas.

Frankie Laine sang "Cry of the Wild Goose," and Tony Martin crooned "Lullaby of Broadway." I never got to see Lili St. Cyr take her famed bubble bath at the El Rancho or Joe E. Lewis tell jokes they deemed were too sophisticated for me.

My all-time favorite second act was The Apache Dancers. They appeared with tomahawks and knives. The male and female dancers threw each other all over the stage in an incredible sadomasochistic fashion. I thought someone would be sliced in two, and the audience was always gasping. After the Indian brave almost killed his Pocahontas, he strangled her with a whip; then she bit him, almost scratched his eyes out, and stomped on his chest with her high heels until he begged for mercy. The music ended with a flourish, and they jumped up cheerily to take their bows, all smiles. Now that was entertainment!

There was a new floor show every two weeks; we would go to the early show opening. I would eat mountains of roast beef and mashed potatoes for dinner. The photo girl always took our pictures, and I had white spots before my eyes because of the flash.

My favorites were the chorus girls with their feather headdresses and magnificent costumes. Oh, I thought, if only I could grow up and be one. "But not a 'walk on,' a pony," my mother would say—not just a tall, big-breasted walker, but a real dancer. Many days at four o'clock after school, when the dancers filed into the showroom to rehearse, I would be sitting in the darkened showroom watching. They'd do their turns, their high kicks (an essential), and strut and sway to the music as I watched in dreamlike fascination. If only!

Dotty Goffstein, wife of hotel owner Ben Goffstein, had been a pony and captain of the line, and she often put them through their paces. I loved her white leather ankle boots. Often, I'd sneak backstage and try on their costumes, fruit-bowl hats, rhinestone tiaras, purple chiffon skirts, sequins, and feathers.

Invariably, one of them would catch me with one of her long, beaded earrings on my left earlobe or a feather bag draped across my shoulders. The makeup lady would untangle a banana earring from my braid, when someone needed it for a Carmen Miranda number. I was quickly dispatched back to the showroom, but I apologized by bringing them Cokes and cigarettes the next day.

THE GORGEOUS CHORUS GIRLS OF VEGAS.

The pool was much more my territory. You couldn't live in Vegas heat and not be in the pool every day. If we didn't go to the hotel, I sat in the plastic inflatable pool in our backyard or asked my mom to hold the hose so I could run through it endlessly.

Usually, my mother and I would hit the pool. She and her friend Dorothy Silvers would wear their stunning one-piece white Catalina suits and their cork wedgies, scarves covering their hair, their toenails flashing red. If they went swimming, they covered their heads with petal-covered swimming caps. My mother ordered iced tea or lemonade for us. She and her friends sat under an umbrella, ate club sandwiches, and played gin rummy.

I would sprint to the high board where I would do my splashy, death-defying cannonballs, yelling "Geronimo." The hotel guests were terrified. When I asked my father to teach me to swim at three, much to my mother's dismay he threw me in the shallow end and said, "Swim to daddy, fight, Susie, fight, come on, come on," as my mother objected from the side. He'd lived his whole life walking a tightrope without a net, and he wanted me to be able to do it, too.

I made it, dog-paddling for my very life to him. He grabbed me when I made it, lifted me out of the water, getting his suit wet, "Good girl, Susie!"

When he had the lifeguard give me swimming lessons the following week, I wasn't afraid of the water anymore. I'd spend hours asking my mother to throw dimes in the deep end, then I'd swim down to the drain holding my breath to retrieve them. I still recall the cool feeling of the water on my descent as my hair glided back from my face.

If I could get away with it, I'd sneak over to the drug store and grab candy or a pool toy yelling "Charge it to Davie Berman," but I always got in trouble with my mother for that. "Just because daddy owns the hotel does not mean you're better than anyone. It's how you act toward others that counts."

My enthusiasm for life matched my young town's. There was always something to do. On Saturday morning, my mother rented horses at the Day Dream Ranch, and we loped across the empty strip that now quakes under the weight of huge buildings. In our specially purchased Western clothes from Smith and Chandler, we explored abandoned silver mines and the ghost towns that surrounded the town, looking for special rocks, agates, and arrowheads.

Some Saturday mornings, our mothers took us on a sunrise ride that included a hay ride at the end. We grilled hot dogs and stuffed ourselves with "somemores" in the desert where Treasure Island now towers. The hotel had a boat for gamblers, and my mother and I fished for catfish off the side on Lake Mead.

My dad and his friends Moe Sedway and Willie Alderman started a synagogue in an old house, Temple Beth Shalom, so we could have a Jewish education. He took me to school there every Sunday and picked me up after his golf game. After a year they built a real Temple Beth Shalom at Thirteenth and Carson, and then we also went to Friday night services.

Then my father decided the town should have a Passover. It became a tradition once a year at the Last Frontier Hotel. My dad had special matzohs flown in from New York, and he'd take me with him to McCarran Airport to pick up the shipment. He'd invite all the Jewish employees and their children and read their names to the rabbi so he could welcome them.

The moment we walked into the Seder dinner, I was overcome with awe. The showroom was absolutely transformed! Our shiksa mothers had decorated with fresh flowers and streamers. Rabbi Leibowitz yelled the Four Questions from the stage. "Why is this night different from all other nights?" We chanted with him. Our Jewish grandmothers clucked in disapproval when they saw that our mothers, trying their best, had strung up Hanukkah or Purim streamers by mistake.

Occasionally, some hotel guests would wander in the showroom by mistake asking why there wasn't a show that night. We kids laughed hysterically at their naiveté. After the dinner, we would all pitch in and take the decorations down off the prickly ceiling because there would be a second show.

As we filed out, giddy from our one cup of wine, we kids would smirk at the tourists lined up. They were visitors, but we were Las Vegas! It was our town!

I remember my grandma Clara's Shabbas dinners better than anything, because they were my father's worst nightmare. I was born on my grandfather David's birthday but he died before I was born; life in the brave new world had never worked for him.

My father bought his mother a duplex near the Fairfax district in L.A. where his sister Lillian could help her. Grandma Clara had little interest in family. She was a compulsive gambler like her youngest son, Chickie, and she was always at the tables in Gardena. Except, that is, for once a month when she visited us, uninvited.

My dad forbade her to come to Vegas because she would gamble in the hotels saying, "I'm Davie Berman's mother, give me credit, he'll pay you." The entire little town was alerted to the problem of Clara Berman. If she showed up, call Davie.

Besides gambling, she had one other interest. She was a cofounder of the Mahnia Silverberg Auxiliary at the City of Hope, an organization that my

THE GANGSTERS GO CHARITABLE. L TO R: WILLIE ALDERMAN, ABE SCHILLER (THE FAMED PR DIRECTOR OF THE FLAMINGO) AND MY DAD PREPARE TO HIT A FEW FOR THE CITY OF HOPE.

father and his friends almost single-handedly supported in the early days by staging constant charity events at my grandmother's suggestion.

Once a month, around three on a Friday, there would be a pounding at our front door. My mother and I would look up fearfully. It was her! Lou Raskin, who lived with us, was in charge of the door. We never had house-keys; mobsters don't carry keys because they can be kidnapped, and rivals can then get into their homes and take their families.

Lou, a gentle, loving man with an extremely high waist and a bulbous nose, sat on an easy chair in our living room and did door. In response to a doorbell or knocking or the usual low-voiced, "It's Davie, Lou," he opened the door.

I usually never heard him utter more than three words. My dad would ask, "Is everything okay, Lou?" and he'd reply, "It's okay, Davie."

On these particular Fridays, no one could mistake the roar of the impending guest.

"It's Clara, open up Lou!" she'd scream. Even Lou was frightened. He'd throw open the door, and a small stout woman in a black dress and a brightly colored shawl carrying two huge, full, needlepoint purses would barrel in.

"Pay the cab," she'd order Lou. Then she'd look at my mother and me with extreme displeasure.

"Hi, Gladys, shiksa!" she'd yell. In defense of my mother, I would run to her and try to kick her, but she was too quick for me, usually kicking me first with a huge black shoe.

She loathed me. My mother would get very upset. "Clara, please, she's a child, she's only four." My grandmother snorted. My mother grabbed my hand and dragged me to my parents' bedroom to try to call daddy to no avail. Because the Bubbie would already be on the phone. We'd listen on the extension as she called all his partners. "Page Gus Greenbaum," she'd bark at the hotel operator, then, "Gus, Clara. Shabbas dinner at sundown, seven, bring gelt." Then she'd dial again, "Page Willie Alderman, it's Davie Berman's mother." Then, "Willie, Clara. Good Shabbas! Dinner's at sundown, bring money." It was another pay-as-you-eat Clara Shabbas dinner.

I'd sneak out into the kitchen to get some junket or chocolate pudding, the only things my mother could cook. Bubbie would be huffing and puffing and emptying the ingredients of an entire Shabbas dinner out of her bags. Her white hair would fall out of her bun in long wisps as she started cooking. She smelled of an old person's rouge but that smell was soon overwhelmed by the wonderful odors of her food.

My mother and I stayed in the bedroom finger-painting or making puppets, our favorite activity, but occasionally I would go back to the kitchen and taste the food against my grandmother's wishes. Chicken, borscht, noodle kugel, poppy seed cookies, rugelah—she even baked! I knew Lucy would have a terrible time cleaning the kitchen the next day.

"Lou, get in here and chop the carrots for the matzoh ball soup," she'd bellow, and Lou would come running. Sometimes, I would stand on my stool and she'd sneer at me and say "Ach, it's you." Or better yet, "*Oy vey*, why didn't Davie have a son!"

After Lou worked for an hour cutting the vegetables, she'd shout, "Not bad for America's guest!" She hated the fact that Lou lived with us and, in her opinion, didn't work. But his job was to protect us with his life, and he would have.

Soon, the sleek black Cadillacs would arrive: Willie, Gus, Joe, Moey, sometimes Mickey Cohen and Nick the Greek even though he wasn't Jewish, and a host of others, men absolutely starved for a Jewish meal. My father always came in last, looking mortified, but he would kiss her dutifully. Even he was scared of her. And my dad wasn't scared of anyone!

He'd come into the back bedroom and ask my mother to come out. Not a chance. She would prefer to read or paint until the entire experience was over, and my dad didn't blame her.

The men I knew as Uncles would start with the chicken soup and inhale it with the gusto of men starved for a matzoh ball. All I heard for half an hour was slurps, "*Vaysmear*, this is good," and "Thank god for Clara."

Halfway through the meal, she would light the menorah. I always wanted to help her say the blessing but she recited it in a sing-song voice so fast that I couldn't keep up. She hovered over my dad's plate, always chiding him for watching his weight. "Whatsa matter, Davie? Can't finish the *tsimmes*? Ulcer bother you?"

"No, Mama, I'm just not that hungry."

"Whatd'ya eat today?"

"I had cottage cheese and...," then he stopped before he fell into her usual trap. No matter what he had eaten, it wouldn't be enough.

"This is great, mama, the borscht is delicious."

"What would you know about borscht? You married a shiksa," she'd bark. As soon as she said that he'd get that thin smile across his face that meant now he was having an ulcer attack. Soon after that, he'd clutch his stomach and go to the refrigerator for a glass of milk.

An hour from the time she covered the table with every kind of delicious Jewish food and poured the men glass after glass of Manischewitz wine, she'd pull out her big, now empty, needlepoint bag and tap Willie on the shoulder.

"I need gelt for the City of Hope; this isn't free, pay up." Each man dug into his pants pockets and dropped hundred-dollar bills in her bag.

"Davie, I want five from you," she said, and my dad dutifully dropped five one-hundred-dollar bills in her purse. She'd examine her take, and if it wasn't enough, she'd shove a fat hand in someone's face and say, "More." She knew her victims.

My embarrassed father said, "Mama, please, you said you wouldn't do this again; I'll give you the money," but he was overruled by exaltations of "Davie, Davie, leave her alone, it was delicious."

Lou would try to give her twenty bucks but she'd say, "America's guest doesn't pay!" humiliating him. She put a rubber band around all the hundred-dollar bills and threw them in her bag.

The Shabbas eve guests then moved as one into the living room and silently smoked dozens of cigarettes and cigars as I waited around to grab the cigar butts. That done, all the mobsters thanked Clara, and patted my dad on the shoulder. They were leaving him with her, thankful that they weren't going to be left alone with her or with their own mothers.

Clara never cleaned up; before the guests were even out, she was on the phone calling a cab. My dad wouldn't give her a ride to the casinos but that didn't stop her.

"Mama, please don't stay out late, come back here, the guest room," he'd beg. I knew it would be a sleepless night for my dad. Usually about four in the morning when he got home from the graveyard shift, someone would call and ask him to come get his mother. He'd bring her home, and she'd be furious. "My son won't even let me gamble. Big shot! Owns a hotel!" She'd call a cab and go back to L.A. before I was even up in the morning. My father would then complain of ulcers for the next four days. He and his friends wound up buying her auxiliary an entire wing for the City of Hope Hospital in Duarte.

My family and the maturing Las Vegas were full of town pride. Every May, the focus of our lives was the Helldorado Parade. It had been started in the 1930s in the Western tradition and now was a showcase for gorgeous hotel floats, high school marching bands, cheerleaders, baton twirlers, the Rotary Club, other town clubs, and champion Appaloosa horses.

Our mothers would dress us for the hotel floats. I was usually a butterfly on the Flamingo Hotel float, my sash tied to a pole that was costumed as a tree, tied tight so I didn't fall off as the float glided down Fremont Street. Our parents took rooms at the El Cortez Hotel so they could watch us and keep filling those ice buckets for their ice tea. I'd always spot my parents and wave frantically, shouting, "Davie, Gladys, it's me!"

The best part was after the parade. They'd lock our dads in the jail called the hoosegow, and our mothers would bail them out, paying a bundle for charity. I loved to see daddy in the paddywagon with the bars on it, what a hoot!

Little did I know he had done seven years of hard time at Sing Sing!

Vegas in the late Forties and early Fifties was young and as full of exuberance as I was. Our fathers, the godfathers of the town, were more than successful in their bid to start new lives. All they saw was a future full of happiness. Nothing could ever go wrong; there was no way the shadows of their former lives could eclipse their future.

GLORY DAYS

I close my eyes and a dreamy reverie overcomes me—dark men, smiling men, squat men in expensive pin-striped suits—always in packs, moving as one, their star-sapphire pinkie rings winking at the chandeliers in the Flamingo Hotel. I only like men in packs to this day. Glossy men, vibrant men, my men—my dad, Willie Alderman, Moe Sedway, Gus Greenbaum.

The Fifties in Vegas were the glory days. My dad and his friends were in big action; they were thrilled. They had been working 16 hours a day for seven or eight years. It was paying off in spades.

I smelled their French cologne, caught their sheer joy in living, "Hi ya Susie!" "What's up Susie?" "Hi, Kiddo!" "How's Davie's favorite girl?" Life was good, it was great, and it could only get better.

"Susie, kings come here, princes, everyone is coming to our town!" my father enthused, continually. He had been proven right. His friends from New York, Chicago, and Minneapolis were all coming to visit, now wanting a piece of the action.

My older sister, Lady Las Vegas, was developing into womanhood while I was gawky. I idolized her, going to all her sparkling events with my parents, who were always supportive and adoring. She was bursting forth with what

WILBUR CLARK AND HIS GLAMOROUS DESERT INN.

seemed like a new hotel a year. Suddenly the Sands, the Sahara, and the Desert Inn sprouted up on the Strip.

My father and his friends were very protective of her, didn't want her to attract the wrong type of suitors. She was universally appealing and didn't discriminate with her favors.

When my mother and I would be in L.A. for the weekend, to see a doctor or a dentist (Las Vegas was still lacking good medical care) or to shop (she loved Saks Fifth Avenue, Haggerty's, and Mildred Moore's, and Pixie Town and Helen Fenton's on Beverly Drive for me), I'd love it, but I'd miss my little town. I would be relieved on Sunday afternoon when Lou would drive us to the airport.

Most of the stewardesses on the Western Airlines planes knew us; they always gave me a gold stewardess pin. I loved looking down as we landed at the jewels of the Strip. Sometimes you could see the searchlights from the hotels.

They'd slide the staircase up to the plane, and I'd want to bound down as soon as I saw my dad. But I restrained myself and held on to my mother's hand. Sometimes I would miss the last step in my fervor to get to him and fell on the hot pavement. My dad rushed to pick me up, but the pavement was so hot, I would get burned.

The sun was always risen. We never had rain or hail storms. I preferred my ice in the ice sculptures at the Thunderbird Hotel buffet "All you can eat for $1.00" breakfasts on Sundays—beautiful ice sculptures of graceful swans, princesses, or angels, or shaved ice in my shrimp cocktail which I had every weekend day for lunch at the Flamingo pool. But not ice falling on my head from the sky!

My dad would take us to the Flamingo Coffee Shop to get a quick dinner before we went home. It was a school night, darn! I sat down with them and ordered a cheeseburger, extra ketchup, and then told my mom I'd be back before it arrived. She would be telling my dad about our trip.

I would leave them in the coffee shop and rush into the showroom to see if the crush of my life, maitre d' Jack Dennison, was there yet. He was devastatingly handsome. He had such gorgeous silver hair that they called him the "Silver Fox," and he promised to marry me if I ever got older than six.

There he was!

"Hi ya Susie! Want to help me do a seating arrangement?" "Sure." He pointed to a diagram of the showroom tables. "Remember the Feins from Amarillo?"

"Yeah, he's a jeweler."

"Party of six, gotta put them somewhere. Durante's on tonight."

"Jimmy? Oh, Jack, can you ask my dad if I can see the show?"

"You know he never lets you stay up late on a school night, Susie." A group of guests came in, took him away. I dashed into the casino, had a couple of errands to do.

"Paging Davie Berman. Paging Davie Berman," rang out as usual. I looked into the pit, didn't see my dad pick up the phone. I dashed to the rim of the casino and put my hand into the silvery mouths of the slots. People would forget some of their change.

I was forbidden to do this by my dad. He had Sheriff Dave Schuman watching me but I always convinced Sheriff Dave to look the other way. I needed money to buy more marbles and rocks at the Last Frontier Rock Shop.

Found fifty cents, pocketed it, took a look at the artist doing pastel chalk drawings of children. She was doing a little blonde girl; I waved. I looked around for Abe Schiller; he was the public relations guy for the hotel and always dressed in Western clothes with boots with silver spurs. He always knew if there was a parade or big outdoor event coming up, and he'd let me ride on the front of his horse if I asked him. No luck, he wasn't there.

I dashed back to the coffee shop; my dad had already gone back to the pit, and my cheeseburger had just arrived. On the way home, I looked out the car window and the pinkish glaze over my Strip. I saw Frank Sinatra's name

LILI ST. CYR, "THE MOST FABULOUS GIRL IN THE WORLD," AT THE EL RANCHO VEGAS.

on the marquis of the Sands. I'd ask p.r. guy Nick Kelly or owner Carl Cohen to get me an autographed picture for my collection. Nobody good was playing at the Sahara or the Desert Inn. Only cowboy groups at the Thunderbird. Lili St. Cyr and Joe E. Lewis were at the Silver Slipper; Lili took a bubble bath but I never got to go. It was considered too risqué for a child.

Driving down Fifth (the Strip) a few blocks before our turn, I saw the wedding chapel where I always tossed money into the wishing well in front and made secret wishes. Finally, we turned on the corner where the Sal Sagev Motel was. As we pulled up in front of our house I saw my mother's purple irises, which were blooming. Then I would fall asleep; Lou must have lifted me out of the car because I'd always wake up the next morning in my bed.

I wasn't the only one having a wonderful time in Vegas in the Fifties. Everybody was coming to play.

"Nobody talked about the backgrounds of the owners; Vegas was like another planet," said Alan King. "All of a sudden things that were illegal all over the country became not only acceptable, it was what drove the town."

Everybody was building hotels on the Strip, hammering and construction was everywhere. Between 1950 and 1958, I watched so many hotels go up: the Desert Inn in 1950, then the Sahara, the Sands; in 1956 the Riviera, then the Dunes, the Royal Nevada, the Moulin Rouge, the New Frontier, the Hacienda, the Fremont and the Mint. In 1958, the Stardust and the Tropicana opened.

Eastern Jewish and Italian mobsters financed the hotels as usual and installed their own front men. Lansky and his Eastern associates controlled the Flamingo (still) and had interests in the Thunderbird and the Sands. Sam Giancanna and Tony Accardo from Chicago controlled the Riviera and the Stardust. Gossip had it that New England's Raymond Patriarcha ran the Dunes.

When Frank Costello was gunned down in New York (he lived), a slip of paper in his pocket contained the amount of the Tropicana's first-month profits. Las Vegas was obviously a source of revenue for the Mafia, and everybody wanted in without fear of territorial reprisals.

Steve Wynn remembers the Vegas of the Fifties. "I was eleven. I was with my father. The Strip was a series of two-story motels with big signs, and in between those buildings was sand. But if you came up the Strip, you'd pass the Sahara Hotel in the middle of the desert. Across the street was the El Rancho Vegas, then you walked along those sidewalks, you walked along a dusty desert road, until you came to the Silver Slipper, the Last Frontier Village."

The man responsible for the famed entertainment of the Fifties was entertainment director Bill Miller. "My first show that I booked there was a tremendous hit—Marlene Dietrich, who I'd never dreamt of being a Vegas act. And she said what should I do to be a novelty—to do something different? So we created the peek-a-boo dress.

"At the Sahara, there was no minimum to see a show. There was no minimum and no cover. You could go into the Sahara and have dinner, which was somewhere around $3.50 or $4.00, see the show, or if you didn't eat, have a Coca-Cola. The Coca-Cola was probably $.50 or so, and you could see any show," says Miller, discussing the impetus to his revolutionary idea of the lounge show.

"I looked at the lounge and there was somebody playing a piano, or

THE OPENING OF THE STARDUST, ALONG WITH THE DUNES AND THE TROPICANA, INITIATES THE RAPID GROWTH OF VEGAS IN THE MID-1950S.

somebody playing something, and here is this beautiful lounge, and I says, 'What do we do with this lounge?' So, I says, 'I think I'll change the format in the lounge. We'll take out all the food. And I'll book a show for the lounge.' I looked around for who I thought would be a great lounge act. Next idea that came to me was Louie Prima. Louie Prima, Keeley Smith, Sam Butera. I says, 'If I book them, they should be tremendous.'"

The Mills Brothers were one of the most popular main room attractions in the Fifties. "We were the first black act to work in Vegas," says Donald Mills. "Songs like 'Paper Doll,' 'You Always Hurt the One You Love,' 'Till Then I'll Be Around,' 'Caravan'. . . now those are the songs that the people remember, like 'Lazy River.'"

Performers remember the Fities fondly. "The Boys were gentlemen at all times to me and treated me like a queen," says Rose Marie. "It was like a family. You could go to any of the hotels, and you didn't pay for anything. If you wanted to go to the bar and get a couple of drinks and they knew you were working the Flamingo, you'd get no check."

"These guys were great," says comedian Shecky Greene. "They would protect you, they would take care of you." People would be talking about "hoodlums" and everything else, but to Greene, "it was a wonderful bunch of people to work for."

The hotel owners brought another time-honored Mob tradition to their new Vegas ventures. Since gambling profits are difficult to track, it was a simple matter for them to doctor their books, "skimming" a fortune in tax-free money off the top.

I was in the counting room. I saw them go, "three for us, one for the government, two for Meyer." I helped them count the bills. They cheated the government. It was a crime, all right, but in the minds of my father and his friends it wasn't a crime like having to kill people.

Bob Stupak, the Vegas casino owner who thought of Vegas World and the Stratosphere, remembers the history of Vegas. "They might have been a little tarnished from Cleveland or Detroit, or whatever. When they came here, they were automatically respected citizens, part of the community."

"In those days, Vegas was a small town, very low, very flat. Land was almost nothing then—a hundred dollars an acre or something. All the hotels were laid out flat," remembers television producer George Schlatter. "The theory was—and it was a good theory—that to get to your room, you had to go through the casino. And to get to the showroom or to get to the taxi cab or to get to a restaurant you had to go through the casino. And then everybody said, 'Wait a minute, this is a pretty good idea.'"

Kay Starr did not know how to gamble. "The other entertainers had said to me, 'If you're going to work in Las Vegas, you have to gamble.' I said, 'Why? What if you don't know how?' 'Oh, you've got to gamble—they expect that and they'll never ask you back if you don't.' Well, it ended up that one night I thought, 'Okay, I'm either going to do it—do or die!'" Starr got together five hundred dollars—"which to me seemed like an awful lot of money"—went over to the tables and started playing." Now all the chips looked alike to me, you know yellow ones were yellow ones, and green ones were green ones. When I put mine down, they would say to me, 'What do you want to do, Miss Starr?' I'd say, 'What do you mean, what do I want to do? Where am I? They heard this for about fifteen minutes, and finally they took me aside and they said, 'Do us a favor, don't gamble.'"

The owners were like family to Alan King. He was in his late teens and, although he had been around the wise guys in New York and Chicago and Miami, he was still quite naive. "I didn't know about the Willie Aldermans and the Davie Bermans and the Moe Dalitzes and, you know, Moey Sedway and Siegel. Well, I knew about Siegel because his reputation preceded him. He was a front-page story. But these guys were like my uncles. Always kidding me." Then an exposé called *The Green Felt Jungle* was published. "I read it in one sitting and said, 'No. This can't be. No. No. No.' They didn't leave any bodies anywhere. I just couldn't believe it. But then, of course, everybody started to look at everybody a little differently."

King remembers working for my dad and his friends as a tremendous experience. "Nobody looked back at the records of some of these guys. But I'll tell you one thing. I worked through a lot of management and this is by no means an apology for the behavior of some of these men in the past, but you didn't need a contract. All you had to do was shake hands with one of them and that was solid," says King.

"I remember I was having trouble, some small legal problem in the city of Chicago, and I was a kid, and I was being taken—in a sense, I was being blackmailed." King went to see Gus Greenbaum, with whom he was very close. "He had a growling voice, you know. I've played these guys in so many pictures because I knew them so well. And he says, 'What do you need, kid?' And I decided to open up, and I said, 'Gus,' and I told him about my problem. I'll never forget it. He hit the phone, said to his secretary, 'Get me Sidney Korshak in Chicago,' and all of a sudden he says, 'Sidney, this is Gus. I got a kid here. We like him. He's got a problem.' I flew to Chicago after the engagement, and they took care of it."

In the beginning, King had his problems hanging on to his paycheck. "I was one of the degenerate gamblers as a young boy because I wanted to sit around and tell stories with the big guys, you know," he remembers. "And there were so many of us that lost our paychecks. Started with the great Joe Louis and up and down the line."

"Walter Winchell, the famed Broadway columnist, wrote a line in his column that the three biggest losers in Las Vegas were Harry Belafonte, Phil Silvers, and Alan King. I don't know how my marriage stayed together. But eventually I was cured. I stayed away from the town for a year because I was almost like an alcoholic; and then finally I realized that if I was going to continue my rise in show business, Las Vegas was a very important part of my career, and I settled down. I never gambled again, and I'm talking about probably 35 years."

Rod Amateau went to Vegas often for entertainment in those years. "The best show I ever saw in Vegas was invariably someone small. The greatest acts I've ever seen, for example, were 'The House Builders' at the Tropicana—Willie West and McGinty. Classic act about 200 years old. These guys come out and start building and the timing is impeccable, and they just miss each other with the lumber and they duck, and they're so good that Jerry Lewis wanted to join the act and they said, 'No thank you, Mr. Lewis, we don't want it because we don't want to photograph our act and give it away. Our great-great-great grandfather came up with it and—and we wouldn't want anybody else to know how to do it.'"

Debbie Reynolds remembers the Boys' gentlemanly ways. "They didn't come near you as a woman, you know what I mean? You were like their family. It was a wonderful time, and they were great bosses. I miss that loyalty, that respect. I don't say I respect how they got the money. It's none of my business anyway. That was for Elliot Ness to handle. No one ever got killed that wasn't supposed to."

Rose Marie worked the Flamingo so often that she was known as the Flamingo Kid. "After opening the room—I worked it maybe four or five times a year—they would always look out after me, they would always say, 'Are you all right, is everything all right?' And I'd say, 'Everything is fine.' I never asked for a penny more in my salary because they would take care of my hotel bill, and if I bought a dress or something in one of the shops I never got a bill, you know, and how dare I ask for penny one. Moey Sedway, who was running the Flamingo at that time, would say to me, 'Are you busy two weeks from now?' And I go, 'No, not that I know.' 'Okay, you're gonna play Cal Neva.' I would say, 'Okay.' And he would say, 'Then you can go to Reno.' 'Okay.' I was really their girl."

The middle Fifties continued the glory days. My dad and his friends bought the just completed Riviera Hotel in 1955 after they sold the Flamingo. Right after that the Dunes, Tropicana, and Stardust went up. It seemed to me that our town doubled in size.

CONSTRUCTION OF THE DUNES, C. 1950.

I remember when my dad built the Riviera. According to gossip, the Riviera had been built in 1954 by "two shoemakers and a designer, opened briefly, had 62 rainy days and lost $8 million." It had cost the Miami investors who built it $11 million.

Greenbaum had sold out of the Flamingo because of health problems. He had wanted to stay in Phoenix. But Chicago gangsters began to put pressure on him to buy it with a group of partners. They wanted an interest in Vegas. At first Greenbaum refused, but when members of his family were threatened he changed his mind and bought into the Riviera. He took 27 percent and gave my father, Joe Rosenberg, and Willie Alderman 7 percent each. New partners were added (Ben Goffstein, who had done publicity, bought in and got 2 percent), but Chicago told my father, "As long as you run the hotel, Greenbaum breathes." My father put a 24-hour-a-day death watch on Gus.

But guests knew none of the back-room drama, and neither did I. I waited all week for Sunday, now that my dad seemed to be working harder and coming home less. On Sunday he took me with his friends to play golf. Neither my dad nor his partners like to lose at card games or golf. They despised losing since they considered themselves winners in life. If they were a gin rummy foursome, one team had to lose, even I knew that. But they didn't seem to expect it. If my father and Willie lost, my father would throw his cards at the ceiling and stalk off. If Gus lost, he would slam his cards into the wall.

When they were on the golf course it was worse. My father and Willie usually played another partner, hotel owner Eddie Barrack, and a revolving fourth. About midway through the game there would always be a dispute in the score. The caddy would be asked to referee. The caddy always looked as if he would give anything to be in another universe at that moment. If my father lost, he would snap the old wood clubs over his knee and stalk off. Other opponents would toss golf balls like baseballs into the trees and throw their bags of clubs on the ground, and by the fifteenth hole the foursome would have stopped speaking. I'd look blasé as I watched the caddy turn pale. I knew that by next Sunday, all this would be forgotten, and my father and three others would be cheerfully heading for another disaster.

My father didn't mind making money off strangers but he didn't want to make money from friends. He hadn't done more than make a minor bet on a horse race in ten years by the time he came to Las Vegas. When he brought friends in from Minneapolis or Sioux City on a junket, he was known to keep tabs on how much they lost. At the end of their stay, he would hand them a hotel check for the amount of their losses and say, "Spend it on your

CELEBRITY GOLFERS BOB HOPE AND BING CROSBY.

family." He never forgot a gambler's face or hometown, and he was in charge of setting all the credit limits. He had an uncanny ability to size up a situation in an instant. He would stand in the back of the casino with that face of his on. When a gambler would motion to him that he wanted to raise his credit limit, my father never had to check his record—he remembered every dollar amount of business in the pit. Instantly he would signal Yes or No. Yes was a silent thumbs-up. For a No, my father would raise his hand, wave and give a slight smile.

To keep with Las Vegas's image as law-abiding, he decreed that no mobsters could carry guns in his casino. Only casino sheriffs were permitted to wear them. In the middle of one active night, my father spotted a gambler with a gun bulging in his jacket pocket. He went over to Greenbaum and said, "Gus, that guy looks like he just got out of the joint. I'm going to get him out of here." But before my father could stop the gambler, he had pulled his gun and started to threaten a whole craps table. My father got to him swiftly and said in a low voice, "You're out of college now, give me the rod." (College was a term for jail.) Stunned, the man handed over his gun, and my father led him outside. At the entrance to the hotel, my father peeled two twenty-dollar bills out of his sterling silver money clip and said, "Buy yourself some dinner and don't come back."

Our favorite vacation was the opening of the Del Mar Race Track in Del Mar, near San Diego, California. My mother would load the chauffeured black Cadillac with hatboxes, and the chauffeur would put sandbag air-conditioners in the windows—they were called swamp coolers. Willie Alderman would bring the betting sheet, and Nick the Greek would chomp on a cigar all the way down and bark out his choices to my father. I knew the stops by heart: breakfast in Barstow, lunch in Victorville.

Occasionally another limousine from Las Vegas would pass us on the lonely stretch of land, and the passengers would roll down the window and yell, "Davie, who you got in the fifth?" I'd watch in terror as the two limousines cruised side by side down the narrow expanse, sure that at any moment another car would come along and demolish the limousine in the wrong lane. After an intense conversation carried on in the desert air, my father would roll up the window and laugh, "Poor Eddie can't pick a horse to save his life."

When we'd go to the track, people would turn around and ask my father if my mother was a famous actress. I'd say proudly, "No, she was a dancer but then she married my dad and had me, and my dad says she has the best shape in town." My mother would blanch and my father would laugh.

Nick or Willie would always take me to the window but I couldn't place a bet. Something about being a child. They always placed bets for my father and he usually won—they all did. Harry James and Betty Grable, who said they owned some of the horses, would lean over from their box and congratulate my father when he won. Midway during the races all three men would stand up and start yelling and punching the air with their fists as if to propel the horses on. Whenever my father won, he'd grab my mother and kiss her hard and say, "We've got *mazel*, baby!"

After the track, we'd take a drive along the beach in La Jolla, which my mother loved. She was attracted to serene quiet places. Sometimes my father would ask the chauffeur to stop, and the three of us would walk along the beach. My mother would kick off her shoes and run ahead telling me that running in the sand was good for our thighs.

On Sunday, it would all be over, and we'd drive back home. My father would always start worrying that he had left his hotel for too long.

CONSTRUCTION OF THE $5 MILLION LAS VEGAS CONVENTION AND VISITOR'S AUTHORITY, COMPLETED IN 1959.

Our hotel drama aside, business was booming in Vegas. The middle Fifties saw the major urban development of Las Vegas as a city in conjunction with the spectacular Strip expansion. The first churches, schools, and subdivisions were built, and Nellis Air Force base was expanded. I remember my father and his friends built an office downtown and then the Las Vegas Bowl off the Strip. My dad predicted that the end of the Fifties would bring many more families to Vegas and the bowling alley was for them.

City fathers came up with the idea of building a convention center to keep the hotels filled on the slow days of the week—Sundays through Thursdays, the slow summers, and the worst week of the year, Christmas. It was to be funded by a room tax levied on all hotel and motel rooms in Clark County. Construction began in 1957 and finished in 1959 when the $5 million Las Vegas Convention and Visitor's Authority opened its doors.

The urbanization of Las Vegas increased the need for the construction of a modern interstate highway to southern California. More and more tourists were coming to Vegas to gamble and to play. The highway was started. The first resort golf course was opened at the Desert Inn, where The Tournament of Champions was established in 1953.

Business had never been better, nothing could possibly go wrong now, reasoned the city fathers. But they were wrong. Something very major threatened to go wrong.

In November 1950, Senator Estes Kefauver had rolled into town, accompanied by his federal Commission to Investigate Organized Crime. Kefauver was determined to make political hay by shutting Vegas down. The mood of the country was patriotic, and the postwar boom was in full swing.

Kefauver was an ambitious senator from Tennessee with an eye on the White House. The mandate of his Kefauver Commission was to link gambling with organized crime and shady law enforcement with illegal gambling. From New York to Los Angeles, he rounded up all the "alleged" crime figures he could subpoena and subjected them to grueling hours of humiliating—if often pointless—interrogation.

On every news program, Kefauver told the nation what he thought the mobsters were like. "The modern day gangster is quite a different person than the gangster of the 1920s during the Al Capone days," he said. "They have put on more respectability, they have more money, they dress better, they try to travel in better society."

The nation was galvanized by the Commission hearings. The following is a transcript from a newsreel that was titled: "Crime Probe: Senate Group Delves Into Gambling Racket."

NEWS ANNOUNCER: The Senatorial Crime Commission shifts to New York, and Frank Costello, alleged overlord of gambling, arrives at the Big Town's Foley Square.

Senator Toby now turns the heat on Costello.

SENATOR TOBY: Has this country come up to your expectations? You must have in your mind something to your credit as an American citizen, if so what is it?

FRANK COSTELLO: Paid my taxes. (Laughter)

NEWS ANNOUNCER: Even a note of glamour is injected into the thrill-packed proceedings by the arrival of Virginia Hill, in whose home the late Bugsy Siegel was killed. She denies any Costello connection.

KEFAUVER: Did you ever get any money from Costello?

HILL: No.

KEFAUVER: And did you ever get any money from Meyer Lansky?

HILL: I never got money from any of those fellas. None of 'em.

Las Vegas historian Hal Rothman believes that the Kefauver hearings scared the leaders of Las Vegas. "They saw a lot of people they knew on television in uncomfortable ways. They heard a lot of talk about Las Vegas and they were afraid it would somehow make their little paradise different."

Sproule Braydon, the Chairman of the New York Anti-Crime Commission, raised the ante. "Of one thing we can be sure. The Costellos, the Adonises, and the rest of this scum are among the Kremlin's best friends and allies. Perhaps in a sense they are even more dangerous than the spies convicted of stealing our atomic and military secrets. Our citizens are aroused. They will relentlessly demand honest and competent officials, who will drive the criminals into prison, out of the country, and into the electric chair."

In November 1950, Kefauver's Commission finally came to Las Vegas itself. He questioned Bugsy's advance man, Moe Sedway; Wilbur Clark and Moe Dalitz of the Desert Inn; Nevada Tax Commissioner William Moore, who was part owner of the Last Frontier; Lt. Governor Cliff Jones; and others.

The Las Vegas trip was one of fourteen that Kefauver committee members took to different cities. Although most of the committee investigations were broadcast, the Las Vegas hearings were conducted behind closed doors. The committee spent just one day in town. Under oath, Wilbur Clark, owner of the Desert Inn, told the committee that in order to finish building the resort, he sold a 74-percent share in the property to reputed Detroit underworld figure Moe Dalitz. The committee interrogated the Flamingo's own Sedway about his previous association with the late Bugsy Siegel and about his Vegas race-book interest. Sedway indirectly admitted ties to organized crime as he was the local representative for the Continental Press Service, which ran the race-wire.

At the conclusion of the hearings in Las Vegas, Senator Charles Toby, a Republican from New Hampshire and one of the committee members, said, "What I have seen here today leaves me with a sense of outrage and righteous indignation. I think it's about time somebody got damn mad and told these people where to get off." Kefauver was more diplomatic. Not only did he thank the state officials, he promised them federal assistance with their "local problems."

But this was a "problem" quickly forgotten. Instead, the Kefauver bill was introduced that would levy a 10-percent federal tax on all wagering that would be collected regardless of whether the casino won the wager. It was a bill that would have discouraged customers and effectively put an end to gaming in Las Vegas. Famed Democratic Nevada Senator Pat McCarran of the Senate Judiciary Committee used all his power to kill the bill. In a Vegas showman coup, McCarran brought a pair of dice to a House member's office and demonstrated the game of craps. By this, he proved that applying a 10-percent tax on each bet would be a crippling mathematical impossibility for the casinos.

Most of the crime figures who testified before the committee, including the Vegas mobsters, painted themselves as former bad boys who were now just trying to make an honest living. In fact, according to Robbins Cahill, administrator of the Nevada Tax Commission, the state agency that regulated gaming during those early years, Vegas's gambling industry could not function without the former mobsters, because only those from illegal gambling understood the games they were offering, since gambling had been illegal before being legalized in Nevada. He said they could keep their gaming licenses as long as they did not engage in any illegal activity.

Although the committee established a link between the underworld and Vegas, ironically Kefauver's investigation ultimately benefited the town. The hysteria created by Kefauver caused crackdowns on illegal gambling nationwide and spurred exiled gambling operators to settle in the West. Black money from all over America poured into Vegas, from the top dons of the New York, Chicago, and Havana Syndicate and from the illegal casino operators in Boston, Miami, New Orleans, St. Louis, Cleveland, Dallas, Phoenix, and Los Angeles. With that came hustlers, small-time hoods, prostitutes, and a wide array of undesirable characters. Vegas found a new source of major capital.

"After the hearings, old bookmakers, black marketeers, loan sharks, a couple of heavy-duty bad guys threw money into these places," says Nick Pileggi. "The financing was about two, three, four million dollars. Six million dollars could build an early casino."

The publicity generated by the Kefauver hearings helped defeat gambling in nearby California and Arizona, much to the relief of most Las Vegas casino owners. Although some quietly supported the measures, in hopes of expanding out of state, most casino owners preferred to keep their financial interests within Nevada. The Las Vegas connection to organized crime was the major factor in gambling being defeated in both of those states.

"I think the defeat of Kefauver emboldened the Vegas mobsters," says historian Hal Rothman. "It made them feel that they had much greater control over this place, had much greater control over the industry than they probably previously realized, and it made them certainly more willing to venture throughout the 1950s."

To Nick Pileggi, "They could very easily have closed down gambling in Las Vegas. If Estes Kefauver had been elected Vice President, you don't think

RONALD REAGAN AND HIS FRIENDS SEND THEIR GREETINGS.

he would have done it? He would have done it in a second. You wouldn't have a Las Vegas."

My father was going to be called along with all his associates. My mother was distraught that I would hear about it and, although only six, would somehow understand what their lives were about. My father tried every maneuver he could to avoid being called and finally three of his friends convinced the committee that he knew only what they did and that my mother's precarious state of health would deteriorate drastically if he were called. In the end, he was never asked to testify.

He was, however, discussed in the proceedings and once was referred to as "a Mob peacemaker." He had supposedly sent an emissary from the Flamingo Hotel to halt a long-standing feud between two Texas gamblers that had resulted in a number of deaths. He was quoted in one FBI-tapped phone conversation as being "Dave Berman, one of the biggest men out there in

Vegas" and the one who demanded that the gamblers "get together and straighten up."

Privately, my father and his friends had joked that the Commission would never shut them down. They had never had respect for politicians since they had made a career of bribing them. In fact, no bookie in town could get anyone to bet that the Commission would win. Although they did not fear the Commission, they were annoyed at the bad publicity it brought their little town. They were into revisionism and sanitization; who needed this dirty laundry aired before the nation?

'*Vaysmear*,' they sighed in Yiddish in unison after it was over. It's no wonder "that politicians never make a buck. They can't do a goddamn thing."

THE FREEWHEELING FIFTIES

There was an ebullience and an exhilaration in the air in the mid-1950s in Vegas. It was as if my town was the center of the universe, and my dad owned it. Maybe my sister was losing some of her charming small-town ways, but she was gaining worldwide fame and a huge bankroll.

It seemed that every other day our black phone would ring, and my dad would answer and say, "Izzy! I've booked a suite for you and the family at the Riv; you'll stay there on me until you find a house. How is it? It's 80 degrees everyday, how bad can it be?" All his friends were moving here.

Las Vegas was beginning to build new schools, and even though we still lived in our little house on South Sixth Street, I was going to be going to a "better" school—the John S. Park Elementary School. Fifth Street Elementary had gotten pretty rough.

My life changed in other ways. The Flamingo was no longer my private sandbox. My dad and his partner sold it. Now I had the $8.5 million Riviera, the only high-rise on the Strip. Gone was my group of green bungalows near my pool.

Debbie Reynolds remembers the heyday of the town. "The Riviera was a beautiful, big hotel, and the stage was wonderful. In those days we had a

20-piece orchestra. You didn't have the expenses that you have today. The hotel picked up a lot of those costs in those days. But not anymore. That's changed."

It seemed bigger. My dad had a new group of partners including Ross Miller from Chicago. He had a great pompadour of hair, wore turtleneck sweaters and was always smiling. I liked him. His son was Bobby Miller; he was the pool lifeguard. He's now the Governor of Nevada.

On the Riviera they had taken a chance. Critics claimed that the porous desert floor was not strong enough to support the nine-story tower. So far they have been wrong. Our new hotel was one of the first to use elevators. It had 250 rooms in a European style, and our showroom, the Clover Room, was 10,000 square feet—"the largest on the Strip," my dad told everyone.

It was beginning to feel like a city.

The Mob godfathers definitely still owned Vegas. Kefauver had come and gone, and his attempt to shut down their desert empire had backfired. The crackdown on illegal gambling elsewhere in the United States attracted millions of dirty dollars that built sparkling new hotels. In addition to the Riviera, there was the Dunes, the Stardust, and the $10 million Tropicana.

In one of the ironies of history, much of the administrative stability behind the casino money machines came from the Mormons. Although gambling is forbidden in the Mormon religion, working in the gaming industry is not. Mormons provided much of the managerial integrity that made the town work and also became prominent bankers and professional people who still lead the town to this day. They had a special relationship with the Mob bosses.

"I'm a very religious person, and I have a lot of respect for how anybody finds God," says Michael Ventura. "That said, structurally—and only structurally—the Mormon organization has a great deal in common with the Mafia. Strictly hierarchical. Great rewards for loyalty. Great rewards for keeping your word. They take care of their own."

To Rod Amateau, the Mormons, in effect, ran the town. "The pit boss who watches you—when he finishes his shift he doesn't drink coffee. He goes home to his wife and 98 children. That's who's succeeding in Vegas because they have a moral center."

The moral center of the Mormons, plus the steady flow of gambling dollars, was part of the equation that made the Mob-run Vegas a paradise. The early gangsters had brought their dream to life. And true to the legacy of the star-struck Bugsy Siegel, the Fifties mobsters were engaged in a love affair with America's favorite entertainers.

"It was like a great theater audience," says comedian Red Buttons. "They were great, great audiences. You'd look forward to working, and the money was enormous. Four weeks in Vegas could buy you a Third World country."

"Those were the days of the Reds," says Rod Amateau. "Red Skelton, Redd Foxx, Red Buttons. And large, heavy, Jewish men with little-boy names: Hennie, Snooky, Youngy, Bickie, Bookie, Bockie. You know, little names. Little names with big guys."

George Schlatter remembers Milton Berle being a huge star. And Buddy Hackett. The comedians in Vegas helped the town to make it.

Perhaps the most celebrated and beloved entertainer to emerge in the Fifties was Liberace, who won the heart of Las Vegas. He was a former child-prodigy pianist from Milwaukee, Wisconsin, who epitomized the spirit of Vegas—spectacle, glitter, and glamour—and took it completely over the top.

"Other people played better piano, but Lee had a charm," says Shecky Greene. "Truck drivers used to come and watch him. They got to love him. After about fifteen minutes, it's like, 'Hey, Mary, you know, this guy's good.' And he did that thing where he'd show off his fabulous jewelry, say a ring, and then say to the audience, 'You like this ring? You bought it for me,' and they'd go crazy."

"He was called 'Mr. Showmanship,'" says Debbie Reynolds. "But more than that, he was a great friend. He was wonderful. We used to stay up late, and we'd go home to his house with his 19 dogs and then he'd make breakfast. 'Oh, I'm just whipping something up, you want scrambled or you want an omelette?' he'd ask. I just loved him."

It wasn't easy for Liberace in Las Vegas in the beginning. He first played the town when he was 23, soon after he started playing commercial piano in the lounge of the Last Frontier Hotel in 1945. He was constantly taunted for his style, especially his hairdo. But he just smiled at the jeers. He earned $400 dollars a week but insisted that one day he would earn "thousands of dollars weekly."

He didn't make it big immediately, wasn't much of a draw until he came up with the idea of wearing his flamboyant costumes and garish jewelry. In 1956, he signed a three-year contract with my dad at the Riviera Hotel for an all-time record of $50,000 a week. And that was just the beginning.

I remember him as a charming man who sang "Happy Birthday" to me from the stage and greeted my dad and me many times when we were in the audience. He was such a consummate performer. The audience would sit in rapt attention as he entered in a rhinestone-lined, full-length, black diamond mink cape and sat down at his glittering piano topped by lit gold candelabras. When he would smile widely and start to play, the audience would melt. In a city of extravagance and outrageous gimmicks, he kept outdoing himself. He earned six gold records, two Emmy awards, and was once entered in the *Guinness Book of World Records* as the world's highest-paid musician—and always, his base was Vegas.

In tribute today, the Liberace Museum is the most popular tourist attraction in Vegas. The main building is full of Liberace's costumes: his 200-pound Neptune costume; his capes; his world-famous red, white, and blue hotpants suit; and his incredible jewelry, including his trademark candelabra ring, complete with platinum "candlesticks" and diamond "flames." There's also a dazzling white-and-yellow-gold, piano-shaped ring, complete with 260 individually set diamonds; his spectacular piano-shaped wristwatch set in a collection of diamonds, rubies, sapphires, and emeralds.

Liberace's exotic cars are on display along with the costumes. There's the "Stars and Stripes," a hand-painted red, white, and blue Rolls-Royce convertible; another Rolls done entirely in mirror tiles and etched with a custom design of galloping horses. And in another building is the re-creation of Liberace's master bedroom from "The Cloisters," his Palm Springs estate.

The other world-famous entertainer associated with Vegas in this era was Elvis Presley, my personal favorite. I had a small red record case of 45s with all his hits, which I carried everywhere. The first time I ever heard of Elvis, my mother and I were in L.A. in 1955. My father called and asked me to watch a television program called "Juke Box Jury." It was a weekly show in which new musical artists performed and the celebrity panel decided whether they would be a "hit" or a "miss."

I watched Elvis do "Don't Be Cruel" and then called my father saying, "He's a hit, hire him, can I meet him?" Although many celebrities had sung "Happy Birthday" to me, I was never more excited than when Elvis did. I still have my autographed picture from that night. That event convinced me that my father was very important in Vegas if he knew Elvis Presley.

Elvis, like Liberace, did not fare well at first in Vegas. He opened in Vegas in April of 1956 at the Last Frontier Hotel for two weeks. He had already recorded the hits "Heartbreak Hotel," "Hound Dog," and "Blue Suede Shoes." The bosses at the hotel were divided as to whether to hire him. Would a kid from Nashville open in Vegas? Would he bring in the craps shooters?

They finally decided to hire him at $8,500 a week, which was the highest fee his agent Colonel Parker could get out of them. Elvis was a flop,

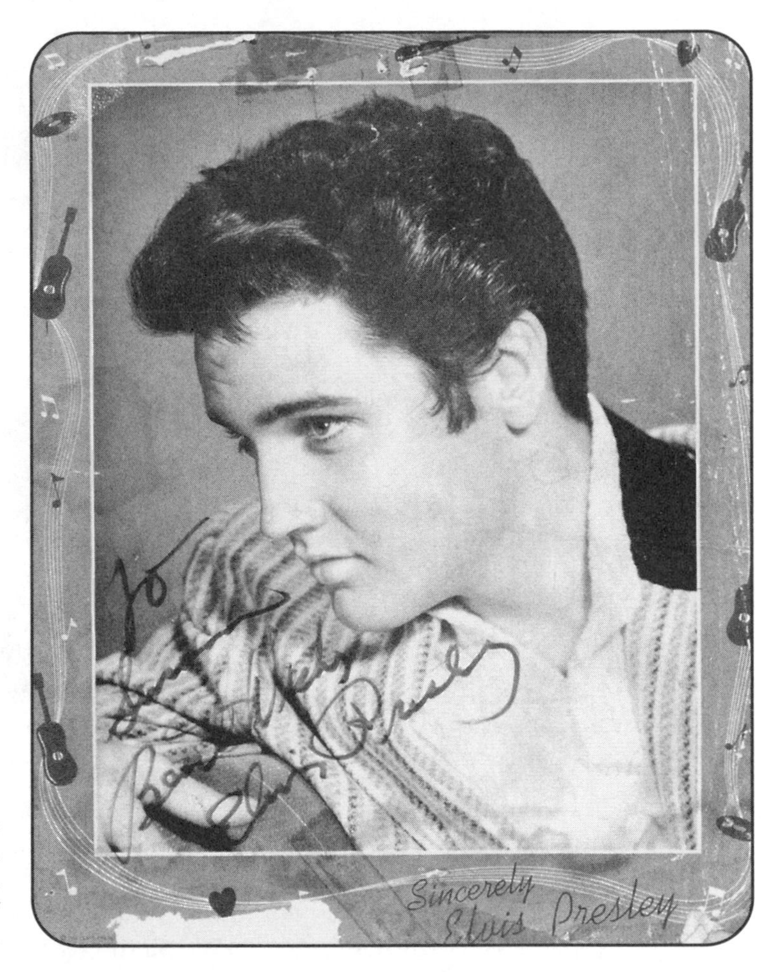

A PRICELESS MEMENTO: "TO SUSAN, BEST WISHES, ELVIS PRESLEY." 1957.

and they fired him after the first week. Colonel Parker threw a fit and said "the next time he plays Vegas, you'll have to pay him ten times more." Thirteen years later, in 1969, entertainment director Bill Miller hired him at Kirk Kerkorian's International Hotel for more than $100,000 a week. By the time he died, he held every record for attendance in a Las Vegas showroom.

"A couple of people called me and said, 'You know, you're making a mistake with Elvis. He's not gonna be as big as you think he is,'" remembers Miller. "And I said, 'Well, I have a great feeling about Elvis, and I'm gonna play him regardless.' And I must tell you, the kind of business that Elvis did. They were standing in line at six in the morning waiting to see Elvis, hoping that maybe somebody wouldn't show. There was never an empty seat for

ELVIS AND PRISCILLA PRESLEY AT THE ALADDIN, 1967.

Elvis Presley. It was just unbelievable." Later, one of the biggest Vegas events was Elvis and Priscilla's wedding at the Aladdin Hotel in 1967. Whether the fact that Elvis married there spawned today's Elvis-impersonator ministers at the wedding chapels is not known. But any couple getting married in Las Vegas today will have no trouble finding an Elvis minister who will sing "Blue Suede Shoes."

Behind my town's glamour in the Fifties, however, lurked a terrible secret, one that caused pain, rage, and humiliation. Las Vegas was racist—it was known as the "Mississippi of the West."

As a child, I knew our maid Lucy Brown lived somewhere else. She just referred to it as the west side. Sometimes I would hear people say, "She lives under the cement curtain," meaning beyond the cement underpass. It separated whites from blacks. I had never been there. My black classmates at Fifth Street Elementary School were bused in from the west side. Since Las Vegas was the only town I knew, it didn't seem odd that no blacks lived in our neighborhood.

In the Thirties and Forties, many of the blacks had come from the South to work in the hotels in the service professions. They lived in humiliating, segregated conditions. The primitive attitudes toward the town's African-American residents began with the Hoover Dam contractors who restricted employment in writing to only "White American citizens." "After the Roosevelt Administration came into power," says historian Dennis McBride, "the government ordered the six companies to hire more black people. You can't even say they hired a percentage. It was an infinitesimal number relative to the number of men who worked on the dam. You could say that virtually no blacks were on the dam. There are a couple of photographs that the six companies took and said, 'Here, see, we have black men working here and we have Indians, Native Americans, working here, we're not racists.' That was for public consumption, but in fact they were very racist."

Many who moved to Las Vegas with the boom of Hoover Dam brought with them prejudices from the South and the Midwest. By the late Forties and early Fifties, hundreds more African-Americans came to town, seeking employment in the exploding hotel industry. According to McBride, "The workers were only allowed to work in housekeeping, cooks—out of sight, out of mind."

Governor Bob Miller, who grew up in Las Vegas, remembers being close friends with a black teenager. "I would go over at various times to pick him up to go to this or that event and socialize with him. It was not common, but it wasn't unheard of to go into a predominantly black neighborhood at the time despite the fact that there was this overt segregation. It just didn't faze me as a young man. I was a teenager, and it didn't occur to me. Perhaps I had been unduly naive, or just sheltered." Hotel and city rules made it impossible for Miller and his friend to swim in the same pool.

When newspaper publisher Hank Greenspun moved to Las Vegas in the late Forties, the city was a Jim Crow town. According to Greenspun's son Brian, "We had wonderful entertainers as the entertainment industry grew and the gaming industry grew. They would bring in Sammy Davis and a number of black entertainers who had to entertain at the hotels and then move out to another side of town called the west side to live. They had to stay there. And blacks were not allowed on the Strip. They were allowed to make the beds and clean up restrooms and do all that, then they had to go home; they were not allowed on the Strip. It was outrageous."

Many of the black performers were among America's most beloved entertainers—the Mills Brothers, Pearl Bailey, Nat King Cole, Louis Armstrong, Harry Belafonte, Lena Horne, Eartha Kitt. They headlined in the glamorous Vegas showrooms, always winning standing ovations from big-spending high rollers. But after the show, they had to make their exits through the hotels' kitchen doors.

ALTHOUGH WELL-LOVED ON STAGE IN THE 1950S, SAMMY DAVIS, JR. AND OTHER BLACK ENTERTAINERS WERE EXPECTED TO ENTER THE HOTELS THROUGH THE KITCHEN.

Donald Mills remembers those times, "You couldn't gamble. You couldn't go in the casinos. You did your show, and then you got out of there."

The west side was a disgrace—run-down public areas, unpaved streets. While white entertainers lounged in their elegant hotel suites, sipping complimentary champagne, it was on the other side of the tracks that the black entertainers were forced to stay.

"There was a couple of individuals who had their homes fixed up like a rooming house, and somehow the word got out. The entertainers generally stayed at those rooming houses when they were appearing in Las Vegas," says James Walker, president of the Moulin Rouge Hotel. "There was also a small apartment complex that served as a motel, but it was certainly inferior in quality and so forth; it was located in west Las Vegas, and the entertainers sometimes stayed there if there were too many of them to stay in these private homes.

"Back in the old days, blacks, or Negroes, as they were called then, were not even allowed to have the traditional black jobs in the gaming industry, such as bellman or waiter. Obviously blacks could not frequent any of the hotels or gaming establishments. It was typical that there was no minority participation in almost all forms of economic or social activities in Las Vegas. So the name of Mississippi of the West was an accurate description."

"It was rotten. Even though I never really talked to many of the black entertainers about it, you could just feel what they were feeling," says Fluff LeCoque, former showgirl. "For us, in the entertainment business, in show business, it was shameful. It was just a crime, the way they were being treated."

Red Buttons remembers that time. "The great Louis Armstrong, the ambassador of goodwill of the United States of America who was revered and cherished all over the world, lived in a trailer before all that was lifted."

There were absolutely no exceptions to the rule, not even for the legendary Sammy Davis, Jr. "Everyone discusses Sammy Davis playing Vegas and sleeping on the west side of town—because he couldn't book into a hotel," says Rod Amateau. "Nat King Cole was told the following, 'Please do not sing to the women—sing above them.' So you get a situation where a man was asked to change his style, his act, and he did it. He did it willingly, because he wanted to play Vegas that badly. He wanted to be asked back."

"Las Vegas was the most controlled society in the world at one point," says George Schlatter, "and black acts could not come into the hotel. You could not come in as an audience. Black performers, whether it was Belafonte or Lena or Sammy or whoever, they did not come in the front door of the hotel. There was a real color barrier in Vegas. They couldn't stay in the hotel. And black people could not come in to see the shows."

George Schlatter remembers that, "Lena was at the Sands, Pearl Bailey was at the Flamingo, and Marlene Dietrich was at the Sahara. When Marlene heard about this color-barrier thing, she said, 'Darling, this is not acceptable.' So after the second show, the three girls got together and they walked the Strip. First they went into the Sahara. It sounds like nothing today, but back then, for two black ladies to walk, not just through the hotel, but through the casino, that was something!"

Popular legend surrounds the end of official segregation on the Las Vegas Strip. It is a matter of debate who first publicly bucked the trend, though Frank Sinatra's boycott of the Sands until Sammy Davis was allowed to stay there was one defining moment.

Performer Sonny Charles remembers how Nat King Cole went to see a show at the Lido in 1960. The management did not want Nat King Cole to sit in the audience. "But he was a big star over there in Europe and all these

A VEGAS TRIO BUT NOT AN ACT—OR WAS IT?
DEBBIE REYNOLDS, EDDIE FISHER, AND LIZ TAYLOR.

European people didn't really understand the segregation thing, so they refused to go on unless Nat King Cole sat front row center. And then when he did, people realized that the audience loved the fact that they were sitting in the same room with Nat King Cole."

Debbie Reynolds remembers how segregation affected Sammy Davis, Jr. "They had very bad rules here about if you were black, you were not allowed in certain clubs. I didn't know this. I said to Sam, 'Let's go to the El Rancho and we'll catch the comics.' He said, 'Uh–oh, Debbie, I can't meet you. I'm not allowed out of the hotel.' I said, 'What do you mean you're not allowed out of the hotel? What's the matter with you?' 'Well, I'm only allowed to stay in the Sands,' he said.

"I didn't understand that. So, I called the El Rancho and I said, 'Excuse me, I have a reservation for tonight and I just wanted to clear something up with you. I'm bringing my friend, Sammy Davis, Jr. That's okay isn't it?' Long pause, then, 'Sorry Debbie.' I said, 'You've got to be kidding. You have to be kidding. Tell me you're kidding. This is a joke.' Wasn't a joke. So I didn't go. I mean, I became crazy then. They couldn't stay in town. It was horrendous. It was horrifying. Frank Sinatra and Sammy Davis and Harry

Belafonte and Lena Horne and myself and Shirley McLaine could not deal with that at all. We helped break that code. We wouldn't work. I said, 'Anybody comes to see my show, any color, any nationality, whoever is allowed in a show.' If they wouldn't do it, then I wouldn't go on."

Anne Jeffreys remembers when Sammy Davis, Jr., first stayed in a Strip hotel. "He was so proud. He was just like a little boy, he was so pleased with the change in politics. That night at dinner, he came down and there were several ladies at dinner. He gave each one of us a little box. And he said, 'As a memento of my opening and the fact that I can stay in the hotel.' He gave each one of us a beautiful gold wristwatch."

It's money that has driven Vegas since her founding days in 1905. And there was no questioning the fact that black performers brought cash in by the bucketful. Eventually, even the most rigidly racist policies had to bend to the reality of economics.

There were no impassioned civil rights marches down Las Vegas Boulevard in those times. But when Hank Greenspun began a campaign against racism in his newspaper, the *Las Vegas Sun*, both black and white performers rebelled in force. On March 26, 1960, Greenspun, Governor Grant Sawyer, Bob Bailey, and Dr. James McMillan, branch president of the local NAACP, spearheaded the signing of an official agreement to end public-accommodations discrimination in southern Nevada. Simple signatures on a contract did not erase overnight such deeply held bigotry, but it was a start.

The story of the black-owned hotel on the west side, the Moulin Rouge, is part of the Vegas legend. Small gambling clubs there, like the Harlem Club, the Brown Derby, and the Cotton Club, catered to those who were unwelcome on the Strip. In 1954, some investors decided to capitalize on Vegas's racial segregation, and they raised the funding for a different kind of hotel casino: one that would be open to both blacks and whites and that would offer first-class accommodations for African-American performers.

In May 1955, Dee Dee Jasmin was a 17-year-old Los Angeles dancer selected for the hotel's chorus line. "You just dream of going to Vegas with all the glitz and the glitter and the bright lights. When we arrived, we had our Sunday best on, believe me. The high-heel shoes on and the hats and the furs and everything," she said. "Then we saw this beautiful hotel. It said Moulin Rouge. Well, that lifted our spirits to no end. We saw the place where we were going to work. My God, it was breathtaking."

The regular Moulin Rouge performers and the hotel staff were housed in a special development, the Cadillac Arms, which far exceeded the usual west-side standards. Young dancers like Dee Dee found themselves living next door to stars like the Platters and Bennie Carter's Orchestra.

AFTER A STAR-STUDDED OPENING, THE MOULIN ROUGE MYSTERIOUSLY SHUT DOWN.

At first, the Moulin Rouge was a sell out. The best black entertainers from all over the country came to perform, and when news of the lavish and exotic production numbers hit the Strip, a third show was added, so performers from the mainstream hotels could drop in after work.

"They found out about the third week it was open, that all the white people were going down there," says George Schlatter. "'Cause it was a lot more fun than being out on the Strip."

"The people that frequented the club, it was star-studded," says Dee Dee Jasmin. "We had Tallulah Bankhead, the Mills Brothers—they were in there every night. And also Harry Belafonte, Milton Berle, naturally Sammy, Frank Sinatra, and Joe Louis who was such a love. He was our official greeter of the Moulin Rouge."

But just seven months after its star-studded opening, the staff of the Moulin Rouge arrived for work to find the club padlocked. The real reason behind the closing remains a classic Las Vegas mystery. Was it pressure from the Strip hotels who feared competition? Was it irresponsible management? Or was the whole Moulin Rouge experiment only a short-term money-making scheme for the investors? Whatever the reason, the short life of integrated entertainment was over for the rest of the Fifties.

One of the most influential men to shape the future of Las Vegas was a former attorney, Hank Greenspun, editor and publisher of the *Las Vegas Sun*. He came to prominence in the Fifties, not just because of his courageous stand against racism, but for his incredible concern for every issue that affected our town. Hank was a good friend of my father's. Every morning at breakfast, my dad opened his copy of the *Sun*, and before he read the headlines, he'd read from Hank's celebrated, "Where I Stand" column. "Let's see what Hank has to say today."

The most famous newspaperman Las Vegas ever saw or probably will see was a former attorney who had driven into Vegas in 1946 and immediately recognized that this was a town that would never have a slow news day. In a town born of crime, he became a beacon of conscience.

Greenspun staked everything on my young town by buying a small newspaper, the *Free Press*, in 1946.

"My dad liked Las Vegas. It was a brand new city then, and he saw an opportunity to be a part of it in a much larger way by having a voice," says his son, Brian Greenspun, now a prominent Vegas citizen. "And he bought the newspaper. I think he paid a thousand dollars down, closed it on a Friday. He borrowed the thousand because he didn't have it. And on Monday, when he went to the bank, he had two thousand dollars in his bank account, so he was off to the races. A short time later he changed the name from the *Free Press* to the *Las Vegas Sun* and took it daily.

"My father's interest was to make sure that as long as there was going to be legalized gaming, Las Vegas would have to grow in a way that the people who came to live and work in and around that industry would be proud of the place where they would raise their children," says Greenspun.

Hank Greenspun went after Joe McCarthy in the Fifties. According to Brian Greenspun, "My dad was having a running feud, one of his many feuds, with Senator Pat McCarran from Nevada, probably one of the most powerful senators at the time in the United States. McCarthy, of course, was an ally. McCarran brought McCarthy out to Las Vegas to attack my father. And my mom and dad were at a rally one night in Las Vegas when McCarthy went out and just zeroed in on my dad and called him all kinds of names and accused him of fostering 'Greenspunism,' you know, like McCarthyism, and accused him of being an ex-Communist.

"Prior to that, because of his involvement with the Israeli War of Independence, my dad had lost his citizenship because he pled guilty to violating the Neutrality Act of the United States. He ran guns and armed shipments and airplanes to Israel and took the heat, basically, for all the people who were caught. He pled guilty, paid a fine, and because of that he lost his civil rights. So McCarthy may have come in here thinking that Greenspun was an ex-convict, but because he was so warped and twisted, he said he's an ex-Communist." Everyone was prepared to lynch the elder Greenspun that evening because no one there liked Communists. "Well, my dad went after him. He got up on the stage and McCarthy ran out of the room. From that time on, my dad went after him in his newspaper. He was the first newspaperman to really go after Joe McCarthy and give cover, if you will, or shelter for everybody else in the country to do the same."

In the early 1950s, Greenspun had another urgent crusade. The Atomic Energy Commission had chosen a portion of the Nellis Air Force Base for America's continental test site for its new nuclear weapons. The AEC assured Las Vegas that the radiation would pose no threat. The first detonation, a one-kiloton device, was in January 1951, 70 miles northwest of Las Vegas.

"When I was a youngster, we lived in Indian Springs, and I can remember in the very early Fifties being woken up," says Sheriff Jerry Keller of the Las Vegas Metropolitan Police. "My dad would put me on top of our trailer house and we would watch the bombs go off. I remember distinctly the clouds and the green streaks through the sky."

"You could see the bombs right over the hill. It was like 60, 70 miles away," says author Michael Ventura. "That's nothing for looking at a mushroom cloud. Those things are tall. And the hotels would organize picnics to go to the hillsides to go look at the bomb blasts."

The atomic tests were the biggest news in town the year they happened. In fact, the town was hoping they would draw tourists from L.A. The *Review Journal* ran articles on how to treat your collectibles during the blast. It was never thought that those blasts could hurt people. The articles only said that atomic fallout was a big danger to your flower vases.

"Now I found something very interesting talking to people who had seen these blasts. No two people told me the same colors," says Michael Ventura. "I would ask, what color was it? It's not the kind of thing you get

KABOOM IN THE DESERT. TESTING THE ATOMIC BOMB.

from books. It's the kind of thing you only get from eyewitnesses because of photographs, color film. Nobody told me the same two colors. Some people just saw white. Some people just saw brown. Some people saw yellow, pink, green, all violet, all the colors of the rainbow. These sometimes describing the same blast.

"So how you see a bomb blast apparently is very subjective. Students who were in high school then were taken out, on class trips, to see the bomb blasts."

"Wilbur Clark's Desert Inn had a beautiful sky room at that time. All the hotel owners went up to the sky room to watch the blast. My father felt that the blasts were very dangerous, and he bundled my mother and me off to Los Angeles so that we wouldn't be in any way hurt by the radiation. But that was an unusual thing, everybody else was totally behind the blasts. Before we went, he covered every item in our house, and when we came back, we shook these sheets out. Atomic dust was on them, and we were shaking them out in our back yard. Just like the way that Vegas has its own take on everything, the atomic blasts were considered tourist events. They even had a Las Vegas chorus girl called 'Miss Atomic Blast.'"

To this day, the lasting effects of the blasts remain unknown.

"That concussion wind is full of plutonium. People in Nebraska in the line of the wind, small towns, became gardens of leukemia," says Ventura. "Somebody else told me that especially after the first few blasts, the horses—and a lot of people had horses around here in those days—the horses wouldn't eat. Cats wouldn't let themselves be scratched. Dogs wouldn't let themselves be touched."

Hank Greenspun was one of the only people in Vegas to object to the atomic testing. According to his wife Barbara Greenspun, now publisher of the *Sun*, "The first nuclear test, they invited all the members of the press including my husband Hank. They were not in any way protected with any clothing of any kind. And that blast went off, and I remember Hank telling me, 'It was like getting kicked in the stomach by a mule, it was such a tremendous blast.'" Greenspun died in 1989, just before his eightieth birthday. Until he died he felt that the exposure that he received might have been the cause of his cancer.

The Vegas of the early and mid-Fifties seemed a gangster's utopia. Former outlaws could show up, shed their pasts like a desert reptile shedding its seasonal skins, and pick up anew as model citizens.

My father kept all the details of his past from me with the greatest of care. With my birth he, too, was reborn in Las Vegas. I later learned that one

MY 11TH BIRTHDAY. LIBERACE SANG "HAPPY BIRTHDAY" TO OUR TABLE AT THE RIVIERA.

time there was a "Talk of the Town" column in the *New Yorker* which said the town was run by former bootleggers. My parents took no chances. My father had all the issues on sale bought out when they arrived at the airport so there would be no chance I could see them and make a connection.

During these years my childhood seemed very safe to me, but there were exceptions. Once my father had to go to Miami for a week. I remember my mother begging him not to go, and I heard the words "not safe." I wondered if that was because Miami had atomic bomb tests like we did.

Later I learned that his partner, Moe Sedway, had had a heart attack and died at the Roney Plaza Hotel there, and he and Willie went to claim the body. There was always a shakeup when anyone died. The whole week he was gone my mother would not let me go to school. I could not even go out of the house. I protested loudly that Lou and gin rummy had ceased to be fun. When my father came back he took me to the SPCA and bought me a puppy, my fondest wish, to reward me.

In 1957, when I was twelve, my dad was sure that Las Vegas was going to be the most incredible boom town that ever came down the pipe.

We were planning to move to the Desert Inn Estates where the new, nicer houses were. I remember so many times he would have arguments with his friends in our living room, and they would say, "Davie, Davie, you know, you're in your 50s. The town is tapped out. Let's move to L.A., let's go back to Minneapolis." My father would say, "This is just the beginning. You are not going to be able to believe what Las Vegas is gonna be. Every piece of property on the Strip is going to be worth $5 million." He knew when he came to Vegas in 1945 that Las Vegas was going to be an incredible mythic place.

It was our Las Vegas, and we were going to live there forever. But things did not work out as my father planned.

On my twelfth birthday, my father gave me a party at the Riviera Hotel. He had invited ten of my girlfriends from owners' families, and Liberace sang "Happy Birthday." My father had a special cake made up, all chocolate, and bought out the hotel gift shop for me. He sat in a booth behind our table to watch the whole extravaganza with pride.

One month later he was dead from a doctor's mistake.

They said my father's funeral was the largest funeral Las Vegas had ever seen. There were thousands of mourners. Pallbearers were Gus, Willie, Uncle Chickie and other Vegas owners.

My father, 54, lay in an open casket while the rabbi intoned, "It is a sad day for all of Las Vegas. Davie Berman, one of our original pioneers, who made this city bloom, is dead. There will never be anyone like him. Davie Berman had a vision. He saw a boom town where others had just seen desert. He was Mr. Las Vegas. Davie Berman, beloved by all of Las Vegas, beloved husband and beloved father, is gone."

Then there was just the Kaddish, which was uttered by all those in attendance, most of whom were crying. It sounded louder than any floor-show orchestra I had ever heard. My voice blended with the others as the rabbi chanted, *"Yitgaddal o'yitkaddash sh'meh rabba."*

After my father's death, the whole town went crazy. First they thought he had been murdered. One man told me, "There was an emergency meeting of all of us. When we heard Davie went down, we were furious. Nobody could kill Davie Berman and get away with it. He belonged to us. He was our mainstay here, he was number one. It was a bad time for us, real bad. I remember that day, men I had never seen shed a tear were crying. In our business we don't really love each other, but we all loved Davie."

Our house was flooded by hotel employees and friends. They all wanted something to remember my father by, a piece of clothing, a book. Since nobody owned a piece of Davie Berman in life, they wanted one in death. Some friends even sent their maids to comfort our maid, Lucy, who was hysterical.

Uncle Chickie fainted in the waiting room of the hospital and went into a diabetic coma. It fell to my cousin, Raleigh Padueen, to tell my mother. When my mother found out, she collapsed, whispering, "Not Davie, not my Davie. Who will take care of Susie and me now?"

Lou Raskin packed a few things in a big brown steamer trunk and called my father's favorite charity, the Variety Club, to come and get all my toys that I didn't want. He sent my dog Blackie to Uncle Chickie's in Idaho, where I was going, and then grabbed my hand and we walked. He locked the house, and we left. Davie Berman and his family didn't live there anymore.

Uncle Chickie and I boarded the plane to go to his home in Lewiston, Idaho. I looked at McCarran Field. Would I ever see my older sister Lady Las Vegas again? How would she and I survive without the man who loved us so?

As the plane ascended, I looked down at my hometown. I could not imagine what my future would be now that my childhood was forever ended. Was there anything beyond my father and Las Vegas? I did not know that day what a pull family and hometown have on a person, how you can never really separate from people and places you love. I did not know that day that every day for the rest of my life I would miss my father and my town and wonder why it all ended much too soon.

Front page, the *Las Vegas Sun*, June 19, 1957:

FUNERAL RITES HERE TODAY FOR DAVE BERMAN, 53

Funeral services will be conducted at Bunker Bros. Mortuary at 11 am today for Dave Berman, 53, one of the pioneers in the Las Vegas casino business, who died of a heart attack yesterday at Rose de Lima Hospital where he was recovering from a glandular operation.

Berman was one of the active owners and operators at the Riviera Hotel where he was associated with Gus Greenbaum, Benny Goffstein, Joe Rosenberg, and Willie Alderman. Moving from the Flamingo to the Riviera, Berman and his associates took over the floundering hotel and made an outstanding success of the venture.

Following the local services to be conducted by Rabbi Arthur B. Leibowitz, Berman's body will be sent to Los Angeles where services will be held at 2 pm tomorrow at the Home of Peace in Boyle Heights. He is survived by his wife, Gladys, his 12-year-old daughter Susan, his brother Charles Berman of Lewiston, Idaho, and sister Mrs. Maurice Minter, of Minneapolis, Minn.

Berman entered the Henderson hospital last Wednesday for major surgery and was making a satisfactory recovery at the time of the heart attack. Doctors said that there was no connection between the heart condition and the surgery. He succumbed about 7 am yesterday.

Berman was well known for his philanthropies—many of them performed anonymously came to light later only by accident. One of them, for example, was the little-known occasion when Berman won a luxurious Cadillac after buying many $100 tickets on a Variety Club drawing. He refused to accept the car, telling the officers to sell the Cadillac and put the money in the club to help handicapped children. He was always willing to help out charitable organizations. In addition to being a member of the Variety Club he was a lifetime member of the City of Hope.

Berman had an outstanding war record. In 1942 he entered the Canadian Army; serving overseas, he fought with distinction at Anzio, Sicily, and throughout the entire Italian campaign. He was honorably discharged in 1945.

Immediately thereafter, Berman came to Las Vegas. He was part owner and associate in four clubs besides the Riviera. In 1945 he was connected with the El Cortez Hotel. In 1946 with the Las Vegas Club and El Dorado (now the Horseshoe), and in 1947 he became interested in the Flamingo Hotel.

Berman watched Las Vegas grow from a fledgling gambling town to one of the world's most glamorous resort centers. It was partly through his vision and industriousness that it became what it is today, according to his close associates.

Berman was born Jan. 16, 1903, in Ashley, North Dakota.

Obituary in the *Los Angeles Times*, June 19, 1957:

LAS VEGAS HOTEL MAN DAVE BERMAN, 53, DIES

David (Dave) Berman, 53, Las Vegas hotel-man and one of the principal owners of the Riviera Hotel there, died yesterday morning after surgery in Rose de Lima Hospital, Henderson, Nev. Mr. Berman had been ill only a week.

Funeral services will be conducted in Las Vegas at 11 am today and a memorial service will be conducted in Los Angeles at 2 pm tomorrow in the Home of Peace Mausoleum Chapel.

Mr. Berman was active in the Nevada hotel business for many years and was one of the group which owned and operated the Flamingo Hotel in Las Vegas prior to his connection with the Riviera.

He leaves a widow, Gladys, and daughter, Susan, 12, of Las Vegas.

THE LADY STARTS A CHECKBOOK

The end of the 1950s would prove as devastating for Lady Las Vegas as for me. Life without my father seemed too painful for either of us to bear. I was sad and desolate, she was broke and saw her reputation ripped to shreds without my dad to protect her. One year after he died, his partner, Gus Greenbaum, and wife, Bess, were decapitated gangland-style. Without my dad to keep the peace, all hell broke loose. Mobsters from everywhere moved to Las Vegas to loot her. They weren't like my dad and his friends, with a vision of the future. These men were carpetbaggers: Get it all, get it now.

The first year after my dad died, my mother was in a mental institution in L.A. She had had a breakdown. I lived with Uncle Chickie in Idaho and went to a private girls' boarding school in Portland, Oregon—St. Helen's Hall, now the Oregon Episcopal School. It was a wonderful school, but I was frozen in grief. When I was in the eighth grade, my mother got briefly well and sent for me. She would be dead six months later.

Lou met me at the airport in L.A. looking much the same, but it was still a shock to see someone from the life I had had just a year and a half before.

When I got off the plane he said, "Hi ya, Susie, how's the gin game?"

Gin! I hardly remembered that I had spent a good part of my first decade playing gin rummy. Did I remember how to call or how to score?

"How's Chickie? In the chips?" he asked.

Chips? I hadn't seen any chips like the chips in Las Vegas. "I didn't see any chips there, Lou, but maybe he had some," I said.

We walked a good distance to the car. I reflected that I had never seen Lou walk more than a block before. He had always just sat in that overstuffed living-room chair in Las Vegas awaiting my father to tell him what to do, and that was usually a sedentary command like, "Stay here 'till I get home, Lou." All my father's friends seemed to have immobile bodies that either sat or stood around.

We drove past the Beverly Wilshire, past the Brown Derby and Armstrong Schroeder's—our old haunts when my dad took us to L.A., and they looked warm and inviting inside. We got to a small street well past this area and parked in front of a building that looked very cold.

I hardly recognized my mother. Her long black hair was now short and streaked with white. And she was so thin. There were two nurses living with her. A room had been decorated for me with dolls and stuffed animals. There were two turtles from the Farmer's Market with names painted on their shells. It was a room for an eight-year-old. Didn't my mother know I stopped being a little girl the day my father died?

I started attending the Chadwick School in Palos Verdes Estates with the sons and daughters of Hollywood; on the weekends I lived with my mother. But she was in such deep grief over my father's death that she barely spoke. By Christmas she had lost her will to live. She hugged me, said good-bye, and sent me to Uncle Chickie. She killed herself six weeks later.

Over the miles, I tried to picture Lady Las Vegas. What was happening to her?

Nothing good, it turned out.

Beneath the surface of their new respectability, Vegas mobsters still backed up their business practices with the barrel of a gun. The Mob needed to keep their guys straight. They didn't want anybody to "fall down" in the Mob terminology, because then that would bring in more supervision from Miami, from New York, from their bosses, from their big partners.

Greenbaum's heroin addiction began affecting his management of the Riviera Hotel. So he was murdered by his bosses. It was theorized that Bess came back early from a hair appointment and thus was killed, too.

Greenbaum's murder was an early sign of more serious problems to come as the freewheeling Fifties drew to a close.

GLITTER GULCH IN THE 1950S.

While the men who founded the Strip had stayed focused on the big picture, many of the mobsters who came as Kefauver refugees were little more than mercenaries, looking for a quick score. They drained the casinos dry with no thought of the future. Organized crime became firmly entrenched, and there was chaos in the managerial ranks. Every mobster who invested capital installed his own front man as pit boss. There was an epidemic of hotel-casino failures, mergers, buy-outs.

The Strip was overbuilt with no new sources of capital. Hotel occupancy plummeted, forcing some to lay off employees, even eliminate the graveyard shift.

"At that particular time, Vegas was absolutely in bankruptcy," remembers Bill Miller. "Even the banks were in desperate trouble."

The artesian wells that gave birth to the meadows had already stopped flowing to the surface. Now, unchecked greed and corruption were poisoning the fountain.

In 1955, the state of Nevada created the Gaming Control Board to oversee licensing and policing procedures. It immediately suspended the license of the Thunderbird Hotel, charging that Jake Lansky, Meyer's brother, had a hidden interest. Then the state felt it needed even more control over gambling to sort out the ever-expanding fiscal disasters, so it created the policymaking State Gaming Commission in 1959.

At this point the ten Strip hotels were fiscal monoliths with hundreds of changing owners who had percentage points. There was also a confusing patchwork of corporations, some owning and others operating the hotels, some holding the real estate and others holding the holding companies.

The state had to walk a thin line between regulating the casinos and facilitating them since gambling was a major source of revenue. Most of the casino bosses had been entrenched for 15 years, and the local regulatory personnel, the sheriff, and the county commissioners protected the action and took a cut. The new gaming commission was weak because it had to safeguard its own interests; it only took a hard line against those it deemed "undesirables."

Robert F. Kennedy, the new attorney general, went after Las Vegas like Kefauver did. He was certain it was controlled by the underworld, which he pledged to eradicate. He had 65 Justice Department agents ready to descend on the town; then-Governor Grant Sawyer deterred them. But the FBI, the Department of Labor, and the Bureau of Narcotics came calling.

Journalists and the media started to rip Vegas to shreds as a town of gangsters. Exposé after exposé was published. Even though tourists were coming and gambling, the foundation was shaking. No new hotels were built on the Strip between 1958 (the Stardust) and 1966 (the Aladdin). State investigators created the famed "Black Book," which listed individuals whom the state deemed undesirable, whose money could cost a casino its license. Most people thought this a public-relations ploy to make it appear that the Strip turmoil was under control. The Black Book went after only the most heinous Mob offenders and did nothing to keep silent partners, out-of-town godfathers, from collecting their clandestine cut of cash.

The neon of the Strip threatened to flicker out. On the eve of the new decade, it looked as if the party in the desert might soon be over.

By the end of the Fifties, the Carrier Air Conditioning Company figured out how to air-condition the casinos. Direct flights to Las Vegas from major cities were put in place at the same time. According to author Nick Pileggi, "As these casinos started going into 2,000- and 3,000-room hotels, there weren't enough gangsters with hidden money in the world to build those kinds of establishments. You had to go somewhere else." But where? Few self-respecting banks and no corporations or Wall Street investors would dare join forces with the shadowy world of gambling.

Vegas leaders would find a new benefactor in an old, familiar friend from the days of Prohibition. Like Las Vegas, the Teamsters union and their president Jimmy Hoffa had a past. And that past was inextricably linked to the Mob. That relationship of the Mob to the labor union grew out of the anti-labor stance of industry, especially the steel industry in the 1930s. The Teamsters had hired the Mob to protect them from the strike-breakers, and a long and solid friendship had ensued.

In the late Fifties, the Mob bosses made a deal with the Teamsters union for a series of sizable loans from the multimillion-dollar Central States Pension Fund. The earliest Teamster loans were unrelated to gambling, and some were made to legitimate developers and local entrepreneurs. Local improvements, like Sunrise Hospital and the Las Vegas International Country Club, were immediately embraced by the community. "Sin City" was finally beginning to look like any other small American town.

The next Teamster loans funded expansions of some existing casinos on the ailing Strip—and began to revitalize Las Vegas. Then the rules changed —and made it possible for men like Howard Hughes to invest.

In the opinion of historian Hal Rothman, when Nevada set up its regulatory structure in the 1950s for regulating casino gaming, it effectively made illegal capital the only capital available to anybody who wanted to develop a resort, because under Nevada law, every casino owner had to be certified by a Gaming Board investigation.

In Rothman's view, "That's one thing if you got a three-person company, but when you're a publicly traded company that has 2 million stockholders, you can't take every one of them in front of the Gaming Board. The result of that was to effectively keep, after 1955, any capital that wasn't private out of the market. The reasons for that were obvious. People feared that the casinos would be held by the people behind the scenes. They would be held by people with criminal records who might cheat, who might do a whole range of things behind the scenes, but the solution that they concocted in effect, codified that very system.

"In 1967, the state of Nevada passed a Corporate Gaming Act and revised it in 1969. After the revision of the Corporate Gaming Act, publicly traded companies could in fact own casinos. What you saw after that was the beginning of a new capital regime, a new source of capital becoming available to Las Vegas."

The first evidence of that was Howard Hughes. Since the 1940s, Howard Hughes had made a name for himself as the world's most fascinating billionaire. The definition of a Renaissance man, this debonair playboy spearheaded giant corporations, flew and designed aircraft, even carved a name for himself as a Hollywood studio boss.

On Thanksgiving eve, 1966, Howard Hughes and his entourage of Mormon bodyguards descended on Las Vegas and moved into the penthouse floor of the Desert Inn Hotel. They announced they would be staying for ten days. Several months later, hotel management told Robert Maheu, then CEO of the Hughes Corporation, in no uncertain terms that they wanted Hughes and company out.

"The owners of the hotel took stock of the situation and said, 'What do we care about room rent, we're in the business of retaining money from gambling, so it's really a lost revenue for us,'" says Nevada's Governor Bob Miller. "Hughes then asked them for a price for the acquisition of the hotel. They gave him one which they thought was inflated, and he paid it."

For a mere $14 million, Howard Hughes had found a place to sleep. But hotel ownership came with an unexpected perk—it solved one of the billionaire's myriad tax problems. "I received a phone call from him one day," says Maheu. "He was laughing on the phone and said, 'How many more of these toys are available?' That's when we started buying."

One by one, other Strip hotels and casinos fell into Hughes's hands. He bought the Desert Inn for $14 million in 1967; four months later he bought the Sands for $23 million, the Castaways for $3.3 million, the Frontier for $23 million, and the Silver Slipper for $5.4 million.

At the time, the Silver Slipper was owned by gambling pioneer Claudine Williams and her husband, Shelby. Hughes was staying at the penthouse of the Desert Inn, which was directly across the street from the Silver Slipper. Williams remembers that Hughes fired off a telegram complaining how that slipper would revolve and the shadows that hit Hughes's window disturbed his rest. Claudine Williams, now CEO of Harrah's, still has the telegram.

Hughes then bought the Landmark for $17.3 million and Harold's Club in Reno for $10.5 million. He imagined an elegant Las Vegas with none of the sleaze: "I like to think of Las Vegas in terms of a well-dressed man in a dinner jacket and a beautifully jeweled and furred female getting out of an expensive car."

When the enigmatic billionaire Hughes wandered into this fantasy wonderland, determined to make it his own, the town needed his cash desperately. And he needed the town. Robert Maheu remembers: "Howard had pointed out to me that he was sick and tired of being a small fish in the growing big pond of Southern California and wanted to be the big fish in the small pond of Nevada."

Brilliant, handsome, and rich, Hughes also was known as a paranoid, unpredictable eccentric who seemed to think ordinary rules didn't apply to him. He was a ladies' man with a reputation for stealing the hearts of the

HOWARD HUGHES SAVED VEGAS BY BUYING IT, STARTING WITH THE DESERT INN FOR $14 MILLION.

silver screen's most sought-after starlets. Actress Terry Moore was among his many conquests. "He arranged an accidental meeting, which I didn't know for ten years that it wasn't an accident," says actress Terry Moore. At one point, he secreted four different starlets in four different Las Vegas hotels, expecting none would find out about the other three. "He had Deborah Paget in one hotel, he had Mitzi Gaynor in another hotel, and he had Jean Peters in another hotel.

"We all found out about it later," says Moore. They used to go to Las Vegas together to gamble. "We could make twenty dollars last, that's how long we used to gamble. But Howard used to like to go downtown because he had gone there years, probably even before I was born. He would go down to the Golden Nugget and the Horseshoe and the Fremont and all those hotels and loved to gamble. He used to like to go down there and people wouldn't recognize him, he'd just fit in with everybody.

"Nobody recognized him. I mean they wouldn't even give him a marker. People didn't know what he looked like. He never dressed up. He had the Texas accent, so they just thought he was a miner or somebody from around there."

During his four-year monarchy, Howard Hughes brought both legitimacy and controversy to Las Vegas. But on the top floor of the Desert Inn, behind the closed doors of his penthouse cell, his reclusive eccentricities were becoming more bizarre. He had armed guards stationed at the entrance to his suite, and installed an air-purifying system, black-out drapes and a special phone service.

Burton M. Cohen, a prominent hotel gaming consultant, remembers the following story. "He loved ice cream, and every day he'd have banana ripple. One day we learned that we were out of banana ripple. To deny Mr. Hughes would cause an eruption of a volcano. So we called Baskin Robbins in L.A. and asked them to send over banana ripple, and Baskin Robbins said they're not making banana ripple anymore.

"We said we had to have banana ripple. They said we would have to take 200 gallons of banana ripple, which they would make specially. So we bought 200 gallons of banana ripple. The next day Mr. Hughes came in and said, 'I think I'll have chocolate marshmallow.' I think to this day, we may still have that banana ripple somewhere around the Desert Inn Hotel."

Many of the properties that Hughes was buying belonged to "The Old Guard"—the Vegas Mob godfathers. With surprising eagerness, they turned over their holdings to the billionaire.

"The Mob began to sell out for a lot of reasons," says Hal Rothman. "First, they'd been under a tremendous amount of heat ever since 1951 in the Kefauver hearings. These guys couldn't get a minute of peace. The second thing was they were getting old, and it wasn't worth the hassle. Here came somebody who could clear them out of it and give them an enormous profit. When they saw Howard Hughes coming, they must have regarded him as the quintessential sucker."

Hughes wound up spending $300 million.

"Howard Hughes was the washing machine. In the public's mind, Howard Hughes wiped out the Mob, kicked the Mob out of the casino business," says Nick Pileggi, "and he had now taken over the casino business. In truth, that's not quite what happened.

"You've got to remember the casinos are run by the men who run the casinos, not by Howard Hughes and his seven Mormons up there in the penthouse. They never went down there; they didn't know what was going on. In a lot of those casinos, skimming continued. Wiseguys still managed to get their girlfriends comped. But publicly, from a public relations point of view, I think Hughes was a tremendous help to the casino business and to Las Vegas as a whole."

Hughes created a whole new era that benefited Las Vegas. Sadly, he was to meet a terrible end. Howard Hughes had a secret—one shared by only a select handful of people. A head injury from a plane crash, plus a bout of syphilis contracted in his youth, were gradually driving the billionaire into madness. Both his body and his mind were deteriorating, and Hughes was determined to keep his condition hidden from the world.

"When I agreed to being his alter ego, maybe I made a serious mistake as far as his world was concerned," says Maheu. "It enabled him the luxury of going into a cocoon with the progression of time—it was very, very difficult for him to understand reality as in fact it was in the outside world. Toward the end of his stay in Las Vegas some of his demands were not reasonable. Unfortunately, I was not aware at that time the extent to which he was dependent on drugs.

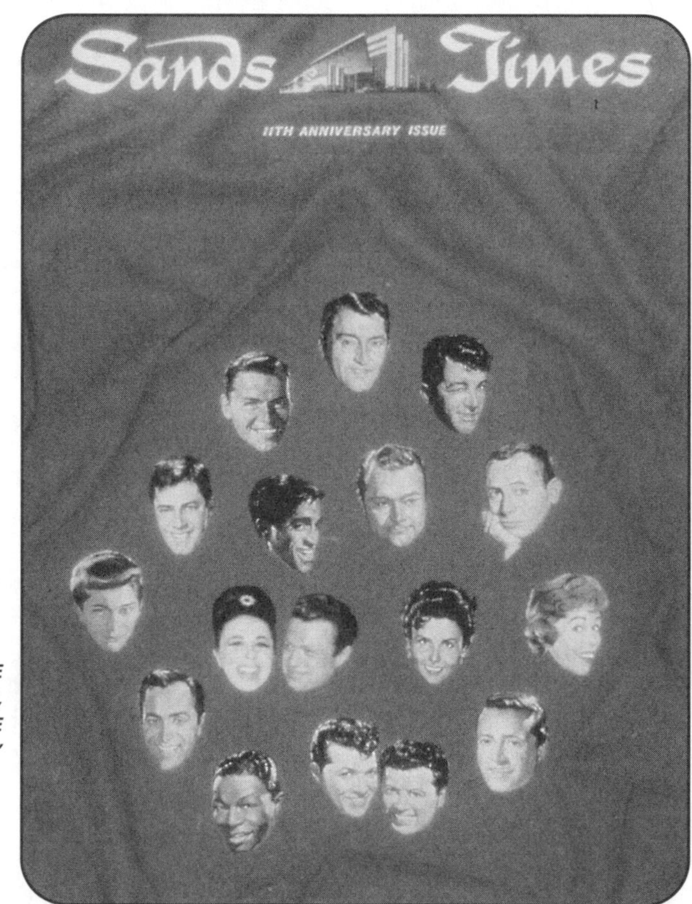

THE 11TH ANNIVERSARY ISSUE OF THE SANDS TIMES, FEATURING MEMBERS OF THE "RAT PACK."

"I felt very bad for this man, though, because I knew that he had an entourage that was encouraging his lack of decision, because it made them more powerful. I thought I could control it as long as he and I could talk. I did not make arrangements, stupidly on my part, for the day that he was too sick to communicate with me. And that's precisely what happened."

On Thanksgiving Day 1970, Hughes's power-hungry entourage mysteriously removed the dying man from the Desert Inn. The richest man in the world was a missing person.

"There is no doubt in my mind that decision was made because they wanted to make sure that they were in control of Howard Hughes. At that point I was fired. I was the last window to the world that Hughes had," says Maheu.

By 1976, Howard Hughes was dead, his corpse unrecognizable from the dashing young man who had taken the business world by storm. Bob Maheu has his own personal view of Hughes's sad end and death. "It was terrible. The same man who created the biggest medical foundation in the world was delivered back to this country with sores all over his body, with broken hypodermic needles in his arm, with holes where teeth should have been. When I read that, I cried like a baby."

Perhaps Howard Hughes had to die for his empire to continue. The Hughes Corporation passed into the hands of a capable relative, William Lummis, who decided to sell off Hughes's holdings in the gaming industry at enormous profits.

Hughes had been a visionary—from behind the darkened windows of his penthouse retreat, he looked out on the desert and saw its unlimited potential. But the limitation of his mind and body kept him from truly leaving his mark.

"He loved to have maps that showed what Las Vegas was like in 1960, and he could see where the growth was going. At times he would say to me, because I'd have to go somewhere to represent him, 'How I wish I could have been there,'" Maheu remembers. "And I'd say, 'Howard, damn it, do it.' And he'd say, 'I can't get myself to do it.' At the completion of these conversations I'd come back, and my wife would say, 'A long conversation, honey?' And I'd say, 'With the poorest man in the world.'"

In 1969, as mentioned above, the Corporate Gaming Act was passed in Nevada, mostly because of the climate Hughes was instrumental in creating. This allowed corporations to own casinos without each stock-holder having to pass a Gaming Board inspection. It took about three years to pass through the legislature, but when it did, it ushered in the beginning of new era, the age of "Corporate Las Vegas," with corporations becoming hotel owners.

DEAN MARTIN AND FRANK SINATRA AT THE SANDS'S COPA ROOM.

The style of hotel ownership changed, but not everyone in town was happy about the changes.

"Howard Hughes, I think, screwed up everything. He let the IRS in the counting rooms," says George Schlatter. "There was a lot of cash activity in Vegas, and there was no way to really track it. But then Hughes opened the counting room, and the IRS came in there and said, 'You're kidding, you're doing that?'"

This era was also famous for the most important entertainment event possibly in Lady Las Vegas's history—a group of entertainers that brought the glittering highway back to life and officially ushered in the decade of the swinging Sixties in Las Vegas. Fans knew them as the "Rat Pack" but the performers themselves preferred "the Summit." They were a band of swinging saloon singers plus a comedian: Frank Sinatra, Dean Martin, Sammy Davis, Jr., and Joey Bishop.

In 1960, they were all heading to Las Vegas to film a new picture, *Oceans 11*. Frank Sinatra, Dean Martin, and Sammy Davis, Jr., had all performed as solo acts in Vegas during the Fifties. They delighted audiences at the Copa Room of the Sands Hotel, run by entertainment director Jack Entratter. Originally, a different member of the group would headline each night, with one or more of the others dropping by. But it wasn't long before the Rat Pack would take the stage together as a team, singing, bantering, and mingling with the crowd. It was impossible to tell who was having the better time—the audiences or the boys up there on the stage.

"They would work all day on the picture, then go in the steam room, come out of the steam room, do the show on stage—where they had an occasional beverage," says George Schlatter. "And then they fainted between shows. Then they went out and did another second show, and then took a nap and got ready to go out to the set of the movie at six the next morning."

Onstage as well as off, their energy was boundless, as was their appetite for practical jokes and misbehavior. "They did some pretty disgusting things. I'll never forget Dean Martin saying to me one time, 'You know, I don't know what we did last night, but I know we're in a lot of trouble,'" says Shecky Greene.

"It was really fun to watch the magnetism that that group of guys had in this town," says singer Kenny Rogers. "When they walked through the casinos, the seas would just part, out of respect. It was really amazing. That was an era when truly they were king."

"The casinos would let them deal at the tables. Dean Martin would tell the gamblers, 'You've got an 18, hit it. Twenty-eight, that's a winner! Dealer has 30, you win with a four,'" George Schlatter remembers. "I mean you just couldn't get into that casino with a shoe horn—and it cost the hotel maybe $20,000 for them to do it."

Sammy Davis fixed breakfast for Vegas. "He said, 'Breakfast is on me, Las Vegas.' Anyone came in the Sands, it was breakfast on Sammy," says entertainer Sonny Charles.

Frank Sinatra was getting into some scrapes of his own. "Frank loved to gamble. And Frank was a big high roller. He would gamble with big stacks of hundred-dollar chips," says former dancer Jeanie Gardner.

In September of 1967, an event occurred in the Sands casino that has evolved into a Las Vegas legend. There are countless versions of the infamous story, which began when Sands Vice President, Carl Cohen, refused to raise Sinatra's marker.

"They got into a big heated argument," remembers Gardner. "The next thing I knew, Carl sprang out of his chair and hit Frank. Well, the blood went flying and Frank's teeth went flying, and I looked down beside me and one of Frank's teeth was on the floor."

Alan King remembers taking up the slack. "I got a call in the middle of the night to get to Vegas from New York, that Sinatra had walked, and I got there the next night, went on stage and I said, 'I'm here to entertain the troops.' It was a war zone."

Soon, the members of the Rat Pack drifted off to separate hotels, but the carefree days of the Summit set off a nonstop party that kept on swinging all through the Sixties.

Jeanie Gardner was courted by billionaires and movie stars—Frank Sinatra, Elvis Presley, and Wayne Newton among them. She was one of the Sands's Copa Girls, the most sought-after beauties in town.

"The Copa Girls had to stay around the hotel between shows and also after the second show 'till about two o'clock in the morning," says Gardner. "We had to be there to decorate the hotel. And decorate the hotel the girls did, because they were all beautiful and beautifully dressed. It was a very, very glamorous era."

In the early Sixties, Kenny Rogers was a musician with a group called The Bobby Doyle Trio, playing the tiny Thunderbird Lounge.

"We did five shows a night, and that was a really wonderful time. It wasn't uncommon for those guys who were headlining to finish their show and come down to our place and come up on stage and play and sing with us," says Kenny Rogers. "It was a strange phenomenon because they were being paid thousands of dollars, and they would come down and play with us for free. But it was just the spirit of the times.

"I guess it's like looking back on your childhood. Some of the stuff you do is dangerous, but it's the danger—if you survive it—that makes it fun."

Some performers lived more dangerously than others. Comedian Shecky Greene was one of the highest-earning performers on the Strip, earning as much as $150,000 a week. But compulsive gambling and drinking helped put much of his salary back into the casinos.

"I was very wild. I was always getting in trouble. As the town got bigger (and we got more police), you couldn't carouse and do the things that I did in a casino. Turn over a table, jump on a table and say, 'I bet my life.' I did some terrible things. I once took my car down the streets of Las Vegas. I was driving 100 miles an hour, completely out of my mind, and I hit a post, careened off the post and went into the fountains at Caesar's Palace. And when the cop came I says, 'No spray wax.' Well, they put me in jail for a long time."

COMEDIAN SHECKY GREENE WAS ONE OF THE HIGHEST-PAID PERFORMERS IN VEGAS.

"I remember the days when they kept a jail cell for Shecky downtown," says Wayne Newton. "He would have too much to drink, and he would just get in a cab and go down and check in. And then when he sobered up, they'd let him out."

The Wild West was back in its modern incarnation—and the action was happening all along the Strip. One of the Vegas stars was too young to join the party when he first arrived in Vegas in 1958. Wayne Newton was then 15 and had to leave the casino whenever he wasn't on stage. By 1964, he was headlining at the Flamingo and was an official member of the Vegas "Set."

"There are so many people who would have thought there was a great battle amongst the performers," says Wayne Newton. "It wasn't that at all. I mean it was nothing for us to get together and party. We really had our own little world here—our own little sandbox."

Las Vegas in the Sixties, world-famous, just like my dad said it would be. I read of Lady Las Vegas's exploits as I went to college, but I said I'd never go back there because, for me, the center of the town was gone and his shadow too big to ignore.

THE LADY DRESSES UP

In the mid-Sixties, I was at UCLA going to college, just a few hours' drive away from my beloved Lady Las Vegas. But I could not visit her, I could never go back, because the last image I had of her was my father's funeral. I had a fantasy of what she would look like now, more elegant and sophisticated, maybe more like New York, maybe L.A., but I could never go back.

I was sitting in my dormitory lounge in 1966 when I heard a newscaster say, "Las Vegas." I looked up, and there on television was the most fantastic hotel I had ever seen; it had just opened and was called "Caesar's Palace." I tried to picture where it was on my Strip. On the opposite side from the Flamingo and the Riviera, but where?

They showed a news clip, and I hardly recognized anything in my town. I had been gone nine years, and my older sister, Lady Las Vegas, had had a total facelift. She looked fantastic. Could that really be her? The glamour of ancient Rome, all gods in her awe. Baby, I knew you when!

This new monument to Caesar dwarfed my dad's hotels, but I was happy for Lady Las Vegas; she was on a roll! During the years that Howard Hughes and others were attempting to turn Vegas corporate, other entrepreneurs, some of them Mob-connected, were using enormous Teamster loans to turn classic Vegas into a theme park.

It all started with the spectacular Caesar's Palace, still an outstanding hotel today. It cost $25 million and was created by Jay Sarno, owner of the National Cabana Motel chain. It was the first new casino to be funded by a loan from the Teamsters' Central States Pension Fund.

"Caesar's Palace was a breakaway property, an enterprise where the building itself was the show," says Steve Wynn. "The idea of the resort being a world unto itself was a very gripping idea."

It was the city's original "theme resort," created on a scale that would have awed Caesar himself. All-powerful gods stand watch at its doorways, then 18 fountains and a 130-foot driveway lead to the grandeur just beyond. Florentine statuary and imported Italian cypress surrounded the swimming pool, designed in the shape of a Roman shield.

"Caesar's Palace was the first explicitly themed casino where they went from the menus through the garb on the cocktail waitresses to the bus boys to the kind of giant rip-off of Roman statues and the Renaissance statues sitting out in the fountain out front," says Steven Izenour, architect and critic.

"The first time I went into Caesar's Palace, I looked around and they had carpets on the ceiling, carpets on the walls. Everything was gilt," says Alan King. "The star suite looked like it was designed by two hookers and a pit boss. I mean, they had a bathtub, a whirlpool, in the middle of the bedroom."

According to Alan Hess's groundbreaking book on Vegas architecture, *Viva Las Vegas*, "Caesar's Palace conjured up a broad yet highly detailed classical environment suited to the large and lavish expectation of Las Vegas gamblers. The first new hotel to be constructed in eight years broke from the roadside tradition to introduce a plan borrowed from baroque cities. The usual frontage parking lot was amended by a long axis of fountains marking an entry drive. The parking lots were pushed to the side for this grand effect. The focus was on a monumental structure with symmetrical wings reaching out to embrace the limousines cruising up to the Porte Cochere."

Steve Wynn credits the Fountainbleu Hotel in Miami Beach with inspiring both him and Jay Sarno. "My father, because of his illness in the Sixties, bought a home in Florida and moved there. My parents sold the house in upstate New York, and they lived in Miami Beach. The Fountainbleu opened there in 1954, built by a man named Ben Novack. All the hotels in Miami were very similar, one to the other, until the Fountainbleu, this magnificent, curved building with no name on it. French, formal gardens, a beautiful pool, a lavish and beautiful lobby—when the Fountainbleu opened up, it changed everything in the hotel business in the world.

THE ALADDIN HOTEL OPENED IN 1966, SHORTLY AFTER CAESAR'S PALACE.

"I got the feeling from looking at Novack strutting around his hotel—that same line from "The History of the World Part I," by Mel Brooks: 'It's good to be king.' I mean, here is this guy in his own world, in his own environment. That hotel and its environment, it was a way of life. It wasn't just a place to stay, it was a very big influence on me as an adolescent.

"It was also an influence on Jay Sarno from Atlanta, Georgia, who came down there. Sarno's dream and his idea of the Fountainbleu is what gave rise to Caesar's Palace. He even had the same men's store and the same builder and the same architect, all those things; he wanted the same people that had created the Fountainbleu to create Caesar's. And Caesar's Palace was to Las Vegas in 1966 what the Fountainbleu had been to Miami Beach twelve years earlier. In those days at the Fountainbleu, Frank Sinatra and Harry Belafonte and Johnny Mathis all sang there, the greatest performing artists of the time, just like they did at Caesar's. But beyond Frank Sinatra, the Fountainbleu itself was the show. Caesar's Palace itself was the show."

High rollers flocked to Caesar's, and theme hotels became the rage. The Aladdin opened in 1966—and in the following year Elvis Presley wed his Priscilla in its ballroom.

In 1968, Jay Sarno had another brainstorm—Circus, Circus. At first, it was a casino without a hotel. Circus acrobats performed in the rigging high above the gambling tables, and guests paid admission at the door.

"The only problem with Jay's vision was that having all of this activity taking place over the heads of the gamblers was not conducive to gambling, so we'd have a crap game going and all of a sudden Norbo the Ape Man would come down a rope with the trainer chasing him, shooting caps off and so on, and of course the crap shooters are looking at this like what the hell's going on," remembers Burton Cohen.

It was also the era of the first colorful gamblers.

Cohen remembers how "one famous gambler would stand at the crap table with a Spanish wine gourd over his shoulder, which had Maalox in it, and as he's shooting, he would tip the gourd up, the Maalox would come out and he'd have his Maalox. Another loved to eat oatmeal through a straw. This was a big, big customer so we took a tube of brass and we made him a brass straw so that he could get his oatmeal anytime. And he would sleep anywhere. One day he was sleeping on the banquettes in the coffee shop. A senior casino executive didn't know who he was, came in, kicked his foot and said, 'Look, we don't allow anybody to sleep in the coffee shop.' From that day on, every time the customer would come in, that executive had to go to L.A. and be out of his sight. The same gentleman bought the underlying property under Circus, Circus because he got mad at Jay Sarno, and he wanted him to have to pay him rent for the land."

During this decade, the Landmark Hotel was built, starting in 1961, then abandoned for three years, then finished with a loan from the Teamsters in 1966. Kirk Kerkorian also opened the International Las Vegas Hilton the same year, even the same weekend, the fourth of July, that the Landmark opened. He invested $60 million of his own money in the construction. Kerkorian bought the Flamingo, my dad's first Strip hotel, in 1967, to use as a "hotel school" to train the International's staff.

The International showcased the ultimate entertainers in its 2,000-seat showroom. Bill Miller, former entertainment director of the International, remembers, "Barbra Streisand, Peggy Lee, and Hair. That was the opening show for the International. And then I followed through with Ike and Tina Turner and Redd Foxx and then I had Elvis."

While Elvis strutted on the International stage, there was a power struggle growing in the rest of Las Vegas—between the pension-fund-dependent owners, and the new, legitimate corporate cowboys. More and more mobsters were selling out to corporate capital.

The growth was good, but Las Vegans were beginning to tire of the negative attention Mob presence was attracting to their town. First there had been Kefauver. Then, Attorney General Robert F. Kennedy attempted to use the Justice Department to uncover corruption in the city. In 1973, past Flamingo Hotel owners pleaded guilty to a hidden interest by mobster Meyer Lansky.

Independent-minded Nevadans had never warmed to government interference. Now it seemed the Mob-connected casinos were attracting more of it than ever before.

"Nevadans are colonial, and like colonized people anywhere, they're drawn to the source of power," says Hal Rothman. "The old source of power no longer serves their purposes and they move on to the next one, which is corporate capital." The situation that developed was one, according to Rothman, of "two-pronged development"—one prong being the Teamsters' money and the profits in the Teamsters' money being skimmed off, and the other the corporate money, which was building like crazy.

Perhaps the incident that best illustrates this tension and the Mob's waning power in Las Vegas is the Stardust Casino scandal. The central characters of the affair were two Midwestern opportunists, Anthony Spilotro and Frank Rosenthal, who were lured to the glittering city by its recent expansion—"two boyhood friends who grew up together in Chicago, who then over time and circumstances found themselves in Las Vegas," says author Pileggi, who profiled the pair in his novel *Casino*. Spilotro was an enforcer for the Mob with secret ambitions to become a Vegas big shot. Frank 'Lefty' Rosenthal was a former bookmaker who came to Las Vegas in the late Sixties and used his Mob connections to land a job at the Stardust Hotel.

For years, there had been an enormous skimming operation at work at the Stardust. A large percentage of money taken in from gambling and the slots was being shipped back to mob bosses in Chicago. "Skimming is a part of Las Vegas and has probably been a part of Las Vegas since the very beginning," says Pileggi. "The early skim started because the casino owners had to pay back a lot of their early investors, and a lot of those investors gave you cash and they wanted cash back. They didn't want any checks."

By 1974, Rosenthal was unofficially running the casino, despite the fact that his shady past had prevented him from obtaining a gaming license. He was soon clashing with the Stardust's newest owner, Allen Glick. A rising young businessman, Glick had naively accepted a $63-million loan from the Teamsters' pension fund to buy both the Stardust and the Fremont hotels. When the FBI raided the Stardust in 1976, chaos was reigning there. Rosenthal was forced out and the eyes of the law—and of the press—once again focused on the Las Vegas Mob.

"All of a sudden there is this tremendous crackdown on the Stardust," says Hal Rothman. The reasons were plain. "First, there is all this legitimate capital in Las Vegas, and they didn't need the Mob capital any more. The second is, the big hotels, the Hiltons, didn't need this kind of stigma in the town."

While Rosenthal fought a losing battle to obtain a license from the Gaming Commission, major indictments came down on Tony Spilotro and his so-called Hole in the Wall Gang. Campaigning for a bigger share of the Las Vegas spotlight, Spilotro had broken a cardinal Mob rule—he had brought dirty street crime and murder inside the city limits. Nevada's Governor Bob Miller was then a district attorney who prosecuted the gang. "Before that time we never had anybody that was associated with organized crime come out and conduct criminal activity at the street level where they were actually conducting burglaries and loan-sharking and other activities."

The Mob bosses didn't take kindly to such blatant bad behavior. Spilotro didn't live to stand trial. He was found buried in an Illinois corn field. Rosenthal barely escaped a car bomb and soon after left Las Vegas permanently. The book and the movie *Casino* depict Spilotro and Rosenthal as powerful Mob figures who personally instigate the downfall of Mob-run Vegas, but history suggests that they were only bit players in a drama that was well into its final act before they even came onstage.

"The irony of *Casino* is that if you think about it, when in the United States do you ever see powerful people blowing each other up in a car? By the 1970s Las Vegas, like everywhere else in the United States, is a place that is run by institutions, not by individuals," says Hal Rothman.

The Sixties and Seventies changed Vegas in other ways as well, according to Wayne Newton. "It became a very entertainment-oriented business. The gaming came a close second. When the big corporations came over, when the publicly held companies came in with Hughes and with Kerkorian, and they brought in, in many instances, people who never had a gaming background, the first thing they decided to do was look at the bottom line, the budget, and that was a big change."

Another change that came to Vegas in the late Fifties and Sixties was the topless shows. I remember Minsky's Follies opening in Vegas in 1957, the year my dad died.

"The topless shows came to Vegas when they got desperate. When they started running out of money and people started not coming," says Rod Amateau. "Imagine the guy who walked in, he says, 'Chief, I got a great idea.

WAYNE NEWTON WITH HIS FIRST WIFE AT THEIR WEDDING.

I don't want every hotel on the Strip to do it, but we get the dames to take off their tops. Heh? How do you like that?'"

Bill Miller, then Dunes entertainment director, got in touch with Harold Minsky, whose bawdy Minsky's Follies had been teasing audiences in New York, Miami, and Chicago.

"I says, 'How would you like to be in Las Vegas forever?'" remembers Miller. "'It'll be the first revue that's played Vegas and stayed there instead of changing every two weeks and the entire show cost $9,000. It stayed there for nine years."

Though risqué for the Fifties, the first topless dancers weren't totally topless. "The girls that were topless wore pasties," says Fluff Lecoque. "Those little sequin tips that they put over the nipples so you don't see them. Even the strippers did that. Nobody worked bare-breasted until the Lido was brought in from Paris."

COWBOY SHOWGIRLS.

In the traditional Vegas spirit of one-upmanship, the Stardust Hotel caused a sensation when it premiered the Lido de Paris show in 1960. This time, the revue featured dancers without benefit of pasties. The show ran an unprecedented 31 years.

When I finally went back to Las Vegas as an adult, it was not to see the magnificent theme hotels of the Sixties and Seventies. No, it was for another reason. Uncle Chickie, my guardian, my father's younger brother, had gone to prison for stock fraud while I was still in college. I had lived with him on and off since I had been twelve; he had sent me to some of the finest schools in America and always stressed education and family.

A bon vivant and charming ladies' man, he had never made a strong stand for life since my father had died. In my sophomore year at UCLA, he called me one day.

"Susie, I've got bad news and I wanted to tell you about it before you read it in the papers. I'm going to be a guest of the government for a while. Do you know what I mean?"

"No."

"I'm going to prison. I go in tomorrow, baby, don't worry about me. I'm too tough to die. The other guys turned state's evidence, and I could have, but I wouldn't—I'm loyal. I'm a fighter. You just be a good girl, take care of yourself, and study hard. I'll write to you if they let me, and one thing, Susie—"

"Yes?"

"If anybody says anything bad about your father or if you ever read anything else, don't even dignify it by a thought. Will you promise me that?"

"Yes, but everybody in Las Vegas loved my father, didn't they?"

"That's right, everybody that ever knew him good loved him."

The next day Uncle Chickie's case was in all the newspapers. The *New York Times*'s headline was: FOUR IMPRISONED FOR STOCK FRAUD—UNITED DYE CASE IS RESTED BY U.S. Charles Berman, forty-nine, had pleaded innocent but had been convicted. "Four brokers and a corporation were convicted Monday of defrauding the public of five million dollars through a conspiracy to sell 400,000 shares of unregistered stock of United Dye and Chemical Corporation. Federal Judge William Herlands said the conviction 'brought to a close the longest trial before a jury in the history of a U.S. District Court in the country.'"

After doing time in Lewisburg Federal Prison, La Tuna and Terminal Island in San Pedro, Uncle Chickie was paroled. I picked him up at Terminal Island. He carried all his possessions in a brown paper bag. He asked me to bring him a corned beef sandwich from Linny's Deli on Beverly Drive, which I did. He ate it gratefully in the car. I took him to the Beverly Hillcrest Hotel on Pico in L.A. Someone there had comped him a room.

He had a work-release job for some old friends answering phones at a little business near the Friars Club on Santa Monica Blvd. When he was young, he had been a famous bookie, maybe he did that, too. For the next few years, he got in more trouble owning and operating pan clubs in Orange County. He was always debonair but broke. Craps was his mistress, compulsive gambling a habit he didn't want to break. When he wasn't in the chips, he'd disappear, and I'd have to track him down. At those times, he didn't want to see me, his humiliation too great.

In the mid-Seventies, I was a reporter for *The San Francisco Examiner* when he called me there. He was broke and had had a heart attack, could I come to him in Las Vegas? I was on the next plane, rushing to the new Sunrise Hospital where he was in intensive care. He looked thin and frail. Where had the time gone? He wasn't going to be able to live much longer, and he was only 68. He gave me the key to his motel room, a place called the Bali Hai off the Strip. He had written me from there many times on their tangerine stationery.

THE GOLDEN NUGGET TODAY.

For the week I was there, I had no spirit to go back to the home I was raised in. I didn't want to see my dad's old hotels. Who would remember us anyway? It had been 20 years since Davie Berman's family had lived there. I just went back and forth to the hospital, hoping to take my uncle home. The motel was built under a TV tower, and every night its red call letters blinked into my window—like the letters of hell were burning into my soul.

I hated my town. Look what it had all come to—naught. I wasn't ready at that time to examine my family's story, to find out the whys and the whatfors. I had lost a father and mother here by the time I was thirteen, and now my nearest living relative who had raised me was destitute and had gambled every penny at the tables. I never wanted to see that fickle older sister of mine again. She had turned her back on her own.

My uncle recovered—but only to lose more food money in crap games for another year. Twice I flew in to take him to a hospital in L.A. He lived in the Fremont Hotel for a while when he was on a winning streak and gambled at his favorite, the Golden Nugget. He'd have me visit him at the tables when I'd fly in for the day to see him and say, "I need to rub my girl Susie's shoulder for luck."

How sad I was, sitting with my uncle hoping he had enough money to live a few more days in a town my dad used to own. Did anybody remember? Did anybody care? Who could help us? Who would?

I remembered no one's name. It was all just a blank of sadness and loss. Loss of family, loss of power, loss of self. Once I went to get Uncle Chickie at a high-stakes crap game at Benny Binion's ranch. It had gone on three days and Uncle Chickie was throwing up blood, but he wouldn't leave. Just one more roll, just one more roll. Luck be a lady tonight! She wasn't; she never was. I barely got him to the hospital in time.

Lady Las Vegas, his other niece, had stolen him from me. He preferred her dark charms to my wholesome ones, and it was with the greatest effort that I finally got him away from her.

He moved to L.A. to be with me for the last year of his life. Even though he was dying and in and out of Cedars Sinai Hospital for that year, he still thought about Lady Las Vegas, I know he did. Oh, he denied it and said I was enough for him, but I know in his heart of hearts he only truly lived where the action was, and she had the edge on me.

I bought Yahrzeit lights to commemorate the lives of my parents and my uncle in a Beverly Hills temple. The rabbi who started the temple, Rabbi Al Maron, had been raised in Sioux City, Iowa, with my father and my uncle; they had all worshiped at the "brown shul" together and had been Bar

Mitzvahed there. My father had given money to Mogen David and Rabbi Maron had faithfully visited Uncle Chickie one Sunday a month at Terminal Island to play bridge with him.

I suppose I took their souls out of Las Vegas. Mine, so it seemed, had never been there.

As soon as he died, I moved to New York. I wanted to get as far away from Lady Las Vegas as I could. I said I would never visit her again. Childhood could be put behind us, I thought; that was then and this is now. It could be possible to jettison a whole part of one's self and throw it into the Atlantic and never deal with it again. The only way I could be strong was to close my own personal borders separating me from my older sister.

THE LADY TAKES A LOVER

Soon I would be called to spend the first chunk of quality time in nearly 40 years with her. I now clung to my autonomy with a desperate fury. It had taken me years of analysis to separate from my mother, to know that I was a very different person than her and that I could be me and choose life rather than death and still be a dutiful daughter to her memory.

But how to approach my sisterly relationship with Lady Las Vegas? Sibling feelings are complicated, binding yet threatening, mirroring yet alienating. The few times I had seen her, for family obligations I could not shirk, hospice visits and funerals, I drifted into town after hours, a little shifty, a little guilty. In a house on the outskirts of town, I hid from the bright of her night so she would not see me, left like a horse thief before her blinding sun rose bold in the sky. I had contacted no one from my past, maybe afraid no one would remember my dad, our family, maybe protecting myself from the cruel fact that time has had to march on. Over the years of separation I had convinced myself that there'd be nothing left of my old town and that it was better that way.

As I prepare to see her again, Lady Las Vegas prepares for me. Although economics has been good to her, public opinion has not always been kind, so she is on guard. She is tired of old-fashioned Mob exposés, articles extolling her bare breasts and titillations, and even more crime books with over-blown godfather operatic illusions and minor sociopathic players given center stage.

If you're serious, so am I, she says, staring me in the eye without flinching. I'm checking you out while you're checking me out, she tells me. I wasn't born yesterday, she says; neither were you.

I cannot do you total justice and meet all your sons and daughters, and I fear there is much about you I will never know. There are people I must meet, some movers and shakers, some not. Some I knew as a child, some I didn't. Some I remember, some remember me. I am not a sociologist, here to evaluate in that way. I have to follow my heart, make my own journey.

As the plane lands in Las Vegas (behind enemy lines?) images of the old McCarran Field overtake me: the small planes that took my family and me to the safety of Los Angeles when there was unrest in Las Vegas, or for joyous occasions like City of Hope functions or shopping sprees and dinners at the Brown Derby (we could hardly move in our Beverly Wilshire Hotel suite, it was so crowded with all the Mission Pak fruit baskets and flowers); planes that took us across the nation for the openings of racing seasons. I can't even believe that the modern jet that carries me to Vegas will have room to land at tiny McCarran.

But of course, McCarran is not tiny anymore, and I am no longer twelve. The plane lands at sunset, the blushing pink dollop of a sun melts into the mountains exactly as it always did. How I loved to look at it through the bubbles I blew with my magic bubble wand.

I drive down the strip during the day. People move a little slower, there's a languid feel; no meaningful action ever happens here except at night. I go into the Flamingo Hilton, it is packed, successful, happening, a well-tuned machine. I'm disoriented—where was our pit? Wasn't our lobby to the right as we walked in? The jewelry stand with the exciting revolving velvet counter was to the left? I imagine my dad standing in the center of the pit, when the only thing preventing me from complete happiness was a velvet burgundy cord with a gold clasp that cordoned off the pit from the rest of the hotel. As soon as I could elude my mother or Lou, I'd rush that rope (children were not allowed in the pit, yeah, right, like that would stop me) and dash under the cord yelling, "Daddy, daddy!" His face would break into a big smile, with that dimple in his cheek, he'd swoop me up, kiss me, and carry me back to my mother.

I'd wave at the sheriffs and the dealers, "Hi Phil, hi Don," and they'd

"THE BRIGHT OF HER NIGHT." MODERN VEGAS.

respond, "Hi ya Susie, how about a gin game later?" There are all new faces now; the owners and pit bosses have their own little girls but I doubt they have their run of the hotel.

I walk around the pool; the green bungalows in the back are gone, as are Fanny's Dress Shop, Gigi's Hair Salon, and the drug store. There is a mall inside this hotel, with many shops; they all look the same. The pool has a nice feel, a few pink ceramic flamingos dot the landscape, and people drink tropical drinks out of red straws. Children play with colorful pool toys, their mothers tan; some things never change.

"Gladys, Gladys, Susie is jumping off the high dive," my mother's friend Dorothy always said to my calm mother as she read a movie magazine, confident I was pool safe and capable of a cannonball when I was four. She'd look up, take off her sunglasses, wave happily. Everything was bright and sunny and warm, then deliciously cool as I hit the water spewing foam on all the hotel guests.

THE RIVIERA,
THEN AND NOW.

I drive to my father's other hotel, the Riviera. Masses of conventioneers stream through the danker than dank interior, eating peanuts, wearing name tags, hitting the tables. I want to shout, "This was the first European-looking high-rise hotel, it was so clean you could eat off the floor; it was the jewel of the Strip!" But who cares today?

Driving down the lavish Strip, there are the giants, the Mirage, Treasure Island, the Monte Carlo, MGM Grand, the International Hilton, the futuristic blue gleaming Bally's. They all stand proud. There's the Hard Rock off the Strip, the baby boomers' rock 'n' roll hotel. The only theme they haven't done is Nazareth, and for all I know that's in the planning stage. Lady Las Vegas is all dressed up, and she has somewhere to go.

I drive through many new suburbs, with opulent mansions behind gated communities, solid-looking suburban middle-class communities. I know people my age who have moved here recently, not for the glamour image of the town or the gambling, but for jobs. Vegas has jobs, Vegas has opportunities. Vegas adapts.

I drive down Sixth Street to my old house. The former middle-class neighborhood is now zoned residential and commercial. Most of the houses, including mine, are now law offices. It still looks the same, that little brown and white Tudor house, but the cottonwood tree out back is gone; it's all paved now. My playhouse is still behind the house, but it's used for storage.

I walk in, introduce myself to the receptionist. She doesn't know the house is a landmark, says I can walk around. The living room still exists but it's now an office. There's our fireplace, the same old bricks, the same grills.

My room is a lawyer's office. My closet is still there but probably not filled with Western clothes, party dresses, and storybook dolls. My parents' master bedroom and my mother's sewing room are law offices. The window in my room is still in the same place, above eye level, where it was raised so that no one could shoot us from outside. There is no kitchen but we hardly ever used ours anyway, except when Lucy Brown made us breakfast.

I used to know people all up and down Sixth but now Sixth only goes four blocks toward the Strip, then it becomes a bigger, unfamiliar street, like my town. I try to picture where Billy Alderman used to live. Is that his house? Was that where the Simms lived, and the Stearns? Weren't the Molaskys down the block?

Beth Shalom was a house when I worshiped and went to synagogue there; the Temple that exists now was built after I left. I drive to that brick synagogue. I've heard the town bought a Yahrzeit light for my dad. I scan the tablets of eternity and there it is! David Berman, son of David, June 18, 1957. And there are my dad's former partners Moe Sedway, Joe Rosenberg, Gus

Greenbaum, and famed publisher Hank Greenspun. And there's my husband, Mister Margulies. Fathers and sons of Vegas, not forgotten in their faith.

The air seems suddenly dense; the molecules of time collide. My time clock does not seem to follow my watch. How long have I spent drifting in the synagogue parking lot thinking about the past? Too long, always too long, however long.

The early years of the Eighties did not begin well for Lady Las Vegas. She was in the depths of a recession, her new rival, Atlantic City, stealing many of her suitors. The bottom had fallen out of her own casinos. The one at the Aladdin Hotel closed; the Stardust and the Sands were in deep trouble. The city had committed itself to construct a major airport and convention center, but could they succeed? What unique charms did Lady Las Vegas still really have to offer?

It's never nice to kick a lady when she's down but that's what happened to her. In the early morning hours of November 21, 1980, fire swept through Kirk Kerkorian's MGM Grand Hotel, the second worst hotel fire in American history. It began with a faulty wire in a lower-level deli, spread in a toxic smoke cloud through air ducts and elevator shafts, then erupted into an inferno raging out of control. The horrible disaster took its toll. Eighty-five people lost their lives.

Things went from bad to worse for my older sister. Hard on the heels of those fiery deaths, more occurred. The International Hilton had a fire in 1981. It seemed that Lady Las Vegas no longer dealt in fantasy; she dealt in tragic reality.

Where once people had come in droves to admire her, now they stayed away, questioning her good intentions. Finally in 1983, the nonstop flights between Las Vegas and New York were canceled. She was lower than low—ready to give up. Her neon heart flickered weakly and then started to skip beats. Just like in the movies, she needed a hero in a white hat to ride in on a white horse and save her.

Las Vegas was down, but not out. She took a deep breath and concentrated her charms. She sensed some interest again from a suitor whom she had known when he was much too young, on a visit from the East. He had briefly flirted with her a few years back but he had had nothing then to offer her. In the intervening years he had acquired sophistication and, better yet, cash.

The visionary who would turn the city around arrived not by horse, stagecoach, or sports car. He came in a jet plane and with Ivy League creden-

THE CONSTRUCTION OF KIRK KERKORIAN'S MGM GRAND HOTEL.
IT WAS DESTROYED BY FIRE IN 1980.

tials, Wall Street backing, and a fire in his heart to make Las Vegas legitimate. His face is now the face of Las Vegas.

I read the beginning of his biography. Stephen A. Wynn, chairman of the board and chief executive officer of Mirage Resorts, Inc. is 54, Connecticut-born, graduated from the University of Pennsylvania, married with two daughters and moved to Las Vegas in 1967. He started his career at the age of 25 as an executive and part owner of the Frontier Hotel, then operated a wine and liquor importing company. The p.r. sheet then lists his first big deal—the famous parking lot he bought from Hughes and got Caesars Palace to buy from him because they did not want a hotel right next door, giving him his first financial score—and how he used that money to buy the Golden Nugget and turn it around.

He walks into our first meeting bold, full of purpose, no entourage. He's fast, he's modern, he's aggressive, immaculately groomed like my dad and his friends were, a black silk shirt with a tiny embossed "sw" on the pocket. He's totally in the minute, ready to talk, full of masculine energy.

He's excited, he's thrilled, he's building the most astounding, the best, the most fantastic, the most fabulous hotel of this century, and you know he will. The Bellagio Hotel, under construction, is within view of the Mirage, "Look at it, it's going to be terrific!" He opens the window. "Listen to the siren song of Las Vegas," he says as her construction sounds fill the room. Cranes and building crews dominate the frame of his office window as the salmon-colored, Tuscan-styled hotel takes shape. You could be in Lake Como, which is the idea.

"There has never been a project like it. My organization has been together for over fifteen years, and now we're ready for the greatest challenge we could imagine; we're ready for it and we're meeting it. Every detail has been examined and reexamined," he says with enthusiasm.

"It is going to be an elegant European hotel here in Las Vegas. We have eleven acres of water in front of it, not just water, a lake! We have a double track monorail coming from the Monte Carlo to the Bellagio!

"Our problem was how to position a new hotel. We already have the Mirage so we had to go one better, make it even more fabulous. This will have even more elegant high roller suites than the Mirage, some specially for the Asians. That part will have a rice kitchen and all the Asian games. The hotel will have a conservatory when you walk in with a two-story glass elevator. There will be an Armani shop, a Hermes store, all the best stores, a Le Cirque restaurant, just like in New York.

"When I first thought of the Bellagio, I was sitting around with my guys, all of them, and I said, 'Where is it written in stone that the best hotel in the world was built in Europe in the 19th century? Where was it written in marble that the greatest hotel in the world had to be old? You couldn't get the best land in New York City to buy it, you can't buy Central Park. You can't buy the best land in London, that's Hyde Park.

"But we owned the best land in Las Vegas right on the Strip, we were the ones!" he says, smiling widely. This is not an anal corporate type; this is an exuberant guy having the time of his life, peppering his enthusiastic sentences with "Oh, my Lord," "Oh, my God," and "Can you believe it?"

He can tell you the year and the amount he paid for every piece of property he ever bought in Las Vegas; he can also tell you what his credit line was, what the interest was, what the deal was, and he wants to! He can tell you what date he made every decision on the Bellagio, what date every part of the Mirage and Treasure Island were finished, and he wants to! He can tell you how many guests have stayed at the Mirage and Treasure Island over the

STEVE WYNN FIRST VISITED VEGAS IN 1953. HE NOW OWNS THE MIRAGE, TREASURE ISLAND, THE GOLDEN NUGGET AND PART OF THE MONTE CARLO.

years, how much each hotel has made, why the guests get major value for their dollars at his hotels, cent by cent, and he wants to! And he can tell you how long each employee has worked at the Mirage and Treasure Island, which ones are going to work at the Bellagio, and he wants to!

He takes a phone call; it's from his friends, Hollywood moguls Billy Friedkin and Sherry Lansing in for the weekend. He's thrilled, loves them. "Billy? You're finally here! Room all right? Are you comfy? I can't wait to see you," he says, enjoying his life and friends. And why not? Hey, my dad would say every morning, "It's 80 degrees outside, how bad can it be?" How can he sustain this level of interest in yet another hotel, considering he already owns the Mirage, Treasure Island, the Golden Nugget and part of the Monte Carlo?

A MODEL OF THE BELLAGIO. THE $1.25 BILLION RESORT IS SLATED TO OPEN IN 1998.

"Do I still have the edge? Of course, I have the edge. I love doing what I'm doing. The water show in front of the Bellagio is going to be incredible; I still have a lot to work out, I just got back from Monaco. I'm trying to bring the Grand Prix Auto Race to the Bellagio."

He's comfortable talking about his career, his family, his background. He's as up front as Lady Las Vegas; he tells you what he thinks, no holds barred, take it or leave it, no apologies but a ton of charm. And he loved his father, you can see that, whom he lost when he was in college. His dad listed his debts on his deathbed, and the good son worked two years to pay them off.

His dad has been dead for over 30 years but it's obvious he's still alive to him, in the ways loving parents never die in the hearts of their children. He's quick to tell you that if his dad had lived he wouldn't be here, he'd be "a professional man, an attorney," but is that true?

Wynn's deep-seated desire to transform Las Vegas has its roots in his relationship with his father, a compulsive gambler. "His name was Mike

Wynn. He was in the bingo business. He was one of the unfortunate people who could not resist the lure of a crap table. And he loved Las Vegas. But he basically liked any place that he could gamble, and he was my best friend."

Wynn first visited Vegas in 1953 when he was eleven, with his dad. They stayed two weeks.

"It was wonderful, in a way, of course much smaller. I think there might have been 60,000 people here, but the Strip was a series of two-story motels with buildings in front of them, all with a big sign; and in between those buildings was sand," Wynn remembers. "There were only two cross streets. If you came up the Strip, you'd pass the Sahara Hotel, which sat in the middle of the desert. Across the street was the El Rancho Vegas, then you walked along those sidewalks; you walked along a dusty desert road until you came to the Silver Slipper, the Last Frontier Village, the Last Frontier Hotel. Across the street was the Desert Inn. There were a few more hotels, but nothing like today.

"If you went a couple miles to the west, you came to Hoot Gibson's Ranch. Between the livery stable and Hoot Gibson's Ranch was a dirt road. And along the sides of that dirt road were things like skulls of burros and cattle that had died. It was just like 'Hopalong Cassidy' Western movies."

Wynn's father gave him his first real taste of Las Vegas. "I started working for my dad when I was fifteen. He gave me jobs to do in the bingo, putting the cards together for the evening's games. Then when I was sixteen, I started becoming an announcer, and I called the numbers. I was a bingo caller, you know, and I stayed—and in case I lose this job, I can go back to that. Gives you something to fall back on," he says.

His initial inspiration for his career came from staying in his parents' cabana at Ben Novack's style-setting Fountainbleu Hotel in Miami—the hotel of that era, when he was in high school.

"Not only did my ideas on hotels come from seeing the Fountainbleu, but I think that deep, visceral emotional things happen to a young person when they see something they would like doing, when—for whatever your adolescent reasons—you form a romantic or irrational reason of why you want to do something."

In the 1970s, after a brief stint as the slot manager at the Frontier Hotel and as the owner of a liquor distributorship, Wynn saw an opportunity and went for it. Encouraged and supported by his friend, prominent Mormon banker Parry Thomas, he managed to talk Howard Hughes into selling a piece of property in Las Vegas—something no one ever did before or after, since Hughes was famous for holding on to land. That piece of property was a parking lot next to Caesar's Palace.

When the parking lot deal was signed, Wynn joyfully announced plans to build a hotel on the spot. Caesar's Palace quickly made an offer on the property to avoid the competition. Wynn's bluff worked. He made a tidy profit and had his first stake.

He then began buying up stock in the Golden Nugget, a downtown casino that had no hotel. He investigated management and found that profits were disappearing because employees were stealing. By 1977, the 30-year-old Wynn had control of the place. He built a hotel to go with the casino and set out to revive Las Vegas's fading downtown.

One of Wynn's first steps was to hire the then-unemployed Kenny Rogers as the Golden Nugget's entertainment director. "The First Edition was breaking up, and I had no clue what I was gonna do with my future," says Rogers. "And I remember I was staying in the Union Plaza Hotel, before I had ever gone to work down there, and I was looking out that window and I was so depressed because when I was working on the Strip, there was always the stigma that once you work downtown you can never work the Strip again. When I walked in the door, Steve met me and said, 'I want you to know, this is going to be the best thing that ever happens to you or me.'"

Following Wynn's lead, Rogers began hiring Strip-quality talent to play the Nugget. Before long, the new hotel had brought "class" to formerly seedy downtown.

"He used the lounge as his drawing card, and he used me and the other people who were there to get people downtown who normally would not have gone downtown. A higher roller, for lack of a term," according to Kenny Rogers.

Wynn fondly remembers starting out in Las Vegas. "It was a wonderful time for a young fellow like me. I was in my 20s—25 to 26 years old. I went in to the wine and liquor distributing business, which gave me a very strong sense of the back of the house, how these places worked. It was a good experience. Then in 1973, I had the opportunity—with the help of my bank—to get control of the Golden Nugget Casino. It had no hotel. Just a little gambling hall downtown.

"When the day came that I got control of the Golden Nugget, I was 30 old. I could step in there and put friends of mine, people I trusted, to work. And in a small casino like that, keep my head above water. For the next two or three years, I operated the place, immediately starting the pattern of a lifetime. The first month that I was there, I closed half the place and remodeled it. My mother was an interior decorator. I'm a born furniture mover. The Golden Nugget immediately prospered, partially because the old management had been very sloppy in controlling the cash. They were at an 8-percent increase in revenue and a 400-percent increase in profits, which meant that there was a lot of money being wasted. Then, with the help of the bank of the Mormon Church, the First Security of Utah, and my Mormon Las Vegas banker, Parry Thomas, who got me $12 million, I built a new garage and a 600-room hotel at the Golden Nugget. In 1978, that was a big deal, because the company went from making $4 million pre-taxes, or about $2.5 million after taxes, to making $12 million pre-taxes, and about $6 or $7 million after taxes. Now that isn't a lot of money, but it did give us a little bit more of a credential."

But the Golden Nugget was just a rehearsal for Wynn's ultimate fantasy—a 3,000-room megaresort that would be a world unto itself. The only obstacle was money. Wynn would need to do more than sell a parking lot to build a hotel estimated to cost nearly $700 million. He needed the kind of venture capital only available from one place—Wall Street.

Wall Street had traditionally shunned Las Vegas, due to her lingering associations with the Mob. But Wynn's stellar track record—in Las Vegas and in Atlantic City with his newest Golden Nugget Hotel—convinced investment brokers to take a chance on the Mirage. He turned to junk-bond king Michael Milken, wedded Wall Street to Las Vegas, and watched the honeymoon profits begin to pour in.

The hotel he built with Wall Street money, the Mirage, is situated on 100 acres, a shimmering landmark in the Las Vegas skyline, with its distinctive Y-shape and crisp white exterior with gold mirrored horizontal bands. As you drive down the Strip in the hot glare of midday, if you blink twice the hotel does seem to appear and disappear just like a real mirage.

As the first Vegas megaresort, it pioneered the concept of free entertainment as part of the structure. The front of the hotel is filled with a lagoon with waterfalls and grottoes as well as a volcano right on the Strip, which erupts every few minutes. There are two natural habitats within the hotel: One is home to the royal white tigers of Siegfried & Roy, and the other is a 2.5 million-gallon dolphin habitat, home for seven bottle-nosed dolphins.

Behind the registration desk is a wall-length, 20,000-gallon aquarium filled with baby sharks, rays, and other sea life. The Polynesian theme is carried out everywhere in the hotel; the pool is designed as a tropical paradise of tree-lined islands. The concept of huge is relative in Vegas, and even though this hotel has 29 floors of guest rooms, you don't feel overwhelmed walking through the halls.

Wynn followed one megaresort with another. Next door to the Mirage is Treasure Island, another Y-shaped hotel. The tall 36-story tower on the Strip features a daily and nightly sea battle in "Buccaner Bay" between the pirate ship *Hispaniola* and the British frigate, the *HMS Britannia,* in which the pirate ship is sunk. The pirate theme is continued inside with the interior done as Buccaneer Bay Village; the facades replicate a thriving Old World business environment including a foundry, a warehouse, a sail repair shop, and a shoemaker.

Cirque du Soleil's "Mystere" show enraptures the showroom audience at Treasure Island. These two theme hotels began a rivalry of one-upmanship among other hotel owners, creating the giant carnival midway that Las Vegas has become today.

In 1993, Wynn imploded the Dunes Hotel to make way for his future fantasy resort, the Bellagio. The $1.25 billion, 35-story, 3,000-room resort is slated to open Labor Day 1998 and will include a twelve-acre artificial lake with a $30 million water ballet attraction. It will feature a VIP check-in area with a private lobby and casino for high rollers, and Wynn even hopes to include a Formula One professional auto race called the "U.S. Grand Prix at Bellagio."

Wynn's implosion of the Dunes had another symbolic meaning to Las Vegas. The Dunes was always known as a "Mobbed-up" hotel, and those fireworks signified very clearly the end of an era in the city's colorful history—and hopefully the demise of Mob power in Las Vegas.

"The original money was the old gamblers and the old bookmakers, and the old Murder, Inc. guys. The middle money came from the Central States Teamsters' Pension Fund. Now it's junk bonds and publicly held corporations," says author Nicholas Pileggi. "You can buy a piece of a Las Vegas casino by simply buying ITT stock or whatever—Marriott or Hilton. That's what it is now."

You wonder if this is the secret dream Mike Wynn dreamed, if his young son Steve was so close to him that he knew it. It was probably never spoken, only felt, his bond to his dad so tight that he imbibed him through his skin. Maybe Steve saw the glint in his dad's eye when he talked about the Fountainbleu Hotel and when he talked about gambling; and maybe the son said someday I can bring these two together, the hotels and the gambling, and I can deliver to my dad everything he loves. Maybe Mike Wynn knew his son Steve was going to try to realize his dream someday so he told him "you can do anything, you can be anything," and it worked.

Who would have thought that a boy from the bingo could go so far no matter how much work? Who would have thought that a boy from the bingo would fantasize about huge hotels on Las Vegas's Strip and within 20 years build them? People like Bob Maheu remember Steve fantasizing 25 years ago

THE DECIMATION OF THE LANDMARK HOTEL.

about what Vegas could be, when he was young, green, and had no track record. And people like Bob Maheu thought Steve was working too hard, not in touch with reality, because how could Vegas ever be that big, that great, a world-class destination resort?

Who would have thought it? Who would have dreamed it? Who would have done it?

People ask everyday, What drives Steve Wynn? What makes him go for the gold? and you see immediately that every step he takes reflects the glory of his father—the bigger, the better, the brighter—and Mike Wynn lives forever not only in the heart of the son but in the world.

Wynn can't sit still for a minute. He's full of kinetic energy, "I'm outta here," and he's outta there. He wants to rush off to a meeting at Atlandia Design, his design firm, which is building the Bellagio. For a minute you forget that this city visionary is slowly losing his sight to a progressive eye disease, because he never mentions it, but goes everywhere with a seeing-eye German Shepherd named Rambas that he loves and kisses on the mouth in exuberance. "Rambas means rambunctious kid in German," he exults, grabbing Rambas and kissing him again.

"I have been a gambler all my life, but not voluntarily. I don't find any particular fascination in flying without a net," he says, seasoned by a lifetime of very hard work.

"I live a very comfortable life, I enjoy it. My wife and family and I enjoy all the things that success and achievement have brought us. I have no interest in testing the proposition of whether, if it was all erased, I could do it all over again. I intend not to find out. I'd like to keep going inward and upward, I'm not interested in going backward."

He's known for his decisiveness. "When you take a step, when you embark on a course of action, it's pointless to have anxiety and to look over your shoulder. It's very productive to recheck yourself. It's a healthy thing to be self-critical and to have self-doubt, but it's a bad thing to be paralyzed by it. You should have a little bit of controlled anxiety and then press on; that doesn't make you a gambler, it makes you sane and mature."

He's into the art of the deal, and he knows everything about the deal and he loves the deal; he could talk deals all day. So he tells you about the deal to buy the land the Dunes was on, and he tells you about the deal with Circus, Circus to build the Monte Carlo; and he tells you about the deal to build the Bellagio, and he is never dealt out.

Now he has to go to the design meeting. Atlandia is near the Mirage, staffed with design consultants. Wynn treats his company like a family business. Everybody's been with him ten, fifteen years, he knows their names and their families. He sits down with his colleagues to discuss the water show that will be featured at the Bellagio, his dog Rambas always at his feet. His architects, designers, landscape architects, hydraulic experts, and others spread plans out before him. He knows if one tiny detail has been changed, because he's totally hands-on.

The discussion revolves around where to put speakers for the sound system for the water show. After an exhausting discussion, Wynn and his consultants come to a consensual decision, Wynn is ecstatic, another piece of the puzzle found. He leaps up, ready to accomplish his next task, picking a rug and a chair. He bounds out of the room, Rambas at his heels, turns right, goes into another office.

"We took two and a half years designing the Bellagio before we touched the ground and started construction. We broke ground in September of 1995. We'll open it Labor Day 1998," he enthuses. "It will be a moment in history without compromise. We don't often get a chance to latch on to an ideal and take it as far as it can go."

"The Bellagio will be staffed by 7,000 people who have already worked for us, in our systems. When we opened the Mirage we had 450 cooks, and only fifteen of them had been with us before. When we open the Bellagio we will have 500 cooks, and all will have been with us in our other hotels.

"What keeps this town happening is the competition. Every new hotel fires people's imaginations and renews their interest in this crazy midway known as Las Vegas. It's probably the world's greatest carnival; it's a party that never stops, a promise that's always kept. Las Vegas is unabashedly itself," he says, plopping down in two chairs.

He's concerned that the chair should be comfortable. "Is this one too flimsy? I think this one is roomier. I want people to feel comfortable," he continues. Then his associate rolls out the carpet samples for the hallways of the Bellagio. He studies the plush carpets. "Too busy? Too complicated? I like this one, it's lush," he says. "What do you think?" She agrees.

But there's a cloud on Steve Wynn's productive sunny day today—well, not really a cloud, but a lack of light. Since the Sands Hotel shut down in the summer of 1996, it is too dark in front of the Mirage volcano. They had basked in the Sands's light. He's worried, has to think of a way to light his side of the street because "whoever thought the Sands would close down?" He's been thinking about this for days, meeting with people, looking for the solution. He'll find it.

He wants me to meet his hotel executives. The CEO of Treasure Island is bursting with zest and goodwill. His name is Bill Hornbuckle, and he came out West to go to the hotel school at the University of Nevada at Las Vegas and worked his way through school by being a busboy at the Jockey Club because the tips were great. "I did quite well with that job," he laughs, uproariously, loving the memory, "then I was a room service waiter at the Flamingo Hotel, and that was great too." Then he met Steve Wynn, and he's been with him ever since.

He takes me on a galloping tour, bounding through his hotel, knowing every inch. We're in the kitchen, then we're in the liquor room where the liquor flows to the bar in long curvy tubes. We're looking at the rooms, then we're in the showroom for "Mystere," and Hornbuckle stoops down suddenly to pick up a bagel because he loves every inch of this hotel and wants it clean.

And he's never been happier. He gets up every morning, spends time with his wife and two daughters whom he adores, then he drives to work (no commuter jams, it's Vegas). Sometimes his job lasts until six and sometimes till midnight and sometimes through the weekend, but he doesn't care. It's hard to keep up with him, "This is a world-class restaurant, and it's small, it's intimate. I call it the nook-and-cranny theory." And "Mystere is fantastic; it was created by the Cirque du Soleil people just for us."

He's showing me the banquet room and the employees' area, and he's so enthusiastic he's sprinting. He knows everybody's name and what they do and smiles at all of them. He's showing me the wedding chapel where they do 35 weddings every Saturday and give the couples a videotape. "We put on the front of the tape, 'You're at Treasure Island,' and people love that." He's showing me the complete gym and the spa, and he knows every service available and raps them down.

I'm thinking to myself, Steve Wynn and Bill Hornbuckle love this town just like my dad and his friends did; they know every single detail of their hotels. I remember my dad being worried about the special crystal globe chandeliers they flew over from Paris for the Riviera in 1955; they were too dark. And how he worried and worried and was going to replace them when my mother suggested someone dust them and saved the day.

"The Mirage has more elegant, more expensive rooms; we service a different clientele here, someone who wants value but who doesn't want to spend as much as they do at the Mirage." And the Mirage tour is as lavish as you would imagine with villas for high rollers to die for.

I think about the Riviera. People say the previous owner Meshluham (Ric) Riklis is a nice guy, but he filed corporate bankruptcy on the hotel and it's a mess. About Las Vegas, like anything that makes money, people tell you: "Yeah, the bondholders own it now, nah, it's not embarrassing, these things happen, and the guy that runs it is turning it around." You just hope so, and goddamit why couldn't Steve Wynn own that one!

Steve Wynn introduces me to the CEO of the Mirage, a former high-stakes poker player, a charming Gary Cooper-type from Tulsa, Oklahoma, named Bobby Baldwin. Steve and Bobby met in a poker game and Bobby doesn't remember who won. The town gossips that everybody was afraid Bobby couldn't handle the job Steve gave him, but Steve had faith in him and he has done a great job.

Bobby Baldwin's eyes are always twinkling with real "gee-whiz charm" when he tells you about planning the Bellagio and about working with Steve and especially about how he won the World Series Championship Poker Game at Benny Binion's Horseshoe in 1978. He won $420,000.

This guy is adorable. He tells you how he was a pool player and a poker player when he was in the seventh grade in Tulsa and how he lost the $60 a month he made delivering the three Tulsa papers after school and on Sunday. Then he started playing "Texas Hold `Em," a form of seven-card stud, and started winning.

BENNY BINION'S HORSESHOE HOTEL AND CASINO.

He came on a junket to Las Vegas when he was 19 in 1969 with $5,000 he had won in a poker game and stayed at the Aladdin Hotel and played at the Las Vegas Hilton.

"And that was the year we landed a man on the moon, and I said to myself, this is fantastic, we have a man on the moon and there's a place like Las Vegas!"

Steve Wynn wants me to meet his wife, Elaine, and come to the Fiftieth Anniversary party of the Golden Nugget Hotel next week, and he's going here, there, and everywhere for the next few hours, do I want to come? I collapse in exhaustion and go back to my "off the Strip" dive, and I think, Lady Las Vegas, if you can keep up with Steve Wynn and his kind, you've bested me again!

"I'M FROM A SMALL TOWN"

As Steve Wynn is now known as the hotel king of Las Vegas, Wayne Newton is equally famous as the premier entertainer. He started performing there as a child, so young he had to be escorted into the casino by an adult, and is still probably Las Vegas's most beloved entertainer.

"I was in Las Vegas the first time in 1958. An agent had come through Phoenix. I had my own local television show there for four years, and he had seen me on television.

"He contacted my parents and he said, 'I would like to take your son to Las Vegas, or at least have him go there to audition for one of the lounges. Do you have a problem with that?'" remembers Newton.

"I thought, in a very childish way I'm sure, that the Flamingo Hotel probably looked like a flamingo, and you took the elevator up the flamingo's leg and the casino was probably hidden in its belly somewhere.

"And that the Dunes was just, you know, a pyramid-kind-of-looking thing, and that the Showboat looked like a showboat. Well, I was about half right. When I got to Las Vegas I remember being not frightened by it because not many things scare me, but I was concerned about the fact that the surroundings were so totally foreign to me. I didn't see any kids my age.

"We auditioned, my brother and I, for a man by the name of Eddie Torres who listened to two songs and got up and walked out of the room. I thought, well, back to Phoenix I go, and he stuck his head back in and said, 'If I can get a permit for you to work, then I'll hire you for two weeks.' Now I had no idea what all of that meant!

"Came to find out of course, in retrospect, it meant that I was very much under age—fifteen years old to be exact—and I had to get a special permit from the State of Nevada just so I could work in the lounge. I was not allowed to be in the place that I was working, which I've never really figured out. I could do the six shows a night, but between shows I had to go out and stand on the street or go to the coffee shop or go to my dressing room."

Newton started his career downtown.

"I played the Fremont Hotel, and out of that first two-week engagement we stayed 46 weeks, doing six shows a night, six nights a week, and we were ultimately there five years. We then started playing what was then known as the Nevada Circuit for lounges, and that was Las Vegas, Elko, Ely, Reno, Lake Tahoe, and Carson City."

Newton's big break finally came, and he catapulted into fame when he went from being a lounge performer to a headliner.

"I had been playing lounges in Nevada for five years, and I had gotten so sick of it that I said to my brother and my then manager, who was our bass player, Tommy Amatto, 'I can't continue to do this, six shows a night, six nights a week.' I had gone through Harrah's casino in Tahoe and into the main room and bumped into the entertainment director. They had been offering a tremendous amount of money—$10,000 a week—to play their lounge. And I said, 'I'm never playing another lounge.' I said, 'But I'll play the main room for you as an opening act at half of that.' His answer to me was, 'Well, I guess you'll never play Harrah's again, period!' Because in those years when you played those lounges and you became important to them in the lounge, that was it. That's where you started, and that's where you stopped.

"I had the opportunity to go to Australia and while we were appearing in Australia, Jack Benny came to see our show, and of course I was thrilled. He came backstage after the show, and he looked and sounded exactly like I had seen him on television. And he said, 'Would you like to come to my concert?' He was playing one of the theaters in Sydney. I said, 'Yes sir, I'd love to.' And so we did. We went to his concert that next afternoon.

"He invited us backstage, and he said, 'How would you like to tour with me?' Now this is before I had a hit record, this is before any of that, and I said, 'You mean tour with you, like as your opening act?' And he said, 'Yes.' And I said, 'I'd be thrilled.'

"He said, 'Wonderful. The first place we'll play will be Harrah's.' Now he didn't know the story so my heart went to my feet, and I said, 'Mr. Benny, I have to be totally candid with you.' I said, 'They don't want me at Harrah's. I've played their lounge and I've played the lounge across the street, and they just do not want me in the main room there.' He looked at me with a little gleam in his eye, and he said, 'If they don't want you, they don't want me.' And that's how I ended up going into the main room in Nevada, and Harrah's was the first one that I played!"

Newton headlined the first time, in November of 1964, at the Flamingo and stayed there until 1967. He remembers everything about the Sixties, including days of the Rat Pack.

"Jack Entratter, who was in charge of the entertainment at the Sands, had a dual deal with all those performers. He paid them under contract, but then they would get another certain amount either to gamble with or—anyway they wanted to handle it. But the contract only showed a specific amount. Well, when Mr. Hughes bought the Sands, he started paying the performers, like Mr. Sinatra, and Dean and Sammy, what the contract called for. He wasn't going to play the other game, because not only was it illegal, it was not something that he wanted to be part of. So that's really what destroyed the Rat Pack, that's really when they started to go their own way. Frank went to Caesar's. Dean went to the Riviera.

"I left the Flamingo in 1967 and went to the Frontier Hotel, but the Frontier wasn't owned by Mr. Hughes then. He bought it between the time that I had signed and the time that I actually played there first. So when I got there, Sammy was in the process of trying to break his contract with the Sands. He did it by saying that he had a point or two in the Tropicana. In those years, he was honoring his contract by showing up at every engagement he was supposed to perform.

"But seventeen times in a row he wouldn't go on. Now in those years, when they were serving dinner, the hotel had to pick up the entire dinner, all the tokens that had been given out, all the drinks, so the performer could really hurt the hotel by doing that. I started to fill in for Sammy, knowing that Sammy would rehearse, and at 7:30, when the show was to go on at eight, Sammy would say, 'I can't go on, I'm sick.' I would stand by. So I ended up there."

Newton did his 25,000th show in January of 1996.

"The thing that hit me most of all was you'd think I'd get it right. The 25,000th show was in a hotel that the general manager swore I would never play again. And I had written something fairly rude on the wall when I left because he and I had a major disagreement, and he told the stage manager to cut that out of the wall. The stage manager didn't. He just put a piece of plasterboard over it and kept it there, and we unveiled it when I was there in January. So it was quite a night."

Newton is honored by the way Las Vegas has adored him over the years.

"Sammy Davis said to me when I went to see him one time at the Desert Inn, 'You have something going that the rest of us don't,' and I said, 'What?' And he said, 'When people come to Las Vegas they see Boulder Dam and Wayne Newton, or Wayne Newton and Boulder Dam, that's a prerequisite.' I must tell you it's a wonderful feeling. It's a wonderful feeling to be in different parts of the world, not only to mention different parts of the United States, and have the people come up to me and say, 'I saw you in Las Vegas.'"

Newton has his favorite "Las Vegas story."

"I was on stage one night and I get a note that says, 'Don't turn up the house lights.' That meant either there was a fight or someone was ill and they needed to get a doctor.

"A terminally ill gentleman had wanted to see my show and came from the East Coast somewhere, with oxygen. And, I believe, on a gurney. And his daughter came with him. They put him on a booth on King's Row and set him up. Halfway through my show the gentleman passed away. Security immediately ran into the room and started to remove the gentleman from the booth, at which point his daughter became very, very upset and said, 'My dad came here to see this show, and he's gonna see this show.' She made them leave him there through the rest of the show, which was about probably another hour. Where else could that happen? Only in Las Vegas, you know, and it was interesting because the security at the hotel, and my own personal security, and the hotel execs all understood. That gentleman stayed in that booth in that state until the show ended and the room emptied, and then they took him to the proper place."

"It's a city that truly raised me. A city that molded a great many of my beliefs, and when I die it's the place I wanna be," says Newton.

In the same way that only Las Vegas allowed Steve Wynn to become Steve Wynn, and Wayne Newton to become Wayne Newton, it has allowed Bob Stupak to become Bob Stupak, although Lady Las Vegas has not yet decided if she's going to commit to him. He first got her attention by starting Vegas World, and then in May 1996 he opened the Stratosphere Tower. The long-awaited observation structure rises close to 1,200 feet just north of the Strip, the tallest building west of the Mississippi.

The multilevel pod near the top has wedding chapels, a revolving restaurant and bar, an outdoor deck, and a conference center. There's a roller coaster at the 900-foot level and a space-shot ride attached to the needle that

VIEW OF THE CITY FROM THE STRATOSPHERE ROLLER-COASTER.

goes up 185 feet under the four Gs of thrust and comes down in free fall. There is an adjacent 1,500-room Stratosphere Hotel.

Unfortunately, by October of 1996, the Stratosphere was not doing well, and Stupak, the founder, was out as the head of it and Lyle C. Berman of Grand Casinos, Inc., was in. Will Stupak, a true Vegas character, survive? He's determined to, and if his life story is apocryphal, he might. He survived a motorcycle accident two years ago against incredible odds.

"I came to Las Vegas on my way to Australia. My father, Chester, ran a crap game in Pittsburgh. It started in 1941 and actually closed in 1991; that was the year he died. So all my life, that's what I was involved with," says Stupak. "My mother was involved in the business, too, 'cause they had lottery, numbers. When I grew up, that's what my dad taught me. How many numbers are on the dice? How many fours? How many sevens? How many sixes? That's what he did. When I was seven or eight, I'd get up in the morning, my mom would get me up. Sometimes a crap game was going on at home. Or my dad and his friends or customers were still shooting crap. I thought that's what big people did, when they grew up. They stayed up all night and threw cubes! That's how I got into it. That's how I understood it. That's all I ever knew. My father liked to use the word 'famous,' because the crap game used to always get raided, and he was always in the paper: 'Chester's crap game raided again.'

"It was not legal at the time, but the last 20 years or so, he didn't have to pay off anybody anymore. Because he became an institution and everybody knew he was there. Anybody else opened up a crap game would be closed in five minutes. That was 'Chester's Place,' so he had a reputation. It was kinda neat.

"I'd like to go back there every once in a while after I was here. I'd get into a cab and always asked the cab driver, 'Any gamblin' in town?' He'd say, 'Yeah. Chester's place down in South Side.' Even the cab drivers knew there was some action down there. That's how I was raised.

"I came here to stay in 1972. I identified with the gamblers who founded Vegas in the Fifties. The original founders might have been a little tarnished from Cleveland or Detroit, or whatever. When they came here, they were automatically respected citizens, part of the community. And that's the way I felt. Like I was part of the community, I was okay. I wasn't an odd character.

"When I came to town, I wanted to do something quick. I wanted to get a handle on Las Vegas. I wanted to get into the casino business, but yet to make a mark; and I was always in a hurry. So I met some people that knew some people, and there was a restaurant here. I opened that restaurant up, and I remember I changed the name of it to Chateau Vegas. I cleaned it up a little bit. I bought some TV spots. They were very expensive. They were five dollars for a 30-second spot. I just bought a whole bunch of them a week, and I remember I wrote the slogan, 'The world's greatest restaurant in the world's greatest city, Chateau Vegas.' And I got into the restaurant business. It was full from the day one. And it was full every night. It was hard to get in the place. Then after the accountants gave me a breakdown of what happened. I think after the first two months, there was no bottom line. Didn't make any money. Well, I said, 'Jeez,' I said. 'Something's wrong with this business. We're so busy. How come we didn't make any money?'

"I wasn't too impressed with the restaurant business. It didn't seem to make any sense because people came in and they brought money and they spent money, but yet, I had to give things back in return. Like food, drinks, you know. I said, 'I didn't come here for this. This isn't what it's all about.' So I wind up selling the restaurant, and I buy another place and put in a casino. I wallpaper the whole place to make magic—the floors, the ceiling, the walls—with money, real money. One-dollar bills, mostly one-dollar bills, because I had a small bank roll. Mostly one-dollar bills, but in strategic places, eye level, fives and tens and, in real, real strategic places, fifties and hundreds. And silver dollars on the floor.

"Then I bought a couple of antique slot machines. And then I put Bugsy Siegel's picture up, real big, with the bullet holes and everything to make it look dramatic. And it said under it, 'Learn the history of cards, dice, and all the gambling games.' Then I had some fun with it. I had a cigarette with some lipstick on it in an ashtray over a little plastic globe. 'This is the alleged cigarette that Marilyn Monroe was smoking when she was playing roulette at such and such a place.' You could use the word alleged. But what's a Marilyn Monroe cigarette? I think I had Jimmy Durante's cigar, when he was shooting craps at the Frontier Hotel.

"And I had at that time the world's largest jackpot. I wanted a million-dollar jackpot if I could raise the million dollars. So I opened up with a quarter-million-dollar jackpot, and the name of the place was 'Bob Stupak's World Famous Million-Dollar Historic Gambling Museum and Casino.'

"People said, 'The name is bigger than the place.' It was a museum, because it was a restricted license. I only had fifteen machines on the location, and the slot machines had to be secondary to your business. So I created the business by calling it a museum. It burned down."

After another business venture, Stupak raised the money to open Vegas World. "In the early Seventies you could just walk into the bank, meet the president of the bank, whatever your deposit was at that time. I mean, you just got acquainted. The first loan they gave me in the early Seventies was $10,000. The last loan they gave me, way later, was $10 million.

"I needed a loan for Vegas World but I kept getting turned down. Every month or two I'd go in and always switch the story a little bit, and always got a 'no, not now.' And a month or two later I'd go in again with another little twisted story and get a 'no.' That just went on and on. It became a pattern. One day I went in and gave the story and they said, 'Yes, okay.' I remember I walked out of the bank a little confused. I walked out of the bank, I got into my car to drive home. I didn't live very far away from the bank where you went up Las Vegas Boulevard and you made a left on Charleston. But all of a sudden I looked up, and I'm passing the Hacienda Hotel, about six miles from my turn-off. You know, I didn't wake up. And, my god, now I got the money. I mean I really have to build a place now? I have to build Vegas World?

"I remember opening up I had a Dixieland band in there. They played, 'When the Saints Go Marching In.' We opened up at six o'clock at night, and

BOB STUPAK'S
STRATOSPHERE
TOWER.

my dad and mom flew into town. They got here about one, and I took them up to the Sahara to get something to eat. My dad said, 'When do you open up, in about a month?' I said, 'About a month? We'll be open in about three and a half hours,' because the place was such a mess. But we opened up immediately. It was still kind of shaky. I remember when the crowd was flowing in—I saw ladders still moving through the crowd to get out of the way. The place was full in the first five minutes!

"Most of the places were a $1,000 limit. Some were even lower, $500 limit. Well, I kicked the limit up to $2,000 and doubled everybody's limit. I came up with the slogan 'The Sky's the Limit,' so I got into big action real quick and had different variations of games. I had a game called double exposure 21, where both dealer's cards were dealt face up. Crap game was called 'crapless craps.' All these things caught on. So it was a tremendous joyride, you know. Every day was fun."

From there, Stupak built on his success to create the Stratosphere.

"I wanted to open a really big casino but I needed a hook, and I was worrying about a hook because I saw all these big places open up. I was losing customers that wanted to go see the volcano, or see some of the other megaresorts that were opening. I was in Australia, in Sydney, having lunch with my daughter, and I was staying at a hotel that overlooked the city of Sydney. I asked her, I said, 'What's that big thing sticking up there?' It was the Sydney Tower. I said, 'Is there a restaurant up there?' She said. 'Yeah, but it's not very good.' I said, 'I don't care, I want to go anyway.' We went there and there were two lines.

"So I approached the guy selling tickets and I said, 'Why are these people in line?' He said, 'Well, they're in line to buy a ticket, and then with the ticket they go over there and they get an elevator ride to go to the top of the tower.' And I said, 'What is the ticket for?' 'The ticket's for the cost of the ride.' I said, 'What ride?' 'The elevator ride.' 'These people pay five dollars to take an elevator ride?' I got friendly with the guy that was selling tickets. I said, 'How many people are going to do this today? Is it going to be a good day?' He said, 'Oh, today we'll do about three thousand.' I said, 'Three thousand what? Three thousand people are going to pay that five dollars to go up there?' He said, 'Yeah.' I said, 'Is this a big day or a regular day?' He said, 'Oh, weekends are bigger and holidays are bigger yet.'

"So I came back to Vegas intrigued. I wanted to find out how tall the Seattle Space Needle was. That was 1,615 feet. I knew of the Eiffel Tower. I knew the Sydney Tower then. There's the Tokyo Tower. I said, 'Call these places. Find out how many people go there as visitors,' and when the figures came back I mean it was just astronomical how many people went and did these various towers, you know. I took a cross section of all the towers and took an average, and it seemed like, my god, this was a home run. This is too easy. In fact, it's so easy, jeez, I'll forget about the casino business. I'll just travel the world, start a company called 'Towers Are Us,' just sell them their tickets. Better than gambling, you don't even give them a chance to win. You just give them a ticket to an elevator. Then I found out the reason this doesn't happen is because there's a lot of regulations—FAA regulations, zoning regulations, what have you. It's not so easy.

"So I thought of the Stratosphere. Everybody just thought I was completely nuts. I mean you don't build a tower in the middle of the desert. For a tower I had the best location in the world, because from the south you saw all of the Strip, not part of the Strip—all of the Strip. And from the north you saw all of downtown. So I built the Stratosphere."

Stupak loves Vegas.

"If you want to drink, go to a bar. If you want to eat, go to a restaurant. If you want to sleep, go to a hotel somewhere. If you want to gamble, come to Las Vegas. If you want to gamble big, come to Las Vegas faster. You want to win big, come to Las Vegas. You want a big jackpot, come to Las Vegas. You want to make a bigger bet, come to Las Vegas.

"Now there's over 30 million people coming. There's going to be 40 million, there's going to be 50 million, you know, and out of the whole country I think it works out that only 15 percent to 20 percent of the people in the whole country have been to Las Vegas. That means there's over 80 percent of the public out there, all the people in Flatsville haven't been there yet, and sooner or later have to show up."

Whether or not Lady Las Vegas returns his affection remains to be seen. The Stratosphere currently teeters to view and all of it is now under financial reorganization.

Besides the hotel owners who run the town, who are its prominent citizens, who does Lady Las Vegas honor? She gives her love to men who have made her tremendously successful and who can afford to take her out in style. Power is an aphrodisiac to her. She validates the women who have been led here by their men, who are at first horrified by her, then accepting, and who have then made a contribution to the fabric of the town.

Who is a true "Las Vegan?" I'm interested in meeting the gentry of Vegas, some of whom I grew up with, and the people they have selected to run their town.

This is a town that does honor its own, and there are jewels among the women. There's Toni Clark, who comes with a solid gold pedigree. For years the dazzling beautiful wife of kindly Desert Inn Hotel owner Wilbur Clark, she came here as his young bride in 1944 and has been here every since. She became the most popular hostess in town. During that time, she was named the best-dressed woman in the United States.

I remember Toni when I was a child, giving luncheons and dinners in the magnificent Desert Inn Sky Room, receiving guests in their lavish home in the Desert Inn Country Club Estates. (They were the most beautiful homes in town in the early Fifties, built on a golf course. It was my mother's dream to live there, and the year my father died he had just bought the property.)

Wilbur Clark started as a bellhop in the Hotel Knickerbocker in San Diego. When he moved to Vegas, he bought the El Rancho and then bought the property to build the Desert Inn for $70,000. He opened that hotel in 1950, and died of a heart attack in 1965.

His gracious widow stayed on. She's just as lovely and feminine as she was in her young years. Many years after Wilbur died, she met screenwriter Larry Pinuf, and they have been together ever since. They live in an elegant gated community. Flowers and antiques adorn the interior.

WILBUR CLARK BUILT THE DESERT INN IN 1950.

"Las Vegas has gotten big; you don't know everyone anymore, it's true, but it still has a friendly small-town atmosphere. When I first moved here with Wilbur, I was shy, but you can't stay very shy in Las Vegas. My early years with Wilbur here were wonderful. He made the Desert Inn world-famous in the Fifties.

"He was known as the goodwill ambassador of Las Vegas," Toni says. She has carefully saved mementos of the old Vegas—original menus from the El Rancho, many pictures of the Desert Inn. Larry, although he has lived here a mere 22 years, is also into the nostalgia of the town. He can tell you the low-down on every hotel through the years.

Barbara Greenspun is another jewel. Hank Greenspun brought her here as a young bride from Ireland. She had the same reaction every other young wife did: what is this place?

"Ireland was so green, so beautiful, this was just desert, nothing here," she remembers, seated in her offices at the *Las Vegas Sun*, which she now runs with her children. Since Hank died in 1989, the Greenspun family has run his empire, which now includes real estate and cable television interests.

They've always been a politically active family, and one of the days I saw them, Brian Greenspun, the oldest son, was hosting a luncheon for President Bill Clinton at his home. Brian's daughter works in Washington for Clinton. It amazes me how my town has political influence now and is a major draw for candidates raising funds.

"I consider myself a Las Vegan now, we've really changed into quite a sophisticated town," says Barbara, soft-spoken, dignified, and articulate. She travels widely and is active in many charitable causes. She and Hank raised their four children here, and now those children are raising families here.

Brian, tall and studious-looking, who heads the Greenspun economic interests, is genial and vivacious. He still cries when he talks of his dad; it's that kind of town, unabashed sentiment.

Claudine Williams, the CEO of Harrah's, would stand out as a powerful executive in any town. She is the only woman to run a major Strip hotel.

"I came here with my husband, Shelby Williams, a gambler from Texas," says Claudine, a well-groomed, handsome woman. "First, we came on our way to California in 1946. We stayed at the El Rancho. The town was so small. Then we came back as Jake Friedman's guests at the Sands in 1952, and we fell in love with the town. We owned a private gambling club in Galveston, Texas, called the Rose Garden. We decided we wanted to move here," she says, seated in her spacious office in Harrah's. The hotel is currently undergoing a major renovation that she's overseeing.

Shelby and Claudine first bought the Silver Slipper on the Strip in 1964.

HOWARD HUGHES BOUGHT THE SILVER SLIPPER FROM SHELBY AND CLAUDINE WILLIAMS BECAUSE THE REVOLVING SLIPPER REFLECTED TOO MUCH LIGHT INTO HIS ROOM AT THE DESERT INN.

The revolving slipper reflected into Howard Hughes's bedroom window at the Desert Inn, so he bought the club from the Williamses. In 1972, they started the Holiday Casino, then Harrah's bought it. After Shelby died, they asked her to stay on as CEO. She's done a legendary job and is recognized worldwide.

"Gambling is so accepted now. In the old days, there was discrimination against me because I was a gambler's wife. People would talk to you at the Kentucky Derby, but they wouldn't invite you to their homes. That's over now; now everyone wants to know hotel owners and executives from Las Vegas."

Elaine Wynn is very popular, another jewel. People perceive her as an activist, issue-oriented and a champion of children. "She could be traveling and going to parties every night on Steve's money, but she stays here and works on educational issues. She's committed to this town," is a sentence you hear often.

"I met Steve on a blind date the Christmas vacation of my freshman year in college. My parents fixed us up. They met him and were crazy about him, and they called me. I was at UCLA," she says, in her office at the Mirage. There are pictures of the Wynn family all over: Steve, Elaine, and their two daughters. Elaine is a tall, attractive blonde with a soft, serious manner.

"Both my parents and Steve's parents lived in Miami, and we had so much in common, the middle-class Jewish values. Our fathers were both gamblers. I didn't know what Steve would do for a living but I had a feeling I'd be with him. In addition to being a charming fast talker, he had a brilliant intellect; I was fascinated.

"His parents owned bingo parlors, so I worked with him for years in the bingo after we got married in Maryland. I didn't even know it was drudgery until much later. His father died when Steve was in college and left debts, gambling debts. Steve paid every one of them off and supported his mother, me, and his ten-year-old brother. Through some of his dad's contacts, he met people in Las Vegas, and we came out here to see it and stayed at the Sands.

"I just hated the place, I thought it was wicked. Maybe I was a bit of a prude but the whole thing was just so threatening. I had no idea that we'd wind up living here. But now, I have a different view, and it's a very different town.

"Once Steve started to be successful here, I said to myself, I've got to look to the community to make a place for myself and my family. I went immediately to the Temple and joined and met friends there who are my best friends even today. I've raised my two daughters here; they've turned out to be very solid, good, wholesome kids.

"And now I'm very honored," she says, smiling happily. "They recently named an elementary school, 'The Elaine Wynn School.' I'm just trying not to go down there everyday to be with the children! I'm thrilled," she says, stopping to take a phone call about the inner-city games in the public schools, which she is helping to organize. Here the days are full of community activity.

One of the original town fathers is Irwin Molasky, a builder with an airy office at Paradise Development. What Del Webb didn't build here, Molasky did. Renderings and pictures of communities, shopping malls, apartment complexes, Sunrise Hospital, and dozens of other large projects that his company built adorn the walls, fighting for space with family pictures.

He and his wife and four kids lived down from us a few blocks on Sixth Street. I remember his wife and my mother taking turns carpooling the kids to the Huntridge Theater on Saturday mornings for the matinees.

Irwin, at 69, still works constantly, hasn't slowed down. He has had many other interests besides those in Vegas. He owned Lorimar, Inc., one of the most successful television-production companies of its day in L.A., and built the world-famous La Costa Hotel and Resort near San Diego. He's currently working on a city-sized, master-planned community in southern California called Ritter Ranch.

"People tell me I'm lucky to have been here in the early Fifties when I started building houses, and I mean doing the construction myself. I was a builder, so happy to have any opportunity. People say that's when it was easy to start out in Vegas, when you could make a deal on the back of a napkin. But it wasn't that easy in those days, it wasn't easy to get financing; this was before Steve Wynn brought Wall Street here. Now it's actually much easier."

Jackie Binion, Benny Binion's son, is the president and chief operating officer of Binion's Horseshoe Hotel and Casino downtown, the famed club that his dad started in 1951. In 1988, the Binions purchased the adjacent Mint Hotel and doubled the size of the Horseshoe.

The first club Benny Binion bought in 1946 when he came from Texas was the El Dorado Club. That's where Jack learned the hotel casino trade working at everything from being a busboy to a dealer. I always liked Benny; he had a fabulous personality and a great sense of humor, and he used to let me try on his white hat all the time. There were five kids, and they lived out on a big ranch on the outskirts of town.

"I remember we saw your dad the day before he went in for that operation that killed him," Jackie says." He was always so nice to me; I was just a kid. My dad says to him, 'If you're having stomach problems it's because your money belt is ingrown,' Your dad laughed. When we found out he had died, we just couldn't believe it."

How does Jackie remember his dad, one of the most famous downtown pioneers?

"My dad just loved people, and it showed; he had a larger-than-life personality. He used to have these sayings that were so true. 'Most people are honest when they can afford to be. Justice is spelled Just-us.'"

Jackie, like the rest of us, didn't stop loving his dad when he went to prison. These are the facts of life we grew up with in the old days. It was getting your family member out that mattered.

"Yeah, they got Benny on income tax evasion. He did three years in Leavenworth, 1953 to 1956. He died in 1989. I really miss him."

Burton Cohen, now retired, and occupying an office near his friend Kirk Kerkorian, came to Las Vegas 30-some years ago from Miami, where he was an attorney specializing in developing airport hotels. His goal was to be a federal judge. He has now been at the top of the Vegas pyramid for a very long time.

"I came out because I was offered a terrific deal to run the Frontier Hotel.

I didn't know anything about gambling but I knew how to run a hotel, so I decided to take it. I figured I'd stay five years, sell my points—that's what we called our positions in the old days—and then go home. Now I'm on my sixth five-year plan," adds Cohen, who is always smiling.

Besides the Frontier, he has run the Flamingo; the Flamingo Hilton; Circus, Circus; and most recently the Desert Inn for ITT. They asked him to stay on but he decided to retire last year. He was recently elected into the Gambler's Hall of Fame.

"I always figured I'd go home to Miami after I retired but then last year I realized this was my home, Las Vegas. It's the only 24-hour town in the nation, and I love it; I'm ecstatic here."

I look for people who are not associated with the hotels that have been here over half a century. There's Ed Von Tobel, whose father started the famed Von Tobel's lumber stores. He grew up to run them with his brother before selling them a few years ago.

"I grew up in a very small town. We knew everyone. We rode our bikes on dirt downtown. The town's had many ups and downs, a couple times when it went into a depression. My dad was one of the only ones who stayed; he stuck it out, and it worked.

"When the Eastern guys came and opened hotels and casinos in the Forties and Fifties, we were happy to see them. They brought business to town and became active in the Elks and the Rotary Club like the rest of us. We didn't look down on them. This town has always been friendly to anyone that brings in business."

There's Thalia Dondero who came here to marry a teacher, stayed, and raised a family. Anybody needs anything done in town, needs to know a political issue, needs to know who can do what, they call Thalia, who runs her own consulting business.

This dynamic matron, Thalia Dondero, sits down for lunch, pulls out a cellular phone, and tells you the history of every educational issue in town. "I'm very glad to live here; it's a city where the citizens are very involved, very concerned about the quality of life here," she says.

There are dozens of people in their 70s and 80s, core people of the town, who have never been associated with the hotels or gambling but who have led very successful family-oriented lives. I had met some of them when I was a child, but didn't really know them. I was a part of the Strip culture, and the hotel people and townies didn't interact that much.

Who moves here now to make a life? A wide diversity of people have in the last five years, reflecting Vegas's modernity and change from a town that just depends on gambling for revenue to a city considered a world-class resort destination.

Hal Rothman, the historian at the University of Nevada, Las Vegas, sits in his book-cluttered office at the college, a fount of information about Nevada's history and just about everything else. He's originally from Louisiana and came here from a professorial job in Kansas.

"UNLV made me an offer I just couldn't turn down," says Rothman, an exuberant, likable, energetic man, who has a picture of his wife and two children on his desk.

"Most other universities do not really help you to go up the ladder. UNLV is just the opposite; it's like Vegas, it gives you incredible opportunities. My students are fantastic, really committed to learning. And remember that families like mine don't live in the eight blocks of the Strip that tourists see. We have a fantastic family life in Henderson," Rothman says.

"My biggest problem in coming out here was that my wife didn't want to. I tried to convince her but she was adamant. Then a friend of mine said to her, 'Why don't you give it a shot, it can't be worse than you think.' So she agreed to give it a try, and it worked out."

There's Deke Castleman, originally from New York. He dedicated his guidebook about Las Vegas to my dad and his friends. He turns out to be a tall, charming novelist who has done every menial job in the classic writer's career so he could write. He is currently working on a science-fiction novel about Vegas in the future. His day job is managing editor for Anthony Curtis' *Las Vegas Advisor*, a monthly consumer magazine that Vegasphiles worldwide subscribe to.

Deke and his wife Virginia and their two sons lived in Reno until two years ago when they moved to Vegas and bought a house. I'm sitting with him in his kitchen as his two adorable sons watch a video, ask for and receive a bowl of Crispix.

Deke is poetic and deep, not sure he will stay with Lady Las Vegas. "There's a lot to do here for a family and a lot of jobs. I love the old Vegas history but they don't value it here. They tear things down; that upsets me. I have a fabulous job. My boss Anthony Curtis knows this town inside out, and I have learned so much from him. You have no idea how fanatical tourists are about Vegas. If the *Advisor* is delayed in the mail for even a day, I get dozens of e-mails asking where it is. They want our Top Ten list, they're ready to come."

Deke has lived a lot of places in his writing career. Will he stay or is this just a tour of duty?

"I haven't decided yet. Virginia likes the small-town atmosphere of Reno better, so I don't know. Vegas isn't a small town anymore," he says, shaking his head sadly.

I think it will always be a small town to me. For how can we separate our childhoods from our hometowns?

Deke has gone to the incredible trouble of finding a Las Vegas phone book from 1956. (So thin! So few of us then!)

"Look, your dad was the only hotel owner who listed his phone number. There you are at 721 S. Sixth Street," he says, kindly. I clutch the pages, thrown back for just a moment into the middle of my loving family, feeling the excitement of a floor-show opening. Oh, but I say to myself, That was then, this is now. Can I integrate the two visions of Las Vegas in my head and in my heart?

I go to the Nevada State Museum and Historical Society to see the Curator David A. Millman.

The museum is a large modern structure with glass cases full of representations of Vegas history. There are photographs of old hotels on the walls. David is originally from L.A., but he went to school here.

"Las Vegas works for me. I love working here. I have a family, they like it. I am a rock climber in my spare time, and Nevada has fabulous rock climbing opportunities," he says, a little craggy-looking with a scruffy beard.

"My hobby is sports betting. I'm quite good at it, and where else but Vegas to do that?" he asks. As I am leaving he asks me if I would consider leaving my family pictures to the museum in my will. I am touched. My family is history; my dad will be remembered.

For a change of pace, I go to see my friend Jed Baron. Jed is an entrepreneur. He does Vegas deals, TV production, real estate, whatever works. He's bright and quick and is always on his cellular phone. His father, now dead, was the famed Al Baron, head of the Teamsters Pension Fund (an attorney whose title was 'Assets Manager' of the fund).

When you ask people in town what Al Baron was like, they all say, "Incredibly bright, never drew attention to himself, and he was the only one that stayed alive through many divorces. Adored his dad, came out to live with him in the Stardust Hotel penthouse when he was sixteen."

"Yeah, Vegas is a big town now," Jed says in his familiar nasal drawl, sitting in the living room of his new house in the exclusive Spanish Trails, which he has built and now has on the market for $6.5 million.

Why is he selling? "Why not?" he asks, with his horse-trader mentality. The two fabulous cars he had last month just sold, too. He built a special six-car garage with a warm-water faucet for washing them, and he only has one car now. He shows me around the house. It is elegant. The pool has two

A PERFECT EXAMPLE OF VEGAS GLITZ.

different light systems, the rooms are huge, the closets are bigger than my whole apartment.

If he sells where will he go? "Plenty of room to build all over Las Vegas," he says, confidently. He drives me around Spanish Trails. The Sultan of Brunei is building a huge residence here—four buildings so far.

"He's only going to be here less that a week a year. Can you believe he's spending all this money? Why doesn't he just stay in a section of a hotel? I would, " Jed says.

We come to two magnificent homes, side by side.

"That guy got tired of having parties that messed up his house so he built a house next to it without bedrooms; it's just for parties," he says, laughing.

I find out that Maury Soss is still alive, in his 80s. He owned Fanny's Dress Shop at the Flamingo. Maury dressed the most fabulous women in Las Vegas.

"My mother, Fanny, came here from L.A. when I was in UCLA and opened a dress shop downtown. We opened the one at the Flamingo later," Soss explains, seated in a yellow chair in his home with the omnipresent air conditioning on.

"I remember when we went to inquire about opening in the Flamingo. Ben Siegel took me around the hotel, and he knew every detail of the place, what a detail mind! He was big on taste and said that my dress shop had to conform to certain standards, be a certain color. That was no problem.

"Our dress shop looked right onto the pool, so we knew who was with whom, when. We knew who was staying in the back bungalows but we never said a word. If a guy would come in and ask us if a certain lady was there, we pretended not to know anything."

He dressed all the greats over the years. Who were his favorites?

"Well, one was Barbara Marx, now she's Barbara Sinatra. She came in and I took her measurements for alterations on a dress she bought, and I realized she had been the model in New York for a pattern we used. She was always lovely and still is, to this day."

I leave, dragging in the humid heat, the usual 108 degrees. I was used to it, not so used to it anymore. I should see the Mayor but I don't have the drive. Mayor Jan Laverty Jones, from a family fortune in L.A., moved here when she married wealthy car dealer Fletcher Jones, Jr. We used to get all our Chevys from his dad, and "Fletcher Jones Chevrolet" was on every Chevy license plate.

I should go see Bobby Miller, he's Governor now. When I knew him he was tall, gangly Bobby Miller, my dad's partner Ross Miller's kid. Ross was from Chicago and came out to be a partner in my dad's Riviera. Ross was a doll, had gorgeous thick hair (most partners were balding), and wore turtlenecks.

I didn't know Bobby well but I remember that he was a lifeguard by the pool and hung around the massage parlor part of Mike Tulane's Health Club on the sixth floor of the Riv, with all the other owners' sons, hoping to get a glimpse of a showgirl coming out.

Most people love him in town. They say he is totally committed to Las Vegas and will probably be a senator. He's an attorney who was head of the National District Attorney's Association and busted bad crime. He refers to himself as a "gambling brat." I see him on the front page of the *Las Vegas Sun* with the Clintons at the National Democratic Convention in Chicago. Go Bobby, make Vegas proud! I do drop by and see Sheriff Jerry Keller in his office downtown. Sheriffs have always been important here, none more so that the famed Ralph Lamb. Such an individual; he busted prostitution, he busted this, he busted that. He's an authentic Western character and a staunch Mormon, still very much alive, out there somewhere, writing a book.

Sheriff Keller is square and Western like all Vegas sheriffs have always been. He's very serious about doing his job well, very concerned about crime statistics, and very well meaning. He wanted to be a teacher, fell into being a policeman, and loves it. He has incredible pride in his job. This is his first term, and you know he'll probably get a second one.

I drop in on Rob Powers, one of the staff who runs the Las Vegas Convention Center. He's tall, genial, laid-back, and seems to be an efficient guy. He came with his family, got his first job as a journalist, and now has his dream job. The number of conventions in Vegas that have to be housed, entertained, maintained, and their exhibits exhibited, must be booked way in advance.

"It's actually not that difficult; we're very organized. This city is just so popular everybody wants to come. We've got the room, we've got the space. It's a great family town, we love it."

Finally, I go to see Autumn Burns, a gorgeous ex-baccarat shill for the Sahara hotel, now retired.

"I moved here from L.A. when I was very young, 18 years old," she says, looking like an ex-showgirl. She is wearing leopard-skin pants and vest, and her house is decorated in a loud wildlife motif. Her husband, Jerry Burns, a Teamster, seems sedate in comparison to the chair he's sitting on.

"I came for a vacation and I couldn't believe it, I fell in love with this town," she says, exuberant and warm. "I didn't even know how to play baccarat but I applied for a job at the Sahara, this was the Sixties, and I learned. The bosses gave us $2,000 to play with in denominations of twenty to start with, because two grand was the minimum bet.

"It was fabulous, the players were great. We used to make a fortune in tips. Our salary was only twenty dollars a shift, but we lived on tips. If a guy wins a fortune, he can throw you $5,000; they'd just toss us a huge roll of dough." Movie-star-like photos of the young Autumn decorate her walls; she still looks the same.

"It was the greatest life. They called us game-starters, rather than shills, because shills had a bad connotation. We were up all night at the tables, slept all day. I got to know the entertainers, the hotel owners. Later I worked at the Stardust," she says. High rollers could only feel good sitting next to the vivacious Autumn.

Unfortunately she doesn't work anymore. She's ill from silicone shots in her breasts.

"I wish I had known what I was doing; I was just so naive. In those days, you figured a doctor wouldn't hurt you; you trusted them. All my friends were showgirls, and they were having silicone shots. The dance captains wanted their breasts to be firm.

"So I wanted the shots, too; I didn't want to sag. It wasn't even implants. They literally took like staple guns and shot you full of silicone. Unfortunately, it's made me very ill. They can't get it out of you. I wish I'd never done it; I'm a very sick puppy from it," she says, sadly.

"But all in all, I've loved living here, I wouldn't live anywhere else, ever. I met my husband years ago, and he said, 'Someday I'm coming for you, Autumn,' and he did." Jerry gazes at her, lovingly, from his chair. You leave adoring her for all her warmth and spirit in the face of tragedy.

She has what is probably a Vegas occupational disease for women of that era. You hope she beats it, and you marvel at Lady Las Vegas's draw and the fidelity that her citizens have for her.

HOUSE OF CARDS

Lady Las Vegas, you amaze me! You're the biggest, the brightest, the most! You have 30 million visitors a year—that's 82,000 people a day housed in your 60 major hotels and 200 motels. With 90,000 places to sleep, your weekend occupancy rate is over 90 percent. Unbelievable! You bring in over 1,000 conventions annually, attended by 2 million people. Fifteen thousand miles of neon lights line your streets.

People rush to you any way they can: by car, bus, and train. Most astounding is that 1,400 daily scheduled flights on 18 major airlines and 19 charter companies service all the people coming to you. You use 300 gallons of water per person per day. In 1995, 30 million people left behind $20 billion. I hear that you perform 80,000 marriages every year. That's 160,000 "I dos!"

In the next three years, there will be 20,000 new hotel rooms, each creating four to five new jobs. The new jobs and the fact that Nevada has the lowest tax rate in the United States attract 4,000 new people each month. Your population just hit 1 million; you're growing fast.

"Whatever it is, we're the fastest," says Governor Bob Miller, "the fastest-growing senior population, the fastest-growing Hispanic population, the fastest-growing school district. Whatever it is, we're the fastest, we're it." *Money* magazine said you were the ninth most livable city in 1995. One of your houses that costs $150,000 is comparable to a $300,000 house in southern California. Who could ever be as plentiful?

Gambling. Gaming. Betting. Handing over your wallet. Call it what you will, but all roads in Las Vegas lead there. The shows, the sex, the sports, the sumptuous meals all add to the allure of gambling.

"In the old days, they used to make the casino like the hub of a wheel. You want to go to the bathroom? Go through the casino. You want to go through the restaurant? Through the casino. Want to go to the elevators? Through the casino," according to George Joseph, Director of Surveillance, Bally's Las Vegas. "I don't think people really understand that it's not just that we throw these things up and hope we're gonna make some money. There's a lot of work in marketing and structure that goes into the town that the average person just never sees.

"Gambling is a legitimate form of entertainment with an ingenious billing system, the house edge; and it's brilliant because it's slight, and it's almost imperceptible," says Anthony Curtis, gaming expert for the *Las Vegas Advisor.*

In the classic era of the mobsters, the main attractions were the tables. Only girlfriends, wives, and tenderfoots lost their nickels in the slot machines. Today, nickel, quarter, dollar, and five-dollar slots are the favorite choice of casinos and patrons alike.

"The good thing about slot machines is that they work 24 hours a day, seven days a week, including Jewish holidays. They don't need uniforms, they don't belong to a union, and you don't have to feed them," says Burton M. Cohen, hotel gaming consultant.

"Somewhere around 70 percent of the revenues earned by casinos now come from slot machines," says Anthony Curtis.

"They are very big on noise, and slot machine manufacturers will actually make trays that make more noise then they need to," says Curtis. "I've actually heard stories about the casinos putting scents and aromas into the air. Not just oxygen, but certain aromas that are supposed to attract you."

Statistics show that club members who win large jackpots eventually pump most if not all of their winnings right back into the machines.

"You go up and down the rows of slot machines. People sit there, they put their money in, they plunk the lever down again and again and again," says Michael Ventura. "They look like they're performing some kind of ritual that's not really giving them what they wanted."

SLOT MACHINES AT THE HARD ROCK HOTEL.

For those who don't crave an automated ritual, there are other games, with live dealers.

"The most popular table game in Las Vegas without a doubt is blackjack," says Curtis. "Blackjack probably provides the chances for the best odds. There's probably no other game that gives the expert player as many opportunities as does blackjack. A perfect basic-strategy player will drop that two percent casino advantage to anywhere from one-half of one percent to, in perfect situations, an even game with the casino. If they were to play on into eternity, there would be virtually no exchange of money. It would be a very even game."

If you prefer more challenging odds, you can throw the dice at craps, take a spin at roulette, or deal yourself in for poker. But the big-stakes game favored by the world's gambling elite, known as high rollers, is baccarat.

"Baccarat players typically are international financiers to whom a $100,000 bet might be the same as a dollar or two bet to the average tourist.

Some of these baccarat players can actually impact a quarterly report for some of these casinos," says Curtis.

For the average Las Vegas tourist, a visit means a little gambling, a show, and a $4.99 buffet. But high rollers with unlimited bankrolls see a completely different city. They are welcomed like royalty and comped with the best that the desert jewel has to offer, courtesy of casino hosts like Toby Dicesare.

Dicesare, a former executive casino host, says, "Casino hosts have been here since the industry started. What we like to offer to high rollers are special suites, complimentary rooms, complimentary shows, complimentary dinners."

The Las Vegas Hilton spent more than $40 million building its three high roller suites. Competing hotels wage a constant battle to win the allegiance and the money of these cash-rich big spenders. When they lose, the casinos even forgive the gamblers some portion of their debts. Why do high rollers merit such extraordinary treatment? Because it's not unusual for them to gamble $5 to $10 million—or more—during one Las Vegas visit.

"If somebody can afford to lose $12 million, needless to say they don't have to go to gamble to try and win money," says Dicesare. "It's got to be more to it. It becomes a challenge, and a little excitement."

"I was discussing one day with a long-time gambler why people gamble and he looks me dead in the eye and says, 'Because if you don't have action, nothing can happen,'" says Curtis.

Different games now produce larger revenues than they did in the old days.

"The games have changed as far as producing for the bottom line. It depends a lot on the hotel. If a hotel is a large people-mover, and a large hotel, the slots contribute a considerable amount of dollars to the bottom line," says Burton Cohen. "And then 21, then would come craps, and then baccarat. At the other hotels, baccarat would be number two or number one in exchange with slots. Craps used to be one of the biggest revenue producers, but it has fallen away to 21. Craps has a tendency to intimidate the new gamer."

According to Cohen, the country of origin of the high rollers has changed over the years. "Initially most of the high rollers, practically all of them, were domestic, Americans. As time went on, marketing expanded to come into Las Vegas, the hotels went after different high rollers who lived in different foreign countries—England, the Arab countries, and, of course, the Far East. I think that the credit for the development of the high roller Asian customer has to be given initially to Caesar's Palace—Billy Weinberger and Hop Louie Woo. Hop Louie Woo was a big customer of Caesar's Palace. He had restaurants in L.A., and he used to come over here and gamble; and he gambled until he lost everything.

"So Billy was the president of Caesar's and he hired Hop. Hop was the one who went to the Orient and induced the Asian customers to start coming to Las Vegas. In the early days, a high roller could be a $5,000 man because you're relating cost of the product to the amount of revenue you could generate from his action. Of course, as cost went up, the definition of a high roller went up from a $5,000 man to $20,000 to $25,000 and so on."

Cohen goes on to describe today's high rollers.

"Domestically a high roller would be considered a man who could wager and lose and put into action $50,000 or better. On the Far East market, it's somebody who could lose or put into action—I hate to use the term 'lose' because we produce a tremendous number of winners—without winners you don't have losers—anything in the amount of $500,000 and above. Now if you take the equation that a $5,000 man was getting complimentary room, food, and beverage, when you got up to the $50,000 man, he would get air fare. And now you had a $500,000 man coming in—he would get approximately three air fares, or better than ten $50,000 men. So you had to not only be able to accommodate the limits: the higher the wagering inclination of the individual—the amount that he could put into action, the higher the limit that he wanted to gamble."

Shills have always been a part of Vegas action, according to Cohen. "Historically we had to put shills into action because nobody likes to go to a game where there are no players. It's like going to a restaurant and there's nobody eating in the restaurant. You're going to turn around and walk out and say, boy, the food must be terrible here. So we brought in shills."

Along with shills, another casino tradition is the "eye in the sky." "In the old days," says Cohen, "we literally had people who lived up in the ceiling. There was a ramp up there, and some of these guys would have a cot and a refrigerator and a hot stove; they were like moles. They would be up there, and they were old-time gamblers who knew every move in the book. There were two-way mirrors, and they could walk down these ramps and look down at the table games. Because sometimes the dealers and the customers would forget that there was an eye in the sky, we made 'em rattle some dust that could fall down to alert everybody that daddy was watching upstairs.

"There was one memorable day when a guy fell out of a catwalk and landed on a craps table face down. Naturally, some guy bet five dollars on his ass," remembers George Joseph.

But the eye in the sky, like everything else in Vegas, is much more modern now. "With the advent of the television camera and the nuances that have been developed, the physical man in the eye is gone. Yet every hotel has the ability if necessary to walk up there and look down on the games," Cohen explains. "So the cameras do that. If you look into a security room where the eye is being taped, it looks like a major television studio. There would be monitors from every game—the ability to bring at least three cameras on a game, down and to each side, and to monitor each dealer. A funny thing happened years ago at one of the hotels. They caught a dealer who yawned a lot, and every time he yawned, he put his hand over his mouth. He was putting a chip in his mouth. A dealer usually works 40 minutes on and 20 minutes off, or 40 and 15. So the eye caught this move, and they didn't break him. He stood there with the chip in his mouth, and he stood there—he couldn't say anything because the chip was in his mouth. Slowly little pieces of sweat were coming down his face, and people were going by and saying, 'Hi Charlie, how are you?' Finally after not getting a break for three hours, he had to cough up the chip. So those things have happened.

THE "EYE IN THE SKY" SURVEILLANCE ROOM.

"We had one dealer in the middle of the summer who used to perspire profusely, and he'd wipe the back of his neck. He was putting chips down the back of his shirt, and inside he was wearing long johns. He had bicycle clips so the chips would run all the way down, and they'd wind up in his pants. Ultimately he was caught. But our biggest concern is not protecting ourselves so much from our own employees, but protecting ourselves from the customer who would corrupt our employee. As for the other checks and balances that you have in the pit in a game—you have the dealer, which is your first line of defense. You have the floor man, which is your second line of defense. You have the pit boss, which is the third line of defense. And you have the shift boss, which is the fourth line of defense. So all of these counter-balances are in there to protect the integrity of the game.

"The cards are all under lock and key with steel bands around them. They're counted in, and they're counted out. And when the cards are not used any longer, we usually cut the corners so that the deck of cards can't come back in. If you notice today when you play 21, in most hotels you don't touch the cards. That is to protect the hotels against daubers, crimpers, and so on. A dauber is a man who would take a small piece of pen or marking and mark a corner, say of the aces or the tens, so that if they came out of the shoe or the dealer's hand, he could see it, or crimp the edge of it. So today the customer doesn't touch the cards," says Cohen.

When a cheater is found, casinos aren't shy. In the high-tech world of gambling scams, millions can be stolen in a matter of minutes. That's where casino security enters the picture.

"'How ya doing? My name's George Joseph. I'm with the casino,'" says Joseph. "'We counted up the chips here. You have $350,000 of our money. And you know what? We're not comfortable with your play. We've notified the Division of Gaming Enforcement. We've also notified your mother. What are you going to say to me now? You want to call me a name? Fine. But you ain't got my money yet. I don't let you out. Not with our money.'"

George Joseph is a former professional card cheat and knows from personal experience how scam artists can drain Las Vegas casinos of millions of dollars every year.

"I've been involved in the investigations in baccarat where $3 million was taken in one play," says Joseph. "So it can get kind of costly, the scams. Most of the thieves today—they have guts. In Arabic we say, 'testicles of a camel.'"

Cheating is a high-risk game of cat and mouse that often attracts brilliant minds and high-tech wizards in the quest to defraud the house.

George Joseph says, "When you get to this era of cheating, they've gone to the covert stuff, which is hidden body computers. I mean hidden computers on the body that analyze the percentages of a 21 game. It gives them perfect card-count strategy. Perfect card-count money management. We have as many as 500 cameras in our surveillance system just looking at gaming and every cash-counting function in the joint. We'll be doing about 12,000 tapes in one week."

These forces are on the lookout for any kind of scam, which can just as easily originate with casino employees as with customers.

"There are tells to every cheating move," according to Joseph. "If we have a videotape of your move, I don't care how good the move is, someone is going to be able to determine what the hell you did."

Joseph travels the world, busting casino scam artists, and familiarizing employees with their tricks.

"Then there's 'pinching a bet.' You know, you got a good hand but you only got fifty dollars, so you try to put fifty dollars on top when the dealer's not looking.

"The last loaded-dice scam I saw was where they switched the dice into the game, where the guy palmed the dice. There was a scam called dice scooting. Sliding the dice, the dice slide, they don't tumble. They'll win as much as three or four thousand on a roll.

"We have the right to ask anybody to leave, for virtually any reason because it's private property. And it's a privileged license. We could approach you and say, your 21 play is a little too strong for us, pal. You're more than welcome to shoot craps or play baccarat or roulette or play the slots or have dinner here, but just rather that you don't play 21. Just back away."

Gambling—gambling—gambling. Lady Las Vegas wants your dollar, ruble, or shekel. No matter where you live, her vistas are always expanding.

"The Far East right now is the hottest area, Malaysia," says Cohen. "At the Desert Inn we had offices in Hong Kong, Taipei, Singapore, Bangkok, Jakarta, Manila, all for the purpose of producing casino customers for the hotel. Europe has changed. At one time the market there was the Arabs, but because of their own economic problems and backlash against the visibility of opulent wealth, the gamblers on that end now are few and far between. But there's always emerging markets for Las Vegas."

Action. Since the earliest days of high-stakes gambling, Vegas has been creating new forms of action to attract big spenders to town. In 1963, when Sonny Liston KOd Floyd Patterson in the first round, the casinos discovered that boxing had serious cash flow potential.

Bob Arum, boxing promoter, says, "In the late 1970s, when the casinos went into this big time, the casinos would pay a set amount of money called the site fee. The fact that Caesar's, Hilton, and later the Mirage and MGM were willing to pay substantial site fees to get the event meant that promoters were very happy to move the action into the hotel casinos."

Muhammed Ali led a list of boxing luminaries who've made Las Vegas a mecca for the world's boxing elite. Some fights gross more than $100 million. But that's not where all the money is made.

"I remember a fight I sold to the Hilton," says Bob Arum. "And the Hilton lost money on the promotion. I got a message that Barron Hilton wanted to see me, so with great trepidation I went to see Barron Hilton. He came over and hugged me and treated me like a hero. I subsequently found out that three Asian gamblers had come in to see Tommy Hearns fight, and they had dropped—the night before and the night of the fight—$23 million."

Boxing leads the way, but other sports play a role in the daily life of Las Vegas.

Lenny Del Genio, former Director of Operations for Race and Sports, Bally's, describes sports betting. "The bookmaker everyone knows is a guy who needs a shave. He's wearing a little hat, and he's smokin' a big stogie, and he's working out of a candy store in Brooklyn. That guy may still be alive and doing very well in Brooklyn, but this is the only place you can legally bet."

While betting on sports events is illegal in the rest of the United States, in 1983 the lowering of a federal tax on Nevada sports betting made the "sports book" the newest gaming explosion in the state.

"The sports book industry really is the most exciting area still left in Las Vegas," says Del Genio. "Between 1976 and 1996, we went from six or seven books to 106 books in the state. The hand went from $3 or 4 million to a $2 billion industry.

"This isn't Siegfried & Roy. It's not magic. If you walk in and pick the right team, you win money. And I'm betting that you can't do it on a regular and consistent basis."

Gambling isn't the only lure in Las Vegas. Customers come for other chancey impersonal pleasures—sex and titillation. Since 1905, easy women with bedroom eyes have urged tourists to come hither and abandon all caution, and in 1996 Vegas's arms are open wider than ever.

Hey, let's face it—my older sister is a tramp, but it works for her.

Almost since its inception, Las Vegas has been branded with the scarlet title of sin city, and that didn't mean just gambling. The red-light district of Block 16 flourished until pressure from the military forced its demise in the 1940s. Since then, prostitution has been illegal in Clark County but out-of-town cathouses sprung up just the same. Roxie's out on Boulder Highway did such a brisk business, even the sheriff helped to keep it open. But *Las Vegas Sun* publisher Hank Greenspun wanted houses of ill repute like Roxie's shut down.

"A key year was 1954," says Guy Rocha, Nevada Historian and State Archivist. "There was a big raid, April 28, 1954. Hank closes Roxie's down, and then we begin to see the high-priced call girl, the street walker, at some of your nightclub venues."

In the Sixties, Sheriff Ralph Lamb, a Mormon, made it his crusade to get the streetwalkers off Vegas boulevards. And though he successfully cleaned up the Strip, the prostitutes never left the city.

From the days of Ben Siegel, sex went along with gambling and was controlled by the hotels. Call girls were connected to the hotels, usually employed in some other capacity, and every pit boss and bellhop knew who to send to high rollers' rooms. With the advent of Howard Hughes, the tight control over working girls in the hotels stopped. The Hughes staff didn't want to run girls. Prostitution became wide open in Vegas, and that period is known as the Great Working Girl Invasion. There were girls offering to turn tricks on every corner of the Strip.

During this time, Joe Conforte, who ran the most famous brothel in the nation, the Mustang Ranch in northern Nevada, began crusading for the legalization of prostitution in Nevada. It has been quasi-legal in Nevada for years. Such houses had been in Nevada for over 100 years, and many rules and regulations governed the brothel business. In 1971, Conforte managed to get prostitution legalized in tiny Storey County, where the Mustang Ranch was located. Subsequently a Conforte-backed politician managed to get an ordinance passed in Las Vegas allowing one brothel to operate in Vegas, in a high-walled security compound.

Conforte opened his Conforte's Mustang Massage immediately. However, lawmakers and citizens organized opposition. They wanted prostitution to be illegal so the ordinance was overturned, and Conforte's place in Vegas closed.

Prostitution was rampant and very visible in Vegas until the early 1980s, when a sheriff won election to Clark County on the platform of ridding the city of prostitution. In the early and mid-Eighties, staggering numbers of prostitutes were arrested both on the Strip and in the hotels. Available girls were then taken off the streets and put back into the well-connected hotel arena.

The system today is pretty much like it was in the Bugsy Siegel days. If you know who to ask at the hotels, you can get what you want. According to Deke Castleman's excellent guidebook *Las Vegas*, "In 1971, the first sex ads appeared in the phone books under 'Escort Services,' then metamorphosed into listings under 'Dating Services,' and most recently were listed under 'Entertainers.' There were 48 pages in 1995."

Let your fingers do the walking, but get the semantics right. Prostitutes, call girls, and sex clubs just like in any other city, and now leaflets advertising sex are handed out on every corner. This is the current Vegas obsession, getting these anonymously published girlie rags with girls in provocative poses and phone numbers off the streets. These fliers are technically illegal; state law prohibits the advertising of prostitution. But illegality never frightened Lady Las Vegas.

"There is still some prostitution here," says Sheriff Keller. "There is prostitution in every city in America. It is not legal here as it is not legal in most cities, and we still actively pursue the crime of prostitution and all of the crimes associated with it as an enterprise here in southern Nevada."

In a town brimming with glamorous performers, stunning showgirls, and exotic dancers, naughtiness is always bubbling on the front burner. High-priced call girls are always available, especially for high rollers.

"It's not always just sex—but it is women," says Guy Rocha. "It's skin."

Some shows are not for family viewing. Like other major metropolitan areas, Las Vegas is home to a growing number of bars and clubs like the Palomino, that offer so-called exotic dancing.

BEAUTIFUL WOMEN HAVE LURED VISITORS TO VEGAS SINCE THE EARLY 1900S.

"I refer to myself as an entertainer," says Aubey, an exotic dancer. "I've been known to call myself a stripper, too, so whatever happens to fit the moment. It is not stripper/prostitute. I am not there to meet a boyfriend. I am there to earn a living. If a man behaves himself in the club, I will do everything to make sure he enjoys that dance and will never forget it. My theory is that the more you behave yourself, the more I'll try to misbehave."

But no one needs to be reminded of neon and sexy women to know that my hometown is a most unusual place. Just take a look at the Strip.

As Las Vegas approaches the century mark, her gambling palaces proliferate, catapulting rapidly outward and upward, rushing to banish vacant space from the cluttered, prosperous Strip.

There is the Circus, Circus venture and Excalibur, a medieval Arthurian-themed resort. There is the Luxor, the world's largest pyramid. Kirk Kerkorian's new MGM Grand is guarded by a lion. And the old MGM Grand, Bally's, entices pedestrians with a state-of-the-art neon entryway.

"Taj Mahal, Pyramid, I don't know. Whatever they call it—the Halls of Montezuma," says comedian Alan King. "They're running out of names now. What should be a ten-minute drive took me fifty minutes. You never saw anybody walking the streets of Las Vegas when I was a kid there. Now it's Broadway."

"I guess the cynical way of calling what Vegas is, is the Jesus Christ factor. You walk into there saying, Jesus Christ, I've never seen anything like this at home in Peoria," says Steven Izenour.

"Now all that land, the buildings are right out on the sidewalk, literally. The casinos are spending most of their time and money with pedestrian access, I mean gigantic moving sidewalks, whatever, right from the corner of their property, that kind of suck you in. Caesar's does that, Mirage does that, that's the new Vegas."

"I call it the seven wonders of the world," says Burton Cohen. "Where else can you go within the radius of a few blocks and walk into the mouth of a lion, see an Egyptian pyramid, a medieval castle, galleons fighting to the death, waterfalls in an erupting volcano, gladiators, and even a circus tent that is built out of concrete and steel? That is the attraction of Vegas."

In June of 1996, the Monte Carlo opened, a joint venture between Mirage Resorts, Inc. and Circus, Circus Enterprises. It brought the French Riviera to Vegas.

Soon New York, New York will bring a scaled-down version of the Big Apple to the desert, including a replica of the Statue of Liberty and the Coney Island roller coaster. Bally's is in the ground-breaking stage of a new theme resort, Paris. Why bother to travel the world? All its "greatest hits" are now headlining in Vegas.

A block south of the Strip, Peter Morton's Hard Rock caters to a younger crowd. Across Highway 91, the all-suite Rio Hotel Casino is the local's favorite, boasting the best buffet and the highest *Zagat*'s travel rating in town.

In 1994 and 1995, ITT Corporation bought the Desert Inn and Caesar's Palace. Residents complain that the corporate hotshots are impersonal and don't know how to run a casino. Nevertheless, the corporation just announced plans to build a Planet Hollywood hotel casino in the near future.

Between the bustling convention center and the Desert Inn on the Strip, the tiny Debbie Reynolds Hotel and Casino—formerly the Paddlewheel—struggles to keep up with the megaresort competition by offering rare movie memorabilia and a more personal approach to the hospitality business.

"After every show I go out and I take pictures and sign autographs, and sometimes it takes me two hours. Two hundred people usually stay," says Debbie Reynolds. "I sign five per person, so that's quite a few autographs every night. I don't mind doing that, because they took the time to come and see me, and there's so many great big shows here to see. I never forget those who have stayed by me all these years, come to see me here in Vegas. It makes my heart feel very good. The husbands leave, but the fans stay."

In 1996, Steve Wynn and the Chamber of Commerce revived the fading Glitter Gulch area with the Fremont Street Experience. Four downtown blocks have been covered with a canopy that at night becomes a spectacular light show.

"It's basically the size of four and a half football fields; it spans four city blocks, has 2,100,000 lights, a 540,000-megawatt sound system, and 100 gigabytes of computer technology," says Mayor Jan Jones.

But as much as Vegas has changed, she will face even more changes in the next few years.

Not yet a century old, Las Vegas has become the site of a prosperity boom that rivals anything the United States has ever experienced. At a time when most U.S. cities are financially struggling, Las Vegas's growth is exponential, and new hotel construction is just the beginning.

"I've lived here 40 years, and I can't think of any of those years in which I didn't hear the statement made, 'We can't possibly fill any more hotel rooms. Who would come?'" says Governor Bob Miller. "So, after about 40 years I'm beginning to think the smart bet is that it's going to continue to grow."

"In the next three years, in the pipeline committed with money are about 20,000 rooms. Our housing is still relatively inexpensive, much cheaper than California. We sell houses for $150,000 you'd have to pay $300,000 for in other communities," says Irwin Molasky, one of the town's most prominent designer builders.

"We have probably the lowest tax rate in the United States. There is no state tax, there is no inheritance tax. A very low property tax, and that's all constitutionally protected so we don't see that changing in the near future," says Mayor Jan Jones.

Those who seek their new life in Las Vegas discover a community that, despite outward appearances, is quite conservative. Once they become accustomed to the 20-hour-a-day schedule, the stop-and-go traffic on the main streets, and the cacophonous slot machines in the grocery stores, new residents discover all the amenities of a traditional American small town or suburb—Boy and Girl Scout troops, recreational sports, even an incredibly active religious community.

It seems everyone has been profiting from the boom, including the original residents of 'The Meadows,' the Paiute Indians. Until the early 1970s, they owned only the ten acres of land deeded them by rancher Helen J. Stewart in 1911. Then they discovered the fact that the state law concerning taxation did not apply to their reservation.

"If a tribe could buy cigarettes wholesale and sell them without having to charge state tax, they could significantly undersell other retailers. In the early 1970s they opened a smoke shop," says anthropology professor Martha Knack.

"We went on to become the largest retailer of cigarettes in the United States, and among the top ten non-gaming businesses in the state of Nevada. With this new-found wealth and economic self-sufficiency, we had the access to creating whatever we wanted to create," says Alfreda Mitre, the Tribal Chairperson of the Las Vegas Paiutes.

In 1983, the Paiute Tribe acquired an additional 4,000 acres of land, 18 miles north of their downtown reservation and, in March of 1995, opened the Nu-Wav Kaiv Golf Course.

In the African-American community, a group of determined Las Vegans are working to further the end of racism, as well as to reclaim a part of their heritage. The Moulin Rouge Preservation Association has an ambitious plan to restore the hotel casino to the condition and status of its six glorious months as Las Vegas's only desegregated nightclub.

"The Moulin Rouge could be a destination resort because there will be a lot of development in the center part of Las Vegas, which is where we are located. They are building a dome stadium in Las Vegas, which we are across the street from," says James Walker.

"Vegas now is totally integrated, but I find that really it's no different from 1955. The prejudice still lingers," says Dee Dee Jasmin. "My goal is to

THE MOULIN ROUGE PRESERVATION ASSOCIATION HOPES TO RESTORE THE HOTEL TO ITS ORIGINAL CONDITION AND STATUS.

make the Moulin Rouge as it was, and better, in 1955. Keep the same flavoring, the tone, the black shows, and the top quality, but the building will be a 22-story high-rise." Las Vegas clearly is not the little railroad stop where everyone knew their neighbors and children rode horses along the Strip. The sawdust town has blossomed into a genuine city—facing the requisite problems of every major American city in this troubled era. Today, as the line between the haves and have-nots widens, as the promise of riches on the Strip heightens the desire for the luxuries money can buy, Las Vegans have become more vulnerable to the crimes plaguing other metropolitan centers—including gangs and illegal drugs.

"We had 6,412 people report crimes who didn't list Nevada as an address," says Sheriff Keller. "We figure that's our tourist crime. That's like having a city four times the size of New York and having three days of crime. We're very, very pleased. We believe, and I believe, that we are the safest tourist city in the world."

Bumper-to-bumper traffic and political and athletic scandals are other woes Las Vegas must cope with as a modern-day city. Then there are the issues that touch the very heart of the desert paradise.

After phenomenal growth in the last two decades, the nationwide expansion of gambling has recently stalled. Gambling industry lobbyists are hoping that the American Gaming Association (AGA), with its influential friends in Washington, will reverse the industry's recent run of bad luck in the states.

The head of the lobby group is Frank J. Fahrenkopf, Jr., a former National Republican Party chairman and a Nevada native. "The gaming industry was one of the few major industries that was not represented in Washington. Every industry from automobiles to pasta companies is represented with a lobbyist or a law office," says Fahrenkopf, Jr. "We're just keeping up with the times and growth of our industry."

The AGA is credited with stopping a congressional proposal to create a commission that would study gambling's impact on surrounding communities. In a study released in June 1996, the Center for Public Integrity, a Washington watchdog group, reported that gambling interests contributed $4.5 million to political parties and candidates at the federal level since 1991. It states, "The gambling industry has moved quickly to accumulate influence and clout in national politics. When it speaks, politicians listen."

During the boom years from 1988 to 1994, 21 states legalized casinos and ten states legalized slot machines or video poker. Americans placed $17 million in legal bets in 1974; in 1994 they bet $482 billion. But over the last two years, anti-gambling forces have won 34 of 36 statewide ballot initiatives involving legislation.

The most pressing issue causing Las Vegans concern is a gambling commission that has been set up to study questions like whether the industry tries to entice pathological and underage gamblers to its tables. Casino owners feared that if the commission has broad subpoena powers, it could force them to produce financial records of high rollers, but the governmental affairs panel recently "scaled back" the commission's subpoena power.

Not everyone is a fan of the expansion of gambling. Foes include, among others, Ralph Reed, president of the Christian Coalition, and Bernie Horn, political director of the National Coalition Against Legalized Gambling.

"I am concerned that the gambling industry is attempting to buy off Washington's leaders," says Horn. "They have only one asset, and that is money. What they lack is public support; what they couldn't do at the ballot box, they're now trying to do by buying politicians in Washington."

Shecky Greene, a former compulsive gambler, warns, "The spread of gambling is the destruction of mankind. It's the fall of the Roman Empire. We're creating compulsive gamblers and sicknesses, and it breaks my heart to see it."

PROFITS FROM THESE SLOT MACHINES ARE DONATED TO THE NATIONAL RESOURCES DEFENSE COUNCIL.

Critics aside, the financial power of Vegas and the gaming lobby is growing daily. Not only did presidential candidates receive record "contributions" from gambling interests in 1996, but Vegas casinos now boast "governmental relations departments" and even conduct polling for candidates.

Perhaps no one has seen the changes in the town more clearly than the man who built a great deal of it, developer Irwin Molasky.

"In 1951, you could buy housing in this area for $25,000 to $35,000. Actually, you could buy quite nice houses. In 1958, when I built Paradise Palm, we were selling a house a day for anywhere from $25,000 to $40,000.

"And in 1951, you could rent an apartment for about $150 a month. There weren't that many of them around, but they were quite nice. They were spacious.

"But there were very few medical facilities here. There was a hospital called Southern Nevada Memorial Hospital, which was a political football in those days. There were no private hospitals. And the people used to go to Los Angeles for medical help because there weren't good facilities here.

"In the Fifties it was really easy to do business—with one exception. The good part was everybody knew everybody. It was like one big family. There wasn't one person in town you didn't know. And everybody trusted you, and your word was like a contract. We grew up in that era of handshakes. The exception was that there was no financing in town. Everybody says to me how lucky I am that I got here in the early days when there was all this opportunity. But people are luckier today because there's financing readily available. In the Fifties if you wanted to develop something or build something, you had to do it with cash. You couldn't borrow anything. People didn't have confidence in this town to loan money out unless you were over-collateralized. Today it's a lot easier to borrow money and to build projects."

Building today is booming in Vegas.

"Our companies today build 600 to 800 houses a year. We build about 300 to 400 apartment units a year. We do industrial parks. We're doing one with Northwestern Mutual Insurance Company that's a million square feet. We do a lot of office buildings, lots of condominium complexes.

"Our housing is still relatively inexpensive, much cheaper than California. We don't have the regulatory entanglements that they have in California. In California where we build it costs you maybe $25,000 to $30,000 before you break ground for clean air act and auto transmissions and all those things. Here it's maybe $5,000. So you get terrific values in housing."

"And there are now seven hospitals in Las Vegas. Sunrise Hospital alone has, I believe, 2,000 physicians on staff. It has 647 beds. It has 16, probably 20 today, surgical sites. It has one of the finest children's pediatric facilities in the world."

And each month someone else announces a plan to build a casino hotel.

"The thing that attracts the new investor to Las Vegas is the cash flow, the ability to build something and to create a cash flow, that, even if you're good managers, would take years to do in any other type of business," says Burton Cohen.

"While the Waldorf in New York will have a cash flow, they don't have slot machines, and they don't have table games. The same thing will take place here in which the customer is staying in a room, he may be paying anywhere from $50 to $90 to $100 where that same quality room in any other city would cost him $200, $300 or $400. He can go to a buffet for $3.95, and in any other city it would cost him $12.95. So that value is here. But all of those things create cash."

With hotels booming and a huge convention center that attracts more conventions to Las Vegas than any other city, the future looks bright. But there are some clouds looming. For one, Vegas may have a major water issue facing her.

"Las Vegas is coming in for a very rude awakening and serious disaster in the next decade if the city doesn't get control over its growth," says Dennis McBride. Under-populated at the time of the Colorado River Compact in 1922, Nevada was given a water allotment that is infinitesimal compared to her present-day needs. As compared to southern California at 4.4 million acre-feet of water and Arizona at 2.8 million acre-feet, Nevada only gets one third of a million acre-feet a year. That's less than the estimated amount of water that evaporates from the Colorado River every year!

Governor Bob Miller says it can be worked out.

"It's a matter of cost. You can get water now from different sources." Outlandish ideas that have been brought to Miller include piping out the Pacific Ocean—from the northwest—and then bringing it across the desert and, taking care of L.A. on the way, coming into Vegas. "All these things are feasible," says Miller, "they're just very costly."

Historian Hal Rothman says water will not be a problem. "Water runs uphill to money. Las Vegas will do what Los Angeles and Phoenix have done, they will beg, borrow, buy, or steal it."

And what of the population boom?

"I have a developer friend who says that there will be 2 million people in this valley by the year 2010, that jobs and construction will taper off. Some people will be thrown out of work and they will leave, and some of those people will be avid gamblers. If he's right, I don't want to be here," says Hal Rothman. "What'll happen at some point is that it'll taper off. People will be thrown out of work."

And there's another potential time bomb ticking on the horizon—a proposed radioactive waste dump to be located at Yucca Mountain, within 100 miles of the Vegas city limits.

And how about economic threats from other gambling resorts?

Alan King says, "Vegas has nothing to worry about. It's a destination resort now. Gambling is only a small part of it because we have gambling in many places now. Steamboats up the river, you know, and Atlantic City. No, I think Las Vegas is unique, and I think that it'll just grow and grow."

Lady Las Vegas is as carefree, giddy, and reckless as ever. She's made it this close to her hundredth birthday, and there's probably nothing that will keep her from celebrating that party.

"It's a promise that's always been kept. It's a party that never stops. God bless this daffy place!" says Steve Wynn.

In less than a century, Las Vegas has made her myth a reality, a triumph of wild imagination and entrepreneurial spirit over a hostile environment and national opposition. Lady Las Vegas requires no penance, just ready cash. Asks for no references, only a credit card. From a dry patch of earth barely nourished by underground springs, she has blossomed into a neon oasis that takes her place proudly among the greatest cities of the world. She earns billions. And she has confidence that she can handle anything. She boasts of her past now and revels in the instant gratification of her present, dancing faster and faster on the flat table of desert where her story began.

YOU CAN GO HOME AGAIN

Hey, Lady Las Vegas, everywhere I turn you're there, hotter than ever. There's been so much speculation about what you do in private over the years, now that you're so much more public, people want all of you. You know how to market your dreams.

You will be even more glamorous and luxurious in the millennium. Not only will the fabulous Bellagio Hotel open in 1998, but Planet Hollywood is building a 3,200-room hotel costing $830 million next to the Sheraton Desert Inn. You're worth it. There will be a new 6,000-room hotel and tower with a Venetian theme where the Sands (good-bye 'Place in the Sun!') was laid to rest. Hilton just spent a fortune to buy Bally's and will improve it. There will be a new Hacienda Hotel and a big joint called Starship Orion soon.

The MGM Grand is planning a $250-million expansion on its $1-billion property. It will resemble a Hollywood studio. The restaurant area will look like a sound stage and have Southland landmarks. The scowling lions will be replaced by six-story lions with 80-foot entertainment walls. People now dangle from perilous heights on your theme park ride, the Skyscreamer, at 250 feet high, the world's largest "swing." And the Rio Hotel is undergoing a $200-million expansion. It will include a $25-million Masquerade Show in the sky.

Every television news program mentions you. You made a rule in the Forties that mobsters couldn't kill one another within your borders, but now gang members from elsewhere prey on you. Famed L.A. rapper Tupac Shakur, who came for a boxing match, was killed gangland-style on one of your bright streets. Presidential candidates visited you many times in their quest for the White House. Founding godfathers would never have believed that you could influence national elections.

The gambling industry is now worth a trillion dollars, and you are her headquarters. You always liked cash money—now you have so much! Although you are now a diversified city with a corporate presence, you'll always have a shadowy past that fascinates.

Novelist Michael Ventura calls Vegas, "the last great mythic city that western civilization will ever create." He says, "Las Vegas has joined the cities of myth. People can be entertained and gamble almost anywhere—if they know where to look. But the world now journeys to Las Vegas at the rate of many thousands a day, for something that can be found only there—the imagery, the pace, the style, the sense of license that is Las Vegas. Both intellectual foreigners and day-tripping tourists say they come to Las Vegas because they feel it is the epitome of all things American. They feel that parts of themselves only wake up in the neon swirl of Vegas.

"When this is a sensation experienced by millions—even vicariously—through movies and other imagery, then a city becomes a part of the collective psyche that is our history. That's what 'mythic' is all about."

Oh, Lady Las Vegas, your ego must be soaring! Amtrak is hoping to bring a new high-speed European train to you soon. It's a Danish-built Flexliner, a self-propelled train that doesn't require a locomotive and can be driven from either end and travels at 112 miles per hour. It would cut travel time from Las Vegas to L.A. from six hours to four. They want to run a Las Vegas–Los Angeles passenger route that features poker, slots, and other table games when it crosses into Nevada.

With an eye to your ever-increasing building boom, Mirage Resorts, Inc., in a joint venture with a major national tour operator, has launched its own company to package and sell vacations to keep all their properties full during slow periods. As if you could have a slow day!

I am at the most packed and popular show in town—Siegfried & Roy. These guys can do no wrong with the audience. It goes on forever, and the audience gets major value for their dollar. I can't quite get the attraction since their German accents are so thick that I can't understand every word, but the white tigers seem to dig them and I'm an animal lover so it's cool. In the lobby are Siegfried & Roy memorabilia of every type, and tourists clamor to buy it. Items sell out.

"Mystere," the show at Treasure Island by Cirque du Soleil, is more my style—melancholy, dark, arty. It haunts me after I leave, like you do, Lady Las Vegas. It is such a strange show for Vegas, yet an absolute sellout. You can't even get a ticket unless you do so way in advance.

This is the circus now, not like the Ringling Brothers Circus that came once a year and was held at the downtown fairgrounds when I was a kid. Oh the lions, the elephants, the clowns, the cotton candy! "Mommy, daddy, how did that clown make that rabbit disappear?" "It's magic, Susie," my dad would say, producing a silver dollar and then making it disappear, too! Magic like my town, like my childhood—magic only Lady Las Vegas can do.

Things change—or do they? My favorite game at Frontier Village in 1950 was a metal claw that was lowered into gravel and could snag a rhinestone bracelet or a plastic toy for a lucky kid. The exact same game is in the video arcade in Treasure Island, only the prizes are different.

I'm enjoying the Copa Cabana dinner floor show at the Rio Hotel, with "young, eager to please performers," as my friend says. Yes, it reminds me of the early Vegas floor shows—dancing and real singing and beautiful, colorful costumes. The dancers even have fruit on their heads and fruit-shaped earrings in their ears!

MODERN VEGAS FLOOR SHOW.

IN THE 1960S, THE LIDO DE PARIS INTRODUCED TOPLESS DANCERS WITHOUT "PASTIES."

I time-travel back to the Dunes "Casino de Paris" show with two dozen nude women playing peek-a-boo behind orange-and-green powder puffs, a tropical samba danced under white latex palm trees, four kissing bears, three Czechoslovakian acrobats, and three Argentinean gauchos beating the floor with bolas while four live stallions gallop about on movable treadmills.

I see the Rat Pack take the stage and talk to the audience. I hear Kay Starr lament the luck of the "Wheel of Fortune." I see Liberace stride out, all sparkles, and play the opening chords of his piano.

I'm at the fiftieth anniversary party of the Golden Nugget. Steve Wynn knows how to throw a party. There are 500 invited guests, chefs in white hats, a gourmet buffet meal. Wynn appears in disguise as Zachariah Wynn, his own ancestor, and welcomes guests and introduces loyal Nugget employees. The Fremont Street Experience light-and-sound show overhead displays highlights of the Nugget, including the old sign that I remember so well. Kenny Rogers, well known as a headliner since his career ignited there in the Seventies, entertains.

People come up to me. "I knew your dad." "He was a great guy." "He was only the best." Two prominent downtown hotel owners say they were my dad's partners in the Forties and Fifties, but someone later tells me that one worked for him then as a bellhop and the other was a cashier. "Everybody wants to say they were your dad's partners, Susie." I remember walking through the lobby with him when the Nugget was just a casino in 1950, watching Uncle Chickie gamble here in the Seventies.

I call my friend Billy Alderman, now living in Hawaii. "What do *you* remember?" I ask Willie's son, who is now a father himself.

"Childhood memories. I remember the trampoline my dad bought me. I remember when my friend and I got in a hotel helicopter and moved it—in the air! I was twelve, my dad flipped, he was so worried! The Easter egg hunts at the Frontier Hotel were fun. I miss the town."

My cousin, Tom Padden, raised next door to my mother in St. Paul, came out to work for my father after World War II. He stayed with us until my father finally picked out the most beautiful dancer in the Flamingo Hotel line, whom he called "the Spaniard" because of her big brown eyes and her exotic looks, and told Tom to marry her. He and Jan lived in Vegas and had two sons.

"I stepped out of a Union Pacific coach car in Vegas in 1946, and there was your mom, my cousin Betty. She was wearing an enormous hat, its brim tied down by a scarf against the blustery wind," says Tom. "She had been there a year with your dad in that little Western town with 16,000 people."

Tom went to work for Ben Siegel and my dad on Fremont Street as a casino cashier in an early operation. For the next 25 years, he observed the town from the inside of casino cages.

"Back when the Golden Nugget opened, everybody condemned it because it was non-yahoo, the 'Million Dollar Golden Nugget.' They said it was a fool's dream and predicted that desert sands would soon blow through its abandoned, bankrupt hulk. Siegel, Davie, Wilbur Clark—they were visionaries. In 1952, Clark told me that in the future, Vegas would have 80 major hotels.

"As Vegas grew, it outgrew something I would call 'the element,' a strange combination of hoods, graduates of the rackets, ex-carnival personnel, bookies, and other specialists in occupations other than work. But there was room for all in Vegas. It's a sort of rehabilitative melting pot. Much of the 'element' wound up dealing the games and then became ordinary, domesticated citizens."

I walk around a popular Vegas graveyard, the Young Electric Sign Company (YESCO), where old neon signs go to die. Just like Hoover Dam, YESCO, although smaller and in a different locale, was on my Brownie Scout tour when I was a kid.

Today, inside, the plant is much larger. They make other things besides neon signs, including elaborate message centers. If I close my eyes, the man before me, shaping a tube, drifts back 40 years, looking just as artistic as he makes one of the Strip signs for a hotel in 1955.

Back outside, that trusty sun beats down on the memories of our past, Lady Las Vegas. There's the CC Anderson sign from the dairy near my house. On our way back home from school, my friends and I would stop for an ice cream cone. There are the big white letters spelling out Sahara Hotel, the sign from the Las Vegas Club, the big red slipper from the Silver Slipper.

No more Dunes, no more Sands, but the signs live on; because you have never lived quietly, Lady, you must announce, you shout. I'm driving later to the Debbie Reynolds Hotel off the Strip. There's a sign by the road with two arrows. One points to Salt Lake City, one points to Los Angeles. But you can go anywhere from my town—all you need is her imagination. The sky's the limit for Lady Las Vegas.

I'm on Jack Kogan's radio program. It broadcasts from the lobby of the hotel. Jack, a kindly old-timer—as he refers to himself—has been here forever. He wears a red alpaca cardigan sweater, hosts his very popular chat hour. Rob Powers calls in from the Las Vegas Convention Center to tell Jack who's in town. Everybody sits around a green felt table, near the bar.

POLISHING THE NEON LIGHTS. TODAY, 15,000 MILES OF NEON STRETCH ACROSS LAS VEGAS.

The guest of honor is Margaret Kelly, who started the famed British dance group, the Bluebells, who danced at the Dunes.

Several former Bluebells are in the audience to pay tribute—these tall, middle-aged women are still some dishes. There is a blonde dancer on the guest panel who dances with the current Vegas icon, Oki, who's on billboards all over town. She's from Canada, used to dance in Tokyo. There's a woman running for City Council, full of earnest Vegas issues.

Jack talks about what's on his mind. He has been asked by Debbie to be a character witness when she tries to get a casino license. He's happy to do it. He says he used to date Bluebells and they liked him because he never tried anything. He thanks each guest a million times for stopping by. Vegas hospitality is still alive.

I walk outside, it's 4 p.m. The outdoors is always a shock to me. But then I'm from a casino culture. Indoors will always be my thing. Inside spells some sense of control to me, the desert outside was just too vast. We were one little town all scrunched up on the Strip, hotels built close for comfort—comfort which became solace.

We were a city carved out of a desert. Our founders came from ghettos. Wide open ranges were to be civilized and controlled. We rushed from hotel lobby to hotel lobby using the air conditioning as an excuse—"Couldn't stand it out there even for a minute, whew!" But it wasn't only the heat that made us anxious—it was the outdoors.

I have a replica of the advertisement for the opening of Ben's Flamingo Hotel in 1946. "Premiere Grand Opening of Las Vegas' Newest $5,000,000 Resort—Thursday and Friday, Dec. 26-27—Starring Jimmy Durante, Xavier Cugat, Rose Marie, Tommy Wonder and the Tune Toppers!" It states that the Flamingo is owned and operated by the Nevada Projects Corporation.

Under "Casino," it says, "The world's finest casino, staffed by an organization gathered from the entire U.S. Special Chemin de Fer gaming room, Craps, Roulette, 21."

THE FLAMINGO ROOM IN 1946.

Then there's the "Restaurant—The Flamingo cuisine will be the finest that money can buy and brains can serve, prepared by a kitchen crew gathered from all parts of the world."

And "Cocktails—A cocktail lounge unsurpassed anywhere, open 24 hours a day—Music and entertainment by the Tune Toppers—Your favorite drinks made to perfection."

My parents attended the opening while I stayed with my grandmother at the El Rancho bungalows where we lived. At a year and a half old, I didn't know what I was missing. Did my dad turn to my mom and say, "Betty, this could be big. Ben's on the wrong track but I'm going to partner up with him after this closes and he opens it again?"

Or did Ben come to him after he failed big and say, "Come on in, it'll work this time?" Or did Meyer say, "Davie, you're Ben's partner now, watch him?"

Those are the stories I'll never know, and if my dad had lived, I still wouldn't know them. Because when he had me at 42, he said good-bye to the life he had before. It was going to be Main Street America now, but lit by neon. There was no past, only the glittering present and a sunrise future. He may have been an immigrant, but I was raised being told I was "100-percent pure American, Susie. You'll be the first Berman to go to college."

After he said that, his friends would guffaw but he would give them a stern look. Later I found out that "college" was the gangster term for being in prison—the joint—but my father wanted to forget all that. To him, college was the ultimate goal for me, symbolizing that this country was mine. He provided for me the one thing he could never have—legitimacy. And you, Lady Las Vegas, made it all possible.

Coming back to reconcile now after half a century, older sister, I realize that you did not seduce my father. You were not my enemy. No, he helped create you, he and his friends made you what you are today. And he had such a task, because in doing so he had to re-create a whole generation of men to parent you, for many reasons, including so that you could then guide me. No, you were never my rival, you were my ally, I just got it wrong.

You were not responsible for my parents' deaths. The years my father lived with you were the happiest years of his life. You gave him a second chance. If you had not existed, he would have had to create you or live his life in racketeering shadows with the hint of hoodlerism always hanging over him. It is true that Vegas is not a woman's town and that my mother might have been happier elsewhere, but how can I know that for sure? She loved my father, they enjoyed something few people do—a passionate love affair. He could not have been him without you. I cannot judge their choices, I can only be grateful that they loved each other so much, because I felt their love and pride in me.

And neither were you a vampire sucking out Uncle Chickie's life blood. His gambling problem ruled his life. He came to you for pleasure, and you gave it to him. Gambling is not my choice because I was raised by my dad, an ex-gambler who made his living off gamblers, and he taught me his lessons well. Every Monday he gave me two dollars. "Here's a dollar for your slot machine, Susie, in nickels. And here's a dollar for your bank account in school. And at the end of the year, tell me which adds up to more," my dad said. At the end of my second-grade year, all the dollars I put in the slot were gone but I had $35 in my bank account.

It's another hot day in Las Vegas. Steve Wynn is in his office at the Mirage, so obsessive about you, Lady Las Vegas, that he cannot stand to hear a bad word about you. He sees you in a white, off-the-shoulder, long silk dress: all virtue, no blemishes, the most expensive, elegant string of pearls around your long thin neck; and a thin diamond bracelet on your narrow left wrist.

Kirk Kerkorian is looking for that ultimate deal where he can build even bigger. New York tycoons are applying for gaming licenses so they can take their place at your buffet. Bob Stupak is looking for his next deal. Corporate CEOs, just relocated here to run hotels, are sure they can handle casinos. "What's to know?" they ask. They're renting houses rather than buying, though—just in case.

The space-age McCarran Airport is full of tourists who can't wait to explore every inch of you. More tourists come by buses and cars, some holding their paper cups of quarters as they enter your portals.

High school graduates arrive with all their possessions in their cars, ready to train for jobs as slot-machine technicians. Beautiful girls arrive to be showgirls, or at least cocktail waitresses. Middle-class job seekers come to you now hoping you will provide the security that California no longer can.

Teenagers, kids, go on your theme-park rides, looking for that adrenalin high. Naturalists climb your rocks and marvel at your terrain. Revelers go to your shows and delight in them.

There are few sins in your town. Thou shalt not be a bad innkeeper! Thou shalt not have a boring time! Thou shalt not eat a dull meal! Thou shalt not cheat at the tables!

Your ethnocentrism is charming, Lady Las Vegas. Both your newspapers examine every issue as it affects you. Your statistics are constantly compared to national stats for everything. You must compare, you must triumph, you must be faster, richer, safer, more desirable.

And, of course, you're a nervous town. Are you still Mob? Who's Mob? Who was Mob? Are you connected? Who's connected? Who was connected? How much longer can your jackpot life pay off—ten years, twenty years, a hundred years, forever?

No matter how far I moved away from you, I kept you with me every day. Since I left you, I have carried my most important possessions in a midnight black velvet evening purse that my mother got as a table favor at your Flamingo Hotel's New Year's Eve party in 1953.

I have carried gum, whistles, marbles, then makeup, homework assignments, dorm keys, pens, and now a driver's license, money, a garage clicker, and house and car keys in that pouch. My key ring is long and gold, it's the one my dad carried. It has a gold medallion that says "DB from Ray Ryan, 1949." I never knew who Ray Ryan was until I recently read that he was a gambler/gangster from Denver who died one of those usual "unfortunate deaths."

We are both maverick desert brats, always searching for ways to make our lives work, fueled by our buoyant imaginations and sure that anything is possible. The same events resonate in our unconscious, bind us. Peace to us is escaping the heat in a hotel pool, diving down, down, down into that cool blue. Can we catch that dime before it rolls down the pool drain? Can we? Can we? Because if we can, everything could change. We believe in magic—we believe in luck. We can take comfort, but will we ever know solace?

I beg to differ with Thomas Wolfe. You *can* go home again. I did. I should have. I'm glad. Lady Las Vegas, you were my parents' Brigadoon, and ever since I left you, I have been seeking you. You and I share a past and a present. And a future? The answer, which I think to be yes, will be written in the hot desert wind and on the drifting sands of Nevada.